THORNTON WILDER was born in Wisconsin in 1897. After two and a half years in China (where his father was Consul-General), he returned to America for schooling at Oberlin, Yale, and Princeton. He spent a year studying archaeology in Rome, and from that experience came his first novel, THE CABALA (1926). He taught French at Lawrenceville School in New Jersey, and English at Chicago University—at the same time lecturing in several parts of the country and writing scripts in Hollywood. In 1927 he wrote THE BRIDGE OF SAN LUIS REY, winning the Pulitzer Prize and establishing himself as a leading novelist of the twentieth century. His other novels are THE WOMAN OF ANDROS (1930), HEAVEN'S MY DESTINATION (1935), THE IDES OF MARCH (1948), THE EIGHTH DAY (1967), and THEOPHILUS NORTH (1973). All are to be published in Avon editions. Among Wilder's plays are the Pulitzer Prize-winners OUR TOWN (1938) and THE SKIN OF OUR TEETH (1942), and THE MATCHMAKER (1954), the basis of the hit musical HELLO, DOLLY. Each will appear in an Avon edition. Mr. Wilder has been awarded honorary degrees from many universities and has been honored by several foreign countries. He lives in Hamden, Connecticut.

THE IDES
OF MARCH

THORNTON WILDER

 BARD BOOKS/PUBLISHED BY AVON

AVON BOOKS
A division of
The Hearst Corporation
959 Eighth Avenue
New York, New York 10019

Copyright © 1948 by Thornton Wilder.
Published by arrangement with Harper & Row, Inc.

ISBN: 0-380-00484-4

First Bard Printing, September, 1975.

BARD TRADEMARK REG. U.S. PAT. OFF. AND
FOREIGN COUNTRIES, REGISTERED TRADEMARK—
MARCA REGISTRADA, HECHO EN CHICAGO, U.S.A.

Printed in the U.S.A.

"Das Schaudern ist der Menschheit bestes Teil;
Wie auch die Welt ihm das Gefühl ver-
teure. . . ."

Goethe: FAUST, Part Two

"The shudder of awe is humanity's highest faculty,
Even though this world is forever altering its values. . . ."

Gloss: Out of man's recognition in fear and awe that there is an Unknowable comes all that is best in the explorations of his mind,—even though that recognition is often misled into superstition, enslavement, and overconfidence.

HISTORICAL reconstruction is not among the primary aims of this work. It may be called a fantasia on certain events and persons of the last days of the Roman republic.

The principal liberty taken is that of transferring an event which took place in 62 B.C.—the profanation of the Mysteries of the Bona Dea by Clodia Pulcher and her brother—to the celebration of the same rites seventeen years later on December 11, 45.

By 45 many of my characters would have long been dead: Clodius, murdered by bullies on a country road; Catullus, though we have only St. Jerome's word for it that he died at the age of thirty; the younger Cato, a few months earlier in this very year, in Africa, resisting Caesar's absolute power; Caesar's aunt, widow of the great Marius, had died even before 62. Moreover by 45, Caesar's second wife Pompeia had long been replaced by his third wife Calpurnia.

A number of the elements in this work which may most seem to have been of my contriving are indeed historical: Cleopatra arrived in Rome in 46, was installed by Caesar in his villa across the river; she remained there until his assassination when she fled back to her own country. The possibility that Junius Marcus Brutus was Caesar's son is weighed and generally rejected by almost every historian who has given extended consideration to Caesar's private life. Caesar's gift to Servilia of a pearl of unprecedented value is historical. The conspiratorial chain-letters directed against Caesar were suggested by the events of our own times. They were circulated in Italy against the Fascist regime by Lauro de Bosis, reportedly on the advice of Bernard Shaw.

The attention of the reader is called to the form in which the material is presented:

Within each of the four books the documents are given in approximately chronological order. Those in Book One cover September, 45 B.C. Book Two, which contains material relevant to Caesar's inquiry concerning the nature of love, begins earlier and traverses the whole of September and October. Book Three, mainly occupied with religion, begins earlier still and runs through the autumn, concluding with the ceremonies of the Good Goddess in December. Book Four, resuming all the aspects of Caesar's inquiry, particularly those dealing with himself as possibly filling a role as an instrument of "destiny," begins with the earliest document in the volume and concludes with his assassination.

All the documents in this work are from the author's imagination with the exception of the poems of Catullus and the closing entry which is from Suetonius's *Lives of the Caesars.*

Source material dealing with Cicero is copious; with Cleopatra, meager; with Caesar, rich but often enigmatic and distorted by political bias. This is a suppositional reconstruction provoked by the inequalities in those records.

THORNTON WILDER

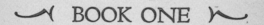

⤙ BOOK ONE ⤚

I   The Master of the College of Augurs to Caius Julius
Caesar, Supreme Pontiff and Dictator of the Roman People.

> (Copies to the Priest of Capitoline Jupiter, etc.; to
> Madam President of the College of the Vestal
> Virgins, etc., etc.)
> [*September 1, 45* B.C.]

To the most reverend Supreme Pontiff:
Sixth report of this date.
Readings of the noon sacrifice:
A goose: maculations of the heart and liver. Herniation of
the diaphragm.
Second goose and a cock: Nothing to remark.
A pigeon: ominous condition, kidney displaced, liver en-
larged and yellow in color. Pink quartz in crop. Further
detailed study has been ordered.
Second pigeon: Nothing to remark.
Observed flights: an eagle from three miles north of Mt.
Soracte to limit of vision over Tivoli. The bird showed
some uncertainty as to direction in its approach toward
the city.
Thunder: No thunder has been heard since that last report-
ed twelve days ago.
Health and long life to the Supreme Pontiff.

I-A   Notation by Caesar, confidential, for his ecclesiasti-
cal secretary.
   Item I.   Inform the Master of the College that it is not
necessary to send me ten to fifteen of these reports a day.
A single summary report of the previous day's observations is sufficient.
   Item II.   Select from the reports of the last four days
three signally favorable and three unfavorable auspices. I
may require them in the Senate today.
   Item III.   Draw up and distribute a notification to the
following effect:

11

With establishment of the new calendar the Commemoration of the Founding of the City on the seventeenth day of each month will now be elevated to a rite of the highest civic importance.

The Supreme Pontiff, if resident in the City, will be present on each occasion.

The entire ritual will be observed with the following additions and corrections:

Two hundred soldiers will be present and will deliver the Invocation to Mars as is customary on military posts.

The Adoration of Rhea will be rendered by the Vestal Virgins. The President of the College will herself be held responsible for this attendance, for the excellence of the rendition, and for the decorum of the participants. The abuses which have crept into the ritual will be corrected at once; these celebrants will remain invisible until the final procession, and no resort will be made to the mixolydian mode.

The Testament of Romulus will be directed toward the seats reserved for the aristocracy.

The priests exchanging the responses with the Supreme Pontiff will be letter perfect. Priests failing in any particular will be given thirty days' training and sent to serve in the new temples in Africa and Britain.

I-B   Caesar's Journal-Letter to Lucius Mamilius Turrinus on the Island of Capri.
> [*For a description of this journal-letter see the opening of Document III.*]

968.   [*On religious rites*]

I enclose in this week's packet a half-dozen of the innumerable reports which, as Supreme Pontiff, I receive from the Augurs, Soothsayers, Sky Watchers, and Chicken Nurses.

I enclose also the directions I have issued for the monthly Commemoration of the Founding of the City.

What's to be done?

I have inherited this burden of superstition and nonsense. I govern innumerable men but must acknowledge that I am governed by birds and thunderclaps.

All this frequently obstructs the operation of the State; it closes the doors of the Senate and the Courts for days and weeks at a time. It employs several thousands of persons. Everyone who has anything to do with it, including the Supreme Pontiff, manipulates it to his own interest.

One afternoon, in the Rhine Valley, the augurs of our headquarters forbade me to join battle with the enemy. It seems that our sacred chickens were eating fastidiously. Mesdames Partlet were crossing their feet as they walked; they were frequently inspecting the sky and looking back over their shoulders, and with good reason. I too on entering the valley had been discouraged to observe that it was the haunt of eagles. We generals are reduced to viewing the sky with a chicken's eyes. I acceded for one day, though in my capability of surprising the enemy lay one of my few advantages, and I feared that I would be similarly impeded in the morning. That evening, however, Asinius Pollio and I took a walk in the woods; we gathered a dozen grubs; we minced them into fine pieces with our knives and strewed them about the sacred feeding pen. The next morning the entire army waited in suspense to hear the will of the Gods. The fateful birds were put out to feed. They first surveyed the sky emitting that chirp of alarm which is sufficient to arrest ten thousand men; then they turned their gaze upon their meal. By Hercules, their cyes protruded; they uttered cries of ravished gluttony; they flew to their repast, and I was permitted to win the Battle of Cologne.

Most of all, however, these observances attack and undermine the very spirit of life within the minds of men. They afford to our Romans, from the street sweepers to the consuls, a vague sense of confidence where no confidence is and at the same time a pervasive fear, a fear which neither arouses to action nor calls forth ingenuity, but which paralyzes. They remove from men's shoulders, the unremitting obligation to create, moment by moment, their own Rome. They come to us sanctioned by the usage of our ancestors and breathing the security of our childhood; they flatter passivity and console inadequacy.

I can cope with the other enemies of order: the planless trouble making and violence of a Clodius; the grumbling discontents of a Cicero and a Brutus, born of envy and fed on the fine-spun theorizing of old Greek texts; the crimes and greed of my proconsuls and appointees; but what can I do against the apathy that is glad to wrap itself under the cloak of piety, that tells me that Rome will be saved by overwatching Gods or is resigned to the fact that Rome will come to ruin because the Gods are maleficent?

13

I am not given to brooding, but often I find myself brooding over this matter.

What to do?

At times, at midnight, I try to imagine what would happen if I abolished all this; if, Dictator and Supreme Pontiff, I abolished all observation of lucky and unlucky days, of the entrails and flights of birds, of thunder and lightning; if I closed all temples except those of Capitoline Jove.

And what of Jove?

You will hear more of this.

Prepare your thoughts for my guidance.

The next night.

[The letter continues in Greek.]

Again it is midnight, my dear friend. I sit before my window, wishing that it overhung the sleeping city and not the Trasteverine gardens of the rich. The mites dance about my lamp. The river barely reflects a diffused starlight. On the farther bank some drunken citizens are arguing in a wine shop and from time to time my name is borne to me on the air. I have left my wife sleeping and have tried to quiet my thoughts by reading in Lucretius.

Every day I feel more pressure upon me, arising from the position I occupy. I become more and more aware of what it enables me to accomplish, of what it summons me to accomplish.

But what is it saying to me? What does it require of me?

I have pacified the world; I have extended the benefits of Roman law to innumerable men and women; against great opposition, I am extending to them also the rights of citizenship. I have reformed the calendar and our days are regulated by a serviceable accommodation of the movements of the sun and the moon. I am arranging that the world be fed equably; my laws and my fleets will adjust the intermittence of harvests and surplus to the public need. Next month torture will be removed from the penal code.

But these are not enough. These measures have been merely the work of a general and of an administrator. In them I am to the world what a mayor is to a village. Now some other work is to be done, but what? I feel as though now, and only now, I am ready to *begin*. The song which is on everyone's lips calls me: father.

For the first time in my public life I am unsure. My actions have hitherto conformed to a principle which I may call a superstition: I do not experiment. I do not initiate an action in order to be instructed by its results. In the art of war and in the operations of politics I do nothing without an extremely precise intention. If an obstacle arises I promptly create a new plan, every potential consequence of which is clear to me. From the moment I saw that Pompey left a small portion of every venture to *chance*, I knew that I was to be the master of the world.

The projects which now visit me, however, involve elements about which I am not certain that I am certain. To put them into effect I must be clear in my mind as to what are the aims in life of the average man and what are the capabilities of the human being.

Man—what is that? What do we know of him? His Gods, liberty, mind, love, destiny, death—what do these mean? You remember how you and I as boys in Athens, and later before our tents in Gaul, used to turn these things over endlessly. I am an adolescent again, philosophizing. As Plato, the dangerous beguiler, said: the best philosophers in the world are boys with their beards new on their chins; I am a boy again.

But look what I have done in the meantime in regard to this matter of the State religion. I have bolstered it by reestablishing the monthly Commemoration of the Founding of the City.

I did it, perhaps, to explore in myself what last vestiges of such piety as I can discover there. It flatters me also to know that I am of all Romans the most learned in old religious lore, as my mother was before me. I confess that as I declaim the uncouth collects and move about in the complicated ritual, I am filled with a real emotion; but the emotion has no relation to the supernatural world: I am remembering myself when at nineteen, as Priest of Jupiter, I ascended the Capitol with my Cornelia at my side, the unborn Julia beneath her girdle. What moment has life since offered to equal that?

Hush! There has just been a change of guard at my door. The sentries have clashed their swords and exchanged the password. The password for tonight is CAESAR WATCHES.

II The Lady Clodia Pulcher, from her villa at Baiae on the Bay of Naples, to the Steward of her Household in Rome.

[*September 3, 45* B.C.]

My brother and I are giving a dinner on the last day of the month. If any mistakes occur this time I shall replace you and offer you for sale.

Invitations have been sent to the Dictator, and to his wife and aunt; to Cicero; to Asinius Pollio; and to Gaius Valerius Catullus. The entire dinner will be conducted in the old mode, that is to say, the women will be present only in the second part of the dinner and will not recline.

If the Dictator accepts this invitation, the strictest protocol will be observed. Start rehearsing the servants now: the reception before the door, the carrying of the chair, the tour of the house, and the leave-taking. Make arrangements to hire twelve trumpeters. Inform the priests of our temple that they are to perform the ceremony suitable for the reception of the Supreme Pontiff.

Not only you, but my brother also, will taste the Dictator's dishes in his presence, as was done in the old days.

The menu will depend upon the new amendements to the sumptuary laws. If they are passed by the day of the dinner only one entree may be served to the entire company. It will be the Egyptian ragout of sea food which the Dictator once described to you. I don't know anything about it; go at once to his chef and find out how it is prepared. When you are sure of the recipe, make it at least three times to insure that it will be perfect on the night of the dinner.

If the new laws have not been passed, we will have a variety of dishes.

The Dictator, my brother, and I will have the ragout. Cicero will have lamb on the spit in the Greek manner. The Dictator's wife will have the sheep's head with roast apples which she praised so highly. Did you send her the recipe as she asked you to? If so, change the preparation slightly; I suggest that you add three or four peaches soaked in Albanian spirits. The Lady Julia Marcia and Valerius Catullus will be offered their choice among these dishes. Asinius Pollio will probably eat nothing as usual, but have ready some heated goat's milk and some Lombardy porridge. I leave the matter of the wines entirely in your hands; watch the laws about it.

16

I am having twenty to thirty dozen oysters dragged under water in nets to Ostia. Some of them can be brought up to Rome on the day of the dinner.

Go at once to Eros, the Greek mime, and engage him for the evening. He will probably make his accustomed difficulties; you may hint to him the quality of the guests I am expecting. When you have closed the interview you may tell him that in addition to his usual fee I will give him Cleopatra's mirror. Tell him I wish him, with his troupe, to perform "Aprodite and Hephaestus" and Herondas's "The Procession of Osiris." Alone, I wish him to declaim Sappho's "Garland-Weaver's Cycle."

I am leaving Naples tomorrow. I shall stop a week with the family of Quintus Lentulus Spinther at Capua. I shall expect a letter from you there telling me how my brother is occupying himself. You may expect me in Rome about the 10th.

I wish to have a report from you on the matter of cleaning up all scribbling about our family in public places. I want this to be very thorough.

> [*What Clodia meant by this last paragraph is best illustrated by a passage in one of Cicero's letters and by some selected graffitti:*]

II-A   Cicero, in Rome, to Atticus, in Greece.
       [*Written in the spring of this year.*]

Second only to the master of us all, Clodia has become the most discussed person in Rome. Verses of unbounded obscenity are scribbled about her over the walls and pavements of all the baths and urinals in Rome. I am told there is an extended satire dedicated to her in the cooling-off hall of the Baths of Pompey; seventeen poets have already put their hands to it; it receives additions daily. I am told that it turns in large part upon the fact that she is widow, daughter, niece, granddaughter, and great-granddaughter of consuls and that her ancestor Appius first laid down the road upon which she now seeks consolatory if not remunerative companionship.

The lady, it is reported, has heard of these tributes. Three cleaning men are engaged nightly in surreptitious erasure. They are overworked; they cannot keep up with their task.

Our Dominie [*Caesar*] does not have to engage workmen to efface calumny. There are scurrilous verses

17

enough; but for every decrier he has three advocates. His veterans have re-armed themselves with sponges.

Poetry has become a fever in our city. I am told that the verses of this new-come Catullus—verses also addressed to Clodia, though in a different vein—are likewise scrawled upon our public buildings. The Syrian pie vendors have got them by heart. What do you say to that? Under the absolute power of one man our occupations are taken from us, or lose their savor. We are not citizens but slaves and poetry is the resource of an enforced idleness.

II-B Graffitti scrawled on the walls and pavements of Rome.

Clodius Pulcher in the Senate says to Cicero:
My sister wouldn't budge; she wouldn't give me a foot,
  he says.
Oh, says Cicero, we thought she was more genrus.
We thought she give you above the knee, he says.

Her ancestors laid down the Appian Way. Caesar
Took up this Appia and laid it down in another way.
Haw, haw, haw.

The Fourpenny Girl is a millionaire, but avaricious
  and no idler;
How proudly she brings in her fifty pennies at dawn.

Monthly, Caesar commemorates the Founding of the
  City.
Hourly, the dissolution of the Republic.

> [*The following popular song, with variants, was found scrawled in public places throughout the world.*]

The world is Rome's and the Gods gave it to Caesar;
Caesar is the decendant of the Gods, and a God.
He who never lost a battle is to every soldier a father.
He has planted his heel on the mouth of the rich man,
But to the poor man he is a friend and a consoler.
By this you know that the Gods love Rome:
They have given it to Caesar, their descendant and a
  God.

Suns set and are able to rise again;
But once our brief light has set
Night is f'rever and must be slep' out.

III   Caesar's Journal—Letter to Lucius Mamilius Turrinus on the Island of Capri.

[*Probably from August 20 to September 4.*]
[*This journal-letter was maintained from the time that the recipient was captured and maimed by the Belgians in 51 to the Dictator's death. The entries offer a wide variety in form; some are written on the backs of discarded letters and documents; some have been written in haste, others with great care; some have been dictated and are in the hand of a secretary. Though they have been numbered serially they are only occasionally dated.*]

958.   [*On the possible etymology of three obsolete words in the Testament of Romulus.*]

959–963.   [*On some trends and events in current politics.*]

964.   [*He gives his low opinion of Cicero's employment of metrical devices in his orations.*]

965–967.   [*On politics.*]

968.   [*On Roman religion. This entry has already appeared in this volume as Section I-B.*]

969.   [*On Clodia Pulcher and her upbringing.*] Clodia and her brother have invited us to dinner. I seem to have discussed the situation of this couple sufficiently in my letters to you, but, like the rest of Rome, I find myself returning to the subject.

I am no longer immediately filled with compassion when I encounter one of those innumerable persons who trail behind them a shipwrecked life. Least of all do I try to find excuses for them when I see that they have found

19

them for themselves, when I see them sitting on the throne of their own minds, excused, acquitted, and hurling indictments against the mysterious Destiny which has wronged them and exhibiting themselves as pure victim. Such a one is Clodia.

That is not the role she performs before her numerous acquaintance; for them she affects to be the happiest of women. It is the role, however, which she plays in her own eyes and before me, for I am, I think, the only person living who knows of a certain circumstance of which she was perhaps a victim and on which she has for over twenty-five years based her claims to being, each day again, a fresh victim.

Another excuse could be found for her and for those other women of her generation whose disorders are similarly calling attention to them. They were born into the great houses of wealth and privilege and were brought up in that atmosphere of noble sentiments and unceasing moralizing which we are now calling "the Old Roman way." The mothers of these girls were in many cases great women, but they had developed a series of qualities they could not transmit. Maternal love, pride of family, and wealth had combined to make hypocrites of them and their daughters were reared in a sheltered world of bland untruths and evasion. The conversation in their home became too full of loud silences, that is of subjects which we do not discuss. Their daughters, the more intelligent ones, on growing older became aware of this; they felt they had been lied to and they promptly flung themselves into a public demonstration of their liberation from hypocrisy. Imprisonment of the body is bitter; imprisonment of the mind is worse. The thoughts and actions of those who awaken to the fact that they have been duped are painful to themselves and dangerous to others. Clodia was the most intelligent, as her behavior is now the most flagrant. All of these girls acquired or assumed a passion for being seen in low company and the ostentation of vulgarity has become a political factor with which I must deal. The plebeian world is ameliorable in itself, but what can I do with a plebeian aristrocracy?

Even the young women whose conduct is irreproachable—like Clodia's sister, like my wife—exhibit the resentment of the awakened dupe. They had been brought up to think that the domestic virtues were self-evident and universal; they had been starved of the knowledge that most attracts the young mind: that the crown of life is the exercise of choice.

In her conduct I see reflected also a matter which I have frequently discussed with you, perhaps too often—the fact that the usage and very structure of our language exhibits and inculcates the belief that we are passive in the presence of life, bound, committed, and helpless. Our language tells us that we are *given* such and such qualifications at birth. That is to say: there is a Great Giver who gave Clodia beauty, health, wealth, high birth, and conspicuous intelligence and to another slavery, disease, and stupidity. She has often heard it and said that she was endowed with beauty [by what endower?] and that another was cursed with a sharp tongue—did God curse? Even if we assume the existence of a God who, as Homer says, pours out from his urns his good and evil gifts, I am amazed at the pious who insult their God by failing to see that as this world is run there is a field of circumstance that is not commensurate with God's providence and that God must have so intended it.

But to return to our Clodia: the Clodias under such a dispensation never receive enough; they are poisoned by resentment against this niggardly Giver who has only given them beauty, health, wealth, birth, and intelligence, who is holding back a million gifts, namely, perfect felicity in every moment of every day. There is no rapacity equal to that of the privileged who feel that their advantages have been conferred upon them by some Intelligence and no bitterness equal to that of the ill-conditioned who feel that they have been specifically passed over.

Oh, my friend, my friend, what better thing could I do for Rome than to put the birds back into the world of birds, thunder back into the phenomena of the atmosphere and the Gods back into the memories of infancy?

I need hardly say we are not attending Clodia's dinner.

IV   The Lady Julia Marcia, a widow of the great Marius, from her farm in the Alban Hills, to her nephew Caius Julius Caesar in Rome.
     [*September 4.*]

Clodius Pulcher and his sister have invited me to dinner on the last day of the month; they tell me, my dear boy, that you will be there. I had not intended coming into town until December when I must take up my duties in connection with the Mysteries [*of the Good Goddess*]. Naturally, I would not think of going to that house without the assurance that you and your dear wife would be there also. Will you return one word by this messenger as to whether you will really be present or not?

I must confess that I am not a little curious to see—after all these years of rustication—how that Palatine Hill society lives. The scandalized letters I receive from Sempronia Metella and Servilia and Aemilia Cimber and Fulvia Manso are not of much help. They are so busy calling attention to their own virtue that I cannot make out whether the daily round at the top of the world is brilliant or trivial.

I have another reason for seeing Clodia Pulcher, also. It may be that, sooner or later, I shall be obliged to have a very serious conversation with her—for her mother's and grandmother's sakes, dear friends of my youth and middle years. Can you divine what I mean? [*As will be seen, Caesar did not grasp this intimation. His aunt was on the Governing Board of the Mysteries of the Good Goddess. If the proposal arose that Clodia be disbarred from participation in the Mysteries, the decision would rest largely with the lay committee and not with the representatives from the College of Vestal Virgins. The final responsibility would devolve, however, upon Julius Caesar himself, as Supreme Pontiff.*]

We country bumpkins are prepared to obey precisely all your laws against luxury. Our little communities love you and give thanks to the Gods daily that you are guiding our great State. There are six of your veterans on my farm. The diligence and cheerfulness and loyalty which they show to me are a reflection, I know, of their worship of you. I try not to disappoint them.

Give my love to Pompeia.

[*Second letter in the same packet.*]

My dear Nephew, this is the next morning.

Forgive my presumption in taking the time of the master of the world, but may I ask you a second question to be answered by this messenger?

Is Lucius Mamilius Turrinus still living? Can he receive letters? Can you give me an address for him?

I have put these questions to a number of my friends, but no one seems to be able to answer them with certainty. We know that he was gravely wounded fighting beside you in Gaul. Some say he is living in complete seclusion in the lake country, in Crete, or in Sicily. Others say that he has been dead for a number of years.

I had a dream the other night—you will pardon an old woman—in which I seemed to be standing by the pool of our villa at Tarentum, with my dear brigand of a husband beside me. Two boys were swimming in the pool—yourself and Lucius. You came up out of the water, and putting his hands on your shoulders my husband looked deep into my eyes and said smiling: "Saplings of our great Roman oak."

How often you both came to our house. You spent the whole day hunting. And what enormous dinners you ate. And do you remember how, at the age of twelve, you used to declaim Homer to me, your eyes flashing. And then you and Lucius went off to Greece together to study, and you wrote me long letters about philosophy and poetry. And Lucius, who had no mother, wrote to your mother.

Oh, the past, the past, Caius.

I woke from that dream weeping, weeping for those lost presences, my husband, your mother, Clodia's father and mother, and for dear Lucius.

Oh, dear, I am wasting your time.

Two answers: Clodia's dinner: and Lucius's address, if he lives.

IV-A Caesar's reply to Julia Marcia, by return messenger.

> [*The first two paragraphs are in the handwriting of a secretary.*]

I have no intention, my dear Aunt, of going to Clodia's dinner. If I thought there were anything of real interest for you there, I would of course oblige you by going. Pompeia, however, joins me in urging you to come to us on that evening. It may be that Clodia has had the effrontery to invite Cicero and he may have had the weakness to accept; if so, I shall steal him from her party and offer him up to you. I think you will like to see him again; he is even wittier than he used to be and he can tell you all about the society on the Palatine Hill. Moreover, do not take the trouble to open your house; the pavilion in our garden is at your disposal and Al-Nara will be delighted to wait on you. While you are in the pavilion, my dear lady, I shall

23

direct that during the night watches the sentrymen refrain from clashing their swords; they shall exchange their passwords in a whisper.

You will see enough of Clodia when you come to town for the Ceremonies. Contemplating Clodia I find scarcely a drop in my heart of that compassion which Epicurus enjoins us to extend toward the erring. I hope you will have those serious talks with her, of which you speak, and I hope you will show me how I may find my way to some sympathy toward her. I am rendered uncomfortable by the dryness within my heart toward one to whom I have been bound by so wide a variety of associations.

[*Here Caesar continues the letter in his own hand*:]

You talk of the past.

I do not let my thoughts dwell on it for long. All of it, all of it, seems of a beauty that I shall not see again. Those presences, how can I think of them? At the memory of one whisper, one pair of eyes, the pen falls from my hand, the interview in which I am engaged turns to stone. Rome and her business become a clerk's task, arid and tedious, with which I fill my days until death relieves me of it. Am I peculiar in this? I do not know. Can other men weave past joy into their thoughts in the present and their plans for the future? Perhaps only the poets can; they alone use all of themselves in every moment of their work.

I think that such a one has come among us to replace our Lucretius. I am enclosing a sheaf of his verses. I want you to tell me what you think of them. This mastership of the world which you ascribe to me is more worth administering since I have seen these examples of what our Latin tongue can do. I am not enclosing the verses which have reference to myself; this Catullus is as eloquent in hatred as in love.

There is a present awaiting you in Rome—though my share in it will cost me some of that application to my present duties which, as I have said, follows upon any return I may make to the past. [*Into the monthly Commemoration of the Founding of the City Caesar introduced a salutation rendered by Rome to the spirit of her husband Marius.*]

As to your second question, my dear Aunt, I am not in a position to answer it.

24

Pompeia sends her love. We await your coming with much joy.

V The Lady Sempronia Metella, in Rome, to the Lady Julia Marcia on her farm in the Alban Hills.
[*September 6.*]

I can't tell you how delighted I am, my dearest Julia, to hear that you are coming to the City. Don't trouble to open your house. You must stay with me. Zosima, who adores the ground you walk on, will wait on you; I can get on very well with Rhodope who is turning out to be a treasure.

Now make yourself comfortable, dear, because I'm afraid this is going to be a very long chat.

First, do listen to an old old friend's advice: don't go to that woman's house. One can go on saying for years that one doesn't listen to gossip, that the absent cannot defend themselves from slander, etc., etc.; but, after all, isn't the provocation of so much gossip an offense in itself? I personally don't believe that she poisoned her husband or that she has had improper relations with her brothers, but thousands do believe it. My grandson tells me that songs about her are sung in all the garrisons and taverns and verses about her are scribbled over all the Baths. There's a nickname for her in everyone's mouth which I won't venture to put down here.

Really, the worst thing one *knows* about her is the influence she has over that whole Palatine set. It was she who began this business of dressing up as one of the people and mingling with the lowest elements of the city. She takes her friends out to the gladiators' taverns and drinks all night with them, and dances for them, and I leave the rest to your imagination. She makes up picnic parties, Julia, and goes to the taverns out in the country among the herdsmen and the military posts out there. These are *facts*. One of the results of this anyone can see: it's the effect on the language; it's now smart to talk pure *pleb*. And there's no doubt that she and she alone is responsible. Her position in society, her birth, her wealth, her beauty, and—for one must confess it—her fascination and intelligence have led society right down into the mud.

But at last she is frightened. And she has asked you to dinner because she is frightened.

25

Now listen: a very serious thing is brewing and one which will finally fall upon your shoulders for a decision.

> [*In the following paragraphs a number of substitute expressions are employed:* The Ox-eyed (*in Greek*) *is Clodia;* The Wild Boar *is her brother, Clodius Pulcher;* The Quail (*a soubriquet conferred upon her by the ladies long before her marriage*) *is Pompeia, Caesar's wife;* The Thessalian (*short for the Witch of Thessaly*) *is Servilia, the mother of Marcus Junius Brutus; and* The Tapestry Class *is both the Mysteries of the Good Goddess and the committee that directed their celebration.* The Weathermaker *is, of course, Caesar.*]

Abandoned though this woman is, I don't believe in debarring her from *certain reunions;* but there's no doubt that her disbarment is going to be proposed. She and *The Quail* were present at the last meeting of the Executive Council which took place just before she went south to Baiae. They asked the Chair—*The Thessalian* was sitting in your chair—to excuse them and they left early; and the minute they were gone groups all over the hall began talking about her. Aemilia Cimber said that if *The Ox-eyed* stood anywhere near her during *The Tapesty Class* she would strike her in the face. Fulvia Manso said that she would not strike her during the rites, but that she would leave at once and submit a complaint to the Supreme Pontiff. And *The Thessalian,* who being in the Chair should not have given any opinion at all, said that the first thing to do was to lay the matter before you and the President of the College of the Vestal Virgins. *Her* indignant tone, I must say, struck me as slightly comical, for we all know that she has not always been as dignified as she now pretends to be.

So there you are! I don't think that you or your nephew would ever let her be disbarred, but what an idea! And what a scandal! You know, I don't think even these older women realize any more what a *scandal* is. Last night I suddenly realized that within my memory there have been only three disbarments and in each case the woman immediately killed herself.

And yet, on the other hand, it is a frightful thing to think that *The Tapestry Class,* which is the most beautiful and sacred and wonderful thing, should include a creature like *The Ox-eyed.* Julia, I have never forgotten what your

26

great husband said about it: "Those twenty hours during which our women draw together are like a column upholding Rome."

It's a great puzzle to all of us: why does *The Weathermaker* [I mean no disrespect, dear, as you know] allow *The Quail* to see so much of her? We are all so surprised by that. Because seeing *The Ox-eyed* inevitably entails seeing *The Wild Boar*, and no woman of principles could ever possible want to see *The Wild Boar*.

But let us change the subject.

I received a great honor yesterday which I must tell you about. *He* singled me out to talk to me.

I went, of course, with all Rome to call on Cato on the day commemorating his great ancestor. Thousands filled the streets near the house, trumpeters, flute players, priests. Inside the house the Dictator's chair had been set up and, of course, everyone was agog. At last he came. And you know, my dear, how unpredictable he is! As my nephew says: he's formal when you expect him to be informal, and informal when you expect him to be formal. He came walking through the Forum and up the hill without the sign of a retinue, just strolling between Marc Antony and Octavius. I tremble for him because it *is* dangerous; but that's one of the things that the people really worship him for; that's *Old Rome*, and you must have been able to hear the shouting from your own farm! He came into the house, bowing and smiling, and went right up to Cato and his family. Now you could hear an ant walk. Well, it's no news to you that your nephew is a perfection. We could hear every word he said. First the gravity and the deference; even Cato was weeping and held his head very low. Then Caesar gradually became more informal; he included the family, and then he became very playful and *very funny* and soon the whole hall was laughing.

Cato answered well, but very briefly. All the agonizing political differences seem to have been forgotten. Caesar accepted one of the cakes that were being passed around and then began addressing one bystander and then another. He refused to sit in the Dictator's chair, but everything he does is so charming that it didn't seem to be a slight on the house. And then, my dear, he espied *me*, and asking a servant for a chair he sat down beside me. You can *imagine* my state.

Has he ever forgotten a fact or a name? He remem-

27

bered having spent four days with us at Anzio twenty years ago, all my relatives and all the guests. He very delicately warned me about my grandson's political activities [but *what*, my dear, can I do about that!]. Then he began asking me my opinion of the monthly Commemoration of the Founding of the City. Apparently he had remarked my presence—think of it, at half a mile distance and while he was marching up and down in that complicated ritual! What portions did I find most impressive, which passages were too long or too obscure for the people? Then he got onto religiion itself, the auspices and the lucky and unlucky days.

Dear, he is the most charming man in the world, but also—I have to say it—isn't he *frightening?* He listens with such total attention to every little thing one struggles to say. And those great eyes are so flattering, flattering and frightening. They seem to say: "You and I are the only really sincere people here; we say what we really mean; we tell the truth." I hope I wasn't a complete goose; but I wish someone had warned me that the Supreme Pontiff was going to ask me how, what, where and when I think about religion, because that is what it finally came to. At last he took his leave and we could all go home. And I went straight to bed.

I ask you in a whisper, Julia: what *must* it be like to be his wife?

You asked me about Lucius Mamilius Turrinus.

Like you, I suddenly realized that I didn't know a thing about him. I assumed that he had died or that he had sufficiently recovered to hold some post in the remoter parts of the Republic. Now in search of information of this kind I have found out that the best thing to do is ask one of our old trusted servants. They constitute a sort of secret society; they know everything about us; and they're proud of all they know. So I consulted our old freedman Rufus Tela, and, sure enough, here are the facts:

In the second battle with the Belgians, at the time that Caesar was almost caught, the enemy captured Turrinus. He had been gone thirty hours before Caesar realized that he was missing. Then, my dear, your nephew hurled a regiment at the enemy's encampment. The regiment was almost annihilated, but it brought back Turrinus *in a pitiable state*. The enemy, in order to extract information from him, was progressively cutting off his limbs and depriving him of his senses. They had cut off an arm and a leg, perhaps more, put out his eyes, cropped his ears, and were about to burst his eardrums. Caesar saw that he received all possible care and since then he has been surrounded by his own wish, with all possible secrecy. Rufus seems to know, though, that he lives in a beautiful villa on Capri, absolutely walled off. Of course, he's still very rich and has a large household of secretaries, attendants, and all that.

Isn't that a simply *heart-rending* story? Can't life be simply *horrifying*? I remember him so well—handsome, rich, capable, obviously destined for the highest places in the state, and so charming. He almost married my Aurunculeia, but his father and all those Mamiliuses were too conservative for me, to say nothing of my husband. Apparently, he is still interested in politics and history and literature. He has an agent here in Rome who sends him all the news and books and gossip, but no one knows who the agent is. He seems to wish to be forgotten by all except a few close friends. Of course, I asked Rufus who goes to see him. Rufus said that he receives almost no one; that the actress Cytheris occasionally goes and reads to him, and that once a year, in the spring, the Dictator goes and stays a few days, but apparently never mentions his visits to anyone.

Rufus, who is pure gold, begged me not to repeat any of this to anyone but you. He's a very remarkable old African and seems to respect something in the invalid's wish to be forgotten. I'm going to do as he wishes and I know you will. I'm *horrified* by the length of this letter.

Come as soon as you can.

VI Clodia, at Capua, to her brother Publius Clodius Pulcher in Rome.
> [*September 8.*]
> [*From the villa of Quintus Lentulus Spinther and his wife Cassia.*]

Brainless:

S. T. E. Q. V. M. E. [*Clodia ironically employs an epistolary convention of the day meaning "If you and your army are enjoying good health, it is well"; by changing two letters she says "If you and your riffraff are well, it is bad."*]

Plucked again. [*Caesar's secret police had again gained access to a letter passing between them. The brother and*

sister arranged, however, that innocuous letters were car-
ried in superficial concealment by their messengers as a
screen for their real letters which were more thoroughly
concealed.]

Your letter was insane nonsense. You say: *They will not live forever.* How do you know? Neither he nor you nor anyone else knows how long he will live. You should make your plans as though he were to die tomorrow or live thirty years more. Only children, political orators, and poets talk of the future as though it were a thing one could know; fortunately for us we know nothing about it. You say: *There have been convulsions weekly.* [*Caesar's attacks of epilepsy.*] I tell you you are wrong and you know my source of information. [*Caesar's wife's maid, Abra, had been recommended to that position by Clodia and was paid by Clodia to keep her informed of all that passed in Caesar's house.*] You say: *Under this Cyclops there is nothing we can do.* Listen, you are no longer a boy. You are forty. When will you learn not to wait for chance but to build on what you have and to use each day to consolidate your position? Why have you never been anything more than Tribune? *Because your plans always begin with next month.* The gulf between today and next month you always try to overleap by the use of violence and your troops of bullies. *Ship's Snout* [*in Greek: this is Caesar*] rules the world and will continue to rule it for one day or for thirty years. You have no career, you are nothing, unless you accept the fact and work in and around it. And I tell you solemnly, any attempt to work *against it* would lead to your destruction.

You must regain your old favor with him. Never let him forget that you were once of powerful assistance to him. I know you hate him; that is of no importance. Hate and love have nothing to do with anything, as he knows well. Where would he have got, if he had *hated* Pompey?

Watch him, Brainless. You could learn a great deal.

You know his weak side: that indifference, that *absence* which people call his magnanimity. I'll wager that he really likes you, because he likes what is spontaneous and uncomplicated, and that he's practically forgotten that you were an idiotic trouble maker. And I'll wager that he was secretly amused that for twenty years you kept Cicero trembling like a field mouse.

Watch him. You might begin by imitating his diligence. I believe it when they tell me that he writes seventy letters and documents a day. They fall over Italy like snow, every day—what am I saying, they fall over the world from Britain to Lebanon. Even at the Senate, even at dinner parties there's a secretary behind him; the very second that the idea of a letter occurs to him he turns and dictates it in a whisper. One moment he's telling a village in Belgium that it can change its name to his and he sends them a flute for the town band, the next moment he's thought out a way of harmonizing the Jewish dowry laws with Roman usage. He gave a water clock to a city in Algeria and wrote a fascinating letter *in the Arab mode*. Work, Publius, work.

And remember: this is the year we conform.

All I ask of you is one year.

I'm going to be the most conservative woman in Rome. By next summer I mean to be an Honorary Votary of Vesta and a Directress of the Mysteries of the Good Goddess.

You can get a province.

From now on we spell our name Claudius. Grandfather curried a few votes by adopting the Plebeian spelling. Tiresome.

Our dinner's a failure. *Ship's Snout* and the *Little Lentil* [*again in Greek; this is Caesar's wife*] have refused. *Hecuba* has not replied. When he hears this, Cicero will probably send a last-minute refusal. Asinius Pollio will be there and I'll fill up the table somehow.

Catullus. I want you to behave nicely to him. I'm gradually getting rid of that. Let me do it my own way. You wouldn't believe it: what goes on! I have as high an opinion of myself as the next woman, but I never pretended to be all the goddesses rolled in one, nor Penelope, to boot. I'm not afraid of anything, Publius, except those horrifying epigrams. Look at those he's hurled at Caesar; everyone's repeating them; they remain on him, like personal disfigurements. I don't want any of those, so let me manage this in my own way.

Do you realize, then, that our dinner's a failure? Put that in your head. No one will come to our house but your Green Mustaches and the roe of Catiline. Yet we are what we are. Our family laid down the pavements of this city and I don't intend that anyone shall forget it.

One more thing, Brainless.

The *Little Lentil* is not for you. I forbid it. Put it out of your mind. I forbid it. There is where you and I have always made our greatest mistakes. Think of what I'm saying. [*Clodia is alluding to her brother's seduction of a Vestal Virgin; and perhaps to her unseemly pursuit through the law courts of the brilliant Caelius, a former lover whom she charged with having stolen her jewelry. He was successfully defended by Cicero in an oration which ransacked the lives of both brother and sister and rendered them notorious and ridiculous in the eyes of the Roman populace.*]

So keep saying to yourself: respectable for one year.

I, your Ox-eyed, adore you. Send me some thoughts on this by return messenger. I shall be staying here four or five days, though on my arriving this afternoon, one look at Quintus and Cassia made me want to hurry north. I shall agitate their complacency, have no fear. Verus and Mela are with me. Catullus will join me here the day after tomorrow.

Send me an answer by this messenger.

VI-A   Clodius to Clodia.
           [*For answer, the messenger was carefully rehearsed in an obscene expletive.*]

VII   Clodia, at Capua, to Caesar's Wife, in Rome.
           [*September 8.*]

Darling:

Your husband is a very great man, but he is a very rude man too. He has sent me a very short word that he cannot come to my dinner. I know that you can persuade him to come. Do not be discouraged if he refuses the first three or four times.

Asinius Pollio is coming and that new poet Gaius Valerius Catullus. Remind the Dictator that I sent him every scrap I had of the young man's verses and that he has neither returned the originals nor sent me copies of them.

You ask me, darling, what I think of the cult of Isis and Osiris. I'll tell you all about it when I see you. Of course, it's very beautiful to the eye, but it's really all nonsense. It's for servant girls and porters. I'm sorry I started taking people of our kind to it. Baiae's so boring that going to the Egyptian cults was just one of those things one does to pass the time. If I were you, I wouldn't urge your husband to let you attend them; it will only vex him and make you both unhappy.

I have a present for you. At Sorrento I found the most wonderful weaver. He makes a gauze so light that you can blow yards of it up to the ceiling and then grow old waiting for it to drift down again. And it's not made of fishes' gills like that shiny material the dancing girls wear. You and I will wear it at my dinner; we'll dress as twins! I've made a design and Mopsa can start work on it the moment I arrive in town.

Do send me a word back by this messenger.

And do drag the ungracious man to my dinner.

I kiss you squarely at the corners of each of your beautiful eyes. Twins! Though you are so much younger than I am!

VII-A   Caesar's wife to Clodia, by return messenger.

Dearest Mousie:

I cannot wait to see you. I am wretched. I cannot go on living as I am. You must advise me. He says we cannot come to your dinner. Every request I put to him he refuses. I cannot go to Baiae. I cannot go to the theater. I cannot go to the Temple of Isis and Osiris.

I want to have a long talk with you. How can I get a little more freedom? Every morning we quarrel and every night he apologizes; but I never make the least real progress, and I never get what I want.

Of course, I love him very very much, because he's my husband; but, oh dear, I wish I could get some pleasure out of life some time. I weep so much that I have grown very ugly and you will hate me.

Of course, I shall keep asking him to come to your dinner, but oh!—I know him. The gauze sounds marvelous. Hurry.

VII   Caesar's Journal—Letter to Lucius Mamilius Turrinus.

[*Probably between September 4 and 20.*]

970. [*On the laws of primogeniture and a passage in Herodotus.*]

971. [*On the poetry of Catullus.*] Many thanks for the six comedies of Menander. I have not been able to read them yet. I am having them copied and shall return the

originals and perhaps some comments of my own before long.

You must, indeed, have a rich library. Are there some gaps that I could help you fill? I am ransacking the world now for a correct text of Aeschylus's *Lycurgeia*. It took me six years to put my hand on *The Banqueters* and *The Babylonians* of Aristophanes, which I sent you last spring. The latter as you noticed was a poor copy; some customs-house clerks in Alexandria had covered it with the inventories of cargoes.

I am putting into this week's packet a sheaf of poems. Old masterpieces disappear; new ones, under Apollo, arrive to take their place. These are by a young man, Gaius Valerius Catullus, son of an old acquaintance of mine who lives near Verona. On the way north in [50] I spent the night at their house and remember the sons and the daughter. In fact, I remembered appraising the poet's brother—who has since died—more highly!

You will be astonished to know that the woman addressed in the poems under the name of Lesbia is no other than Clodia Pulcher to whom you and I have written poems in our day. Clodia Pulcher! By what strange chain of significances has it come about that this woman who has lost intelligible meaning to herself and lives only to impress the chaos of her soul on all that surrounds her should now live in the mind of a poet as an object of adoration and should draw from him such radiant songs? I say to you in all gravity that one of the things in this world that I most envy is the endowment from which springs great poetry. To the great poets I ascribe the power to gaze fixedly at the whole of life and bring into harmony that which is within and that which is without them. This Catullus may well be of that company. Are these sovereign beings then subject to the deceptions of the lesser humanity? What disturbs me now is not his hatred of me but his love of Clodia. I cannot believe he is addressing merely her beauty, and that the beauty of the body is sufficient to evoke such triumphs in the ordering of language and idea. Is he able to see in her excellences which are hidden from us? Or does he see the greatness that undoubtedly was within her before she wrought on herself the havoc which now arouses detestation and laughter throughout the city?

For me these questions are connected with the first

34

questions which one puts to life itself. I shall continue to inquire into them and shall report my findings to you.

972. [*On politics and appointments.*]

973. [*Concerning certain reforms introduced into the Mysteries of the Good Goddess. See Document XLII-B.*]

974. [*On some casks of Greek wine Caesar is sending as a present.*]

975. [*On Cleopatra's request that when she is in Rome she be permitted to attend the Mysteries of the Good Goddess. See Document XLIII-A.*]

976. [*Recommendation of a servant.*]

977. [*On the enmity felt toward him by Cato, Brutus, and Catullus.*] I called on Cato on the day commemorating his great ancestor's services.

As I have told you before, writing to you has a strange effect on me; I find myself examining matters which I do not otherwise consider. The thought that came to my pen that moment and which I was about to reject is this:

Of the four men whom I most respect in Rome three regard me with mortal enmity. I mean Marcus Junius Brutus, Cato, and Catullus. It is very likely that Cicero would also be pleased to miss me. There is no doubt about all this; many letters reach me which were not intended for my eyes.

I am accustomed to being hated. Already in early youth I discovered that I did not require the good opinion of other men, even of the best, to confirm me in my actions. I think there is only one solitude greater than that of the military commander and of the head of the state and that is the poet's—for who can advise him in that unbroken succession of choices which is a poem? It is in this sense that responsibility is liberty; the more decisions that you are forced to make alone, the more you are aware of your freedom to choose. I hold that we cannot be said to be aware of our minds save under responsibility and that no greater danger could befall mine than that it should reflect an effort to incur the approval of any man, be it a Brutus or a Cato. I must arrive at my decisions as though they were not subject to the comment of other men, as though no one were watching.

And yet I am a politician: I must play the comedy of extreme deference to the opinion of others. A politician is one who pretends that he is subject to the universal hunger for esteem; but he cannot successfully pretend this unless he is free of it. This is the basic hypocrisy of politics and

35

the final triumph of the leader comes with the awe that is aroused in men when they suspect, but never know for certain, that their leader is indifferent to their approval, indifferent and a hypocrite. What?—they say to themselves—: what? can it be that there is absent from this man that serpent's nest which is lodged within us all and which is at once our torture and our delight—the thirst for praise, the necessity of self-jurisdiction, the assertion of one's self, cruelty, and envy? My days and nights are spent amid the hissing of those serpents. I once heard them in my own vitals. How I silenced them there I do not know, though the answer to that question, as put to a Socrates, exceeds all other questions in interest.

It is not by reason of such serpents' nests, I think, that I am hated by a Marcus Brutus, a Cato, and by this poet. It is indeed from their minds that they hate me and from their views of government and freedom. Even if I brought them up to the place I hold and showed them the world stretched out as one can only see it from here; even if I could split open my skull and show them the experience of my lifetime, so many hundredfold closer to men and government than theirs has been; even if I could read with them, line by line, the texts of the philosophers to whom they cling, and the histories of the countries from which they draw their examples; even then I could not hope to clear their eyes. The first and last school-master of life is living and committing oneself unreservedly and dangerously to living; to men who know this an Aristotle and a Plato have much to say; but those who have imposed cautions on themselves and petrified themselves in a system of ideas, them the masters themselves will lead into error. Brutus and Cato repeat liberty, liberty, and live to impose on others a liberty they have not accorded to themselves—stern, joyless men, crying to their neighbors: be joyful as we are joyful; be free as we are free.

Cato is not educable. Brutus I have sent to Hither Gaul as governor, to school. Octavius is beside me, seeing all the traffic of state; I shall soon send him out into the arena.

But why should Catullus hate me? Can great poets generate indignations out of sentiments acquired in old textbooks? Are great poets stupid in everything except poetry? Can they form their opinions from the table conversation of the Aemilian Draughts and Swimming Club?

I confess, my dear friend, that I am astonished by a

36

weakness that I feel awakening in me, a delirious weakness: oh, to be understood by such a one as Catullus and to be celebrated by his hand in verses that would not soon be forgotten.

978. [*On a principle of banking.*]

979. [*On some conspiratorial activities in Italy agitating for his assassination. See our LXI.*]

980. Do you remember where Redhead Scaevola asked us to go hunting with him the summer we returned from Greece? The second wheat there promises very well. [*This is a financial tip, obliquely stated in order not to alert their several secretaries.*]

981. [*On the poverty of adjectives which discriminate color in the Greek language.*]

982. [*On a possible abolition of all religious observances.*] Last night, my noble friend, I did something which I have not done for many years: I wrote an edict; reread it; and tore it up. I indulged an uncertainty.

These last few days I have been receiving unprecedentedly absurb reports from the disembowelers of birds and the auditors on thunder. Morcover, the Courts and the Senate have been closed for two days because an eagle let fall an untidy mess within an arrow's flight of the Capitol. My patience was drawing short. I refused to perform myself the ceremonial of propitiation, to mime the frightened self-abasement. My wife and my very servants looked at me askance. Cicero deigned to advise me that I should comply with the expectations of popular superstition.

Last night I sat down and wrote the edict abolishing the College of Augurs and declared that henceforward no days were to be regarded as unlucky. I wrote on, giving to my people the reasons for this action. When have I been happier? What pleasures are greater than those of honesty? I wrote on and the constellations glided before my window. I disbanded the College of Vestal Virgins; I married the daughters of our first houses and they gave sons and daughters to Rome. I closed the doors of the temples, of all our temples except those of Jupiter. I tumbled the gods back into the gulf of ignorance and fear from which they came and into that treacherous half-world where the fancy invents consolatory lies. And finally the moment came when I pushed aside what I had done and started to begin again with the announcement that Jupiter himself had never existed; that man was alone in a world in which no voices were heard than his own, a world neither friendly nor unfriendly save as he made it so.

And having reread what I wrote I destroyed it.

I destroyed it not for Cicero's reasons—not because the absence of a state religion would drive superstition into clandestine forms and still baser practices (that is already taking place); not because so sweeping a measure would disrupt the social order and leave the people in despair and dismay like sheep in a snowstorm. In certain orders of reform, the dislocations caused by gradual change are almost as great as those caused by a total and drastic alteration. No, it was not the possible repercussions of the move which arrested my hand and will; it was something in and of my self.

In myself I was not certain that I was certain.

Am I sure that there is no mind behind our existence and no mystery anywhere in the universe? I think I am. What joy, what relief there would be, if we could declare so with complete conviction. If that were so I could wish to live forever. How terrifying and glorious the role of man if, indeed, without guidance and without consolation he must create from his own vitals the meaning for his existence and write the rules whereby he lives.

You and I long since decided that the Gods do not exist. Do you remember the day that with finality we agreed upon that decision and resolved to explore all its consequences—sitting on the cliff in Crete, throwing pebbles into the sea, counting porpoises? We took a vow never to allow our minds to offer entrance to any doubt upon this matter. With what boyish lightheartedness we concluded that the soul was extinguished at death. [*The English language cannot reproduce the force of this phrase in Caesar's Latin where the very cadence expresses a poignancy of renunciation and regret. The recipient of the letter understood that Caesar was referring to the death of his daughter Julia, the wife of Pompey, the overwhelming loss of his life. Mamilius Turrinus was with him when the news of her death reached Caesar's headquarters in Britanny.*]

I thought I had not relapsed from all the strictness of these assertions. There is only one way, however, to know what one knows and that is to risk one's convictions in an act, to commit them in a responsibility. In drawing up the edict last night and in foreseeing the consequences that would ensue, I was driven to examine myself most strictly. All the consequences I would most gladly face, certain

38

that the truth would ultimately fortify the world and all that are in it, but only if I were certain that I was certain.

Some last hesitation arrests my hand.

I must be certain that in no corner of my being there lingers the recognition that there is a possibility of a mind in and behind the universe which influences our minds and shapes our actions. If I acknowledge the possibility of one such mystery, all the other mysteries come flooding back: there are the Gods who have taught us what is excellent and who are watching us; there are our souls which are infused in us at birth and which outlive our death; there are the rewards and punishments which furnish a meaning to our slightest action.

Yes, my friend, I am not accustomed to irresolution and I am irresolute. You know how little I am given to reflection; whatever judgments I arrive at I arrive at I know not how, but instantaneously; I am not adept at speculation, and since the age of sixteen I have regarded philosophy with impatience, as a tempting but fruitless exercise of the mind and as a flight from the obligations of immediate living.

It seems to me that there are four realms in which, with dread, I see in my life and in the life about me, the possibility of this mystery:

The erotic—have we not explained away too easily all that accompanies the fires that populate the world? Lucretius may be right and our jesting world wrong. I seem to have known all my life, but to have refused to acknowledge that all, all love is one, and that the very mind with which I ask these questions is awakened, sustained, and instructed only by love.

Great poetry—poetry is indeed the principal channel by which all that most weakens man has entered the world; there he finds his facile consolations and the lies that reconcile him to ignorance and inertia; I count myself second to no man in my hatred of all poetry save the best—but great poetry, is that merely the topmost achievement of the man's powers or is that a voice from beyond man?

Thirdly, a moment that accompanies my illness and whose intimation of greater knowledge and happiness I cannot hastily dismiss. [*This sentence is evidence of the unbounded confidence that Caesar felt in his correspondent. Caesar never permitted any reference to be made to his attacks of epilepsy.*]

And finally, I cannot deny that at times I am aware

39

that my life and my services to Rome seem to have been shaped by a power beyond myself. It may well be, my friend, that I am the most irresponsible of irresponsible men, capable long since of bringing upon Rome all the ills that a state can suffer, but for the fact that I was the instrument of a higher wisdom that selected me for my limitations and not for my strength. I do not reflect, and it may be that that instantaneous operation of my judgment is no other than the presence of the *daimon* within me, which is a stranger to me, and which is the love which the Gods bear to Rome and which my soldiers worship and the people pray to in the morning.

A number of days ago I wrote you in arrogance; I said that, respecting no man's good opinion, I was not interested in any man's advice. I come to you for counsel. Think over these things and give me all your thought when I see you in April.

In the meantime I scan all that passes without and within me, and particularly love, poetry, and destiny. I now see that I have been putting these questions all my life, but one does not know what one knows, or even what one wishes to know, until one is challenged and must lay down a stake. I am challenged; Rome is requiring some new enlargement of me. My time grows short.

IX Cassia, wife of Quintus Lentulus Spinther, from her villa at Capua, to the Reverend Maid, Domitilla Appia, Clodia's cousin, a Vestal Virgin.
[*September 10.*]

For the sake of our long friendship, my dear Domitilla, I feel I must write you at once about a decision I have taken. I intend to ask for the disbarment of Claudilla [*Clodia Pulcher*] from the Mysteries of the Good Goddess.

I realize all the gravity of what I shall do.

Claudilla has just stayed at my house for three days on her journey from Baiae to Rome and some events have taken place which I feel I must recount to you in detail.

On arriving she showered us with endearments. She has always pretended that she loved me, my husband, and my children; she has assumed that we love her; but I have long known that she has never loved any woman, not even her mother, nor any man either.

As you know, to receive Claudilla as a house guest is like receiving a proconsul returning from his province. She arrives with three friends, ten servants, and a dozen outriders.

Now my husband and I have long known that any view of another's happiness is repugnant to your cousin. In her presence we may not exchange understanding glances; we may not caress our children; we may not point out improvements to the villa; we may not take pleasure in the works of art which my husband has collected. The immortal Gods, however, have given us much happiness and we are not clever at dissembling, even when the laws of hospitality enjoin us to appear contentious and discontented.

Claudilla is always at her best at beginnings. The first day she was gracious to all. Even my husband conceded that she talked brilliantly. After dinner we played "portraits" and she did, he said, the best portrait of the Dictator that could conceivably be made.

Now the things I am going to tell you may not seem as decisive to you as they do to me, several of them may even seem to you to be trifles.

The second day she decided to create havoc about her. That she insulted me I pass over; that she made my husband unhappy fills me again this moment with rage. My husband takes a great interest in genealogy and great pride in the achievement of the Lentulus-Spinther family. She began making fun of them: "Oh, my dear Quintus, you can't really, etc. . . . a few mayors up in the Etruscan country . . . but no one actually believes they were even noticed by Ancus Martius . . . a respectable family, of course, Quintus." I don't know anything about such things; of course, she has everybody's cousin's name right back to the Trojan War. She knew she was lying and she just did it to *poison* my husband, which it did.

Without telling us, she had invited the poet Gaius Valerius Catullus to join her here. We were glad to see him, particularly my children, though we would much have preferred to see him alone. When she's around he's either in the heavens or in hell. This time he was in hell, and soon we all were.

Now, Domitilla, I do not stay awake to find out what visits my guests may be paying in one another's rooms; but I do not like to feel that my house has been selected to be the scene of a cruel indignity. Since your cousin invited Valerius Catullus to join her here I was ready to assume that she looked favorably on a love which has been sufficiently widely celebrated in his verses which I think are very beautiful. But apparently not: she chose my home in which not only to bar the door to him but to bar herself in with another man—that wretched little poet Verus. My husband was awakened during the night by noises in the stable and there was the poet borrowing a horse in order to depart at once for Rome. He was beside himself with rage; he tried to apologize, he stammered; he sobbed. Finally my husband took him to our old villa across the road and watched over him until morning. Even a Vestal, dear Domitilla, can understand how shameful, how derogatory to our whole sex, her behavior was—how contemptible. The next morning I spoke to her about it. She looked at me coldly and said: "It is quite simple, Cassia. I will not permit any man, any man, to think he has any rights over me whatever. I am a completely free woman. Catullus insists he has a claim on me. I had to show him quickly that I did not recognize any such claim. That is all."

I could think of no answer then, but I have thought of a thousand since. I should have trusted to my impulse and have asked her to leave the house at once.

As we were finishing dinner that afternoon my children came into the court with their tutor, visiting the altars for their sunset prayers. You know how devout my husband is and all our household. Claudilla, in their hearing, began scoffing at the salt ceremony and the libations. I could endure it no longer. I stood up and asked everyone else to leave the court. When we were alone I told her to take her party and go. There is an inn four miles up the road. I told her that I would apply for her disbarment from the Mysteries.

She looked at me a long time in silence.

I said: "I see you do not even see wherein you have been offensive. You may leave in the morning, if you prefer," and I left her.

In the morning she was most correct. She even apologized to my husband for any words which may have appeared unsuitable. But I have not changed my mind.

X   Clodia, on the road to Rome, to Caesar.

[*From the Inn at the 20th Milepost, south of Rome.*]
[*September 10.*]
[*This letter is in Greek.*]

Son of Romulus, descendant of Aphrodite:

I have received the expression of your contempt and of your profound regret that you cannot be present at my brother's dinner. It appears that you are engaged on that afternoon with the Spanish Commission. This you tell to me who know—who better?—that Caesar does what he wishes and that what he wishes is accepted without demur by the Spanish Commission and by the trembling proconsuls.

You have long since made it clear to me that I may never see you alone and that I may never come to your house.

You despise me.

I understand that.

But you have a responsibility toward me. You made me what I am. I am your creature. You, a monster, have made me a monster.

My claim has nothing to do with love. Beyond love, far beyond love, I am your creature. In order not to importune you with this thing they call love I have done what I have done: I have brutified myself. You who understand everything [for all your pretense at being noble and blank] you understand that. Or does your public and ostentatious stupidity forbid you to know the things that you know?

Tiger! Monster! Hyrcanian Tiger!

You have a responsibility toward me.

You have a responsibility toward me.

You taught me all that I know; but you stopped short. You withheld the essential. You taught me that the world has no mind. When I said—*that* you remember and why I said it—that life was horrible, you said no, that life was neither horrible nor beautiful. That living had no character at all and had no meaning. You said that *the universe did not know that men were living in it.*

You do not believe that. I know, I know that there is one thing more that you have to tell me. Anyone can see that you behave as though something for you holds reason, holds meaning. What is it?

43

I could endure my life if I knew that you were wretched also; but I see that you are not so and that means that you have one more thing to tell me—that you *must* tell me.

Why do you live? Why do you work? Why do you smile? A friend—if I can be said to have friends—has described to me your behavior at the house of Cato. It seems that you were gracious, that you charmed the company, that you set it laughing, that you talked interminably with—who can believe it?—Sempronia Metella. Can it be possible that you live by vanity? Is it enough for you that you hear the City now and—beyond the City—your future biographers describing you as magnanimous or charming? Your life did not use to be a series of postures before a mirror.

Caius, Caius, tell me what to do. Tell me what I must know. Once, let me talk to you, let me listen to you.

Later.

No, I will not be unjust to you, though you are unjust to me.

It was not you alone who made me what I am now, though you completed the work.

It was that monstrous thing that life did to me. You are the only person living that knows my story—that is a responsibility. Such another thing life did to you also.

X-A   Caesar to Clodia.
[*Not by return messenger, but some four days later.*]

My wife, my aunt, and I are coming to your dinner; do not speak of it until you receive my formal acceptance.

You write me of things I told you. Either you are deceiving yourself or me, or your memory is faulty. I hope that arising from the conversation of your guests—who include, I am told, Cicero and Catullus—some matters will be touched on that you have known, but have forgotten.

The degree of my admiration for what you were is known to you. Its restoration, like so much else, is in your power. I have always found it difficult to be indulgent to those who despise or condemn themselves.

[*September 13. From his offices, at eight in the morning.*]

I hope, my dear wife, that you have thought over the injustice of your charges against me this morning. I ask your pardon for having left the house this morning without answering your last question.

It makes me very unhappy to refuse you anything. It makes me doubly unhappy to refuse you the same request over and over again, refurnishing reasons which on earlier occasions you have told me you understood, you agreed with, and you accepted. Since it is these repetitions which try my patience and do an injustice to your intelligence, let me put some of them down in writing.

I can do nothing for your cousin. The record of his cruelty and corruption on the Island of Corsica becomes more widely known every day. It may develop into an enormous public scandal; my enemies may finally render me responsible and it may take a great deal of time which I should be giving to other things. As I told you, I can give him any post, within reason, in the Army; I will not appoint him within five years to any administrative position.

I repeat that it is most unsuitable that you attend the ceremonies at the Temple of Serapis. I know that many remarkable things take place there for which it is not easy to furnish an explanation, and I know that the Egyptian rites arouse strong emotion and send the votaries away in states of mind which they and you describe as "happier" and "better." Believe me, my dear wife, I have studied them closely. Those Egyptian cults offer particular dangers to our Roman natures. We are active; we believe that even the smaller decisions of the daily life have a moral importance; that our relation to the Gods is strictly related to our conduct. I have known women of your position in Egypt. From time to time they visit their temples in order to prepare their souls for immortality after death; they roll on the floor and howl; they take long imagined journeys during which they are "washing their souls" and passing from stage to stage of divinity. The next day they return to their homes and are again cruel to their servants, deceitful to their husbands, avaricious, noisy and quarrelsome, self-indulgent, and totally indifferent to the misery in which the mass of the people of their country live. We

45

Romans know that our souls are engaged in this life, and the journeys they make and the washing we give them are nothing more than our duties, our friendships, and our sufferings if we have them.

As to Clodia's dinner I ask you to trust my judgment. In these other matters I am willing to furnish arguments; I could do it in this case also, but this letter is already long and we both have more profitable things to do than to rehearse the history of that couple. They might have become outstanding friends of the Roman good, as their ancestors were, instead of laughingstocks to the people and a consternation to patriots. This they know well. They do not expect us to accept their invitations.

You tell me that my appointees are everywhere enriching themselves at the expense of the State. I was surprised this morning to hear you say this. I do not think, my dear Pompeia, that it is a wife's business to taunt her husband with inefficiency or reprehensible neglect on the basis of rumors she has picked up in general conversation. It is more suitable that she ask him for an explanation of charges which affect her honor as much as they affect his. If you lay before me an example of such profiteering I shall give you an answer. It could not be a short one, for I would have to open your eyes to the difficulties inherent in administering a world, the extent to which one must compromise with the greed of capable men, to the antagonism always present in one's subordinates, to the differences that distinguish conquered lands from those long incorporated in the Republic, and to the methods one employs in assisting headstrong men to plunge to their own ruin.

Your frequent charge that I do not love you connot be repeatedly answered without humiliating us both. No amount of protestation could assure you of my love, if you were not aware of it in every moment of our life. I return to you daily from my work with the most affectionate expectation; I pass with you all the time that is not devoted to my official duties; the very refusal of your requests is evidence of my concern for your dignity and greater happiness.

Finally, you ask me, my dear Pompeia: *Are we to have no enjoyment in our life?* I beg you not to ask me that question lightly. All wives inevitably marry also the situation in which their husbands find themselves. Mine does not admit of the leisure and freedom that many enjoy; yet your position is one which many women envy. I shall do

46

what I can to afford you a greater diversity of recreation; but the situation is not easily alterable.

XII   Cornelius Nepos: Commonplace Book.
[*The great historian and biographer appears to have kept an account of the events of his own time, information gathered from the most varied sources, as material toward some future work.*]

¶ The isster of Caius Oppius tells my wife that at dinner Caesar discussed with Balbus, Hirtius, and Oppius the possible transfer of government to Byzantium or Troy. Rome: inadequate port, floods, extremes of climate, disease from the now uncorrectable overcrowding. Possibility of campaign into India?

¶ Dinner again with Catullus at the Aemilian Draughts and Swimming Club. Very pleasant company, young noblemen, representatives of the most illustrious houses of Rome. My chagrin in questioning them about their ancestors—their ignorance concerning them and I, must add, their indifference.

They have elected Catullus to be their honorary secretary, I think out of tactful consideration for his poverty. Thus he is provided with an attractive apartment overhanging the river.

He seems to be their adviser and confidant. They bring him their quarrels with their fathers, their mistresses, and their money lenders. Three times during dinner the clubhouse door was flung open and a distraught member rushed in shouting "Where's Sirmio?" (this nickname seems to be derived from his summer lodge on Lake Garda) and the two retired to a corner for a whispered consulation. His popularity does not appear to be based, however, on any indulgence toward them; he is as severe as their fathers and, although extremely licentious in conversation, is little short of austere in his life and attempts to inculcate "the Old Roman Way" in them also. Curious.

He seems to have chosen his best friends among the less cultivated members or, as he calls them to their faces, the Barbarians. One of these members told me that he never talks literature, except when drunk.

He appears to be both stronger than he looks, and more frail. On the one hand he can outdo almost any member of the Club in those feats of strength and balance that arise so naturally toward the end of drinking parties—crossing the ceiling by swinging from rafter to rafter, or swimming the Tiber with a cat upheld in one hand, the cat howling but dry. It was he who stole the golden porpoise from the roof of the Tiburtine Rowing Club which figures so largely in the song he wrote for his own fraternity. On the other hand his health is undoubtedly frail. He seems to suffer from some weakness of the spleen or bowels.

His love affair with Clodia Pulcher. Surpise to all. Inquire into it.

¶ Marina, a sister of our second cook, is a servant at the Dictator's house. She talked freely to me. There have been no attacks of the Sacred Malady for some time. The Dictator spends every evening at home with his wife. He often rises in the middle of the night and goes into his study overhanging the cliff and works. He has an army pallet there and often falls asleep in the open air.

Marina denies he has fits of temper. "Everybody says he has rages, sir, but it must be in the Senate and the Courts. I've only seen him in a rage three times in all five years, and never at servants, even when they make enormous mistakes. My mistress is often in a temper and wants us whipped, but he only laughs. We all tremble like mice in his presence, sir, but I don't know why because he is the kindest master in the world. I think it's because he looks at us all the time and really sees us. Mostly his eyes are smiling as though he knew what a servant's life is and what we talk about in the kitchen. We all understand very well that cook who killed himself when the stove caught fire. There were important guests and the House-master did not want to tell the Dictator so he made the cook go in and tell him. So the cook went in and told him the dinner was spoiled and the Dictator only laughed and said 'have we some dates and salad?' and the cook went and killed himself with the vegetable knife in the garden. He was angry, oh, it was terrible, when he discovered that Philemon who was his most favorite amanuensis and had been with him years, tried to poison him. It wasn't like anger it was like weight, sir, just weight. You remember he wouldn't let him be tortured, but directed that he be killed quickly. And the Chief of Police was very angry because he wanted to torture him to find out who was behind it. But what he did was worse than torture, I think. He called us all into the room, about thirty of us, and for a long time he looked at Philemon in silence and you could hear an ant walk. And then he talked about how we are all in the
48

world together and how bits of trust begin to grow up between people, between husband and wife, and general and soldier, and master and servant; and I think it was the worst rebuke anybody ever got in the world, and while it was going on two girls fainted. It was like as though there were a God in the room, and afterwards my mistress vomited.

Octavius is home from school at Appolonium. He's a very silent boy and never talks to anybody.

The secretary from Crete was heard saying to the secretary from Rimini that maybe the Queen of Egypt is coming to Rome, that's Cleopatra the witch.

My mistress can do anything with him. Whenever she weeps, he becomes like a distraught person. We cannot understand that, because he is always right and she is always wrong.

Cicero to dinner. Much coquetry: his life is over; the ingratitude of the public, et cetera. On Caesar: "Caesar is not a philosophical man. His life has been one long flight from reflection. At least he is clever enough not to expose the poverty of his general ideas; he never permits the conversation to move toward philosophical principles. Men of his type so dread all deliberation that they glory in the practice of the instantaneous decision. They think they are saving themselves from irresolution; in reality they are sparing themselves the contemplation of all the consequences of their acts. Moreover, in this way they can rejoice in the illusion of never having made a mistake; for act follows so swiftly on act that it is impossible to reconstruct the past and say that an alternative decision would have been better. They can pretend that every act was forced on them under emergency and that every decision was mothered by necessity. This is the vice of military leaders for whom every defeat is a triumph and every triumph almost a defeat.

"Caesar has cultivated this immediacy in everything that he does. He seeks to eliminate any intermediary stage between impulse and execution. He carries a secretary with him wherever he goes and dictates letters, edicts, laws, at the moment they occur to him. Similarly he obeys any impulse of nature at the moment he is aware of it. He eats when he is hungry and he sleeps when he is sleepy. Time after time in the weightiest councils and in the presence of the counsuls and the proconsuls who have crossed the

49

world to confer with him he has left the meeting with a smiling apology and withdrawn briefly into the next room; but which of the calls of nature it was we could not know, perhaps it was to fall asleep, to eat a stew, or to embrace one of the three child-mistresses he keeps always at hand. I will say on his behalf that he accords these liberties to others as well as to himself. I shall never forget his consternation at one such reunion when he learned that an ambassador had foregone his dinner and was hungry. And yet—for there is no end to that man—in the siege of Dyrrhachium he starved with his soldiers, refusing the rations that had been reserved for the commanders. His unusual cruelty against the enemy when the siege was lifted was, I think, merely the delayed irritation of his hunger. He elevates these practices into a theory and declares that to deny that one is an animal is to reduce oneself to half a man."

Cicero does not enjoy discussing Caesar for long at a time; but he is not averse to retouching a portrait of himself with materials from that of Caesar. I was able to bring him back to the subject once more.

"Every man must have an audience: our ancestors felt that the Gods were watching them; our fathers lived to be admired of men; for Caesar there are no Gods and he is indifferent to the opinion of his fellow men. He lives for the opinion of aftertime; you biographers, Cornelius, are his audience. You are the mainspring of his life. Caesar is trying to live a great book; he has not even enough of the artist in him to see that living and literary composition cannot furnish analogies to one another." Here Cicero began to shake with laughter. "He has gone so far as to introduce into life that practice inseparable from art which is erasure. He has erased his youth. Oh, yes, he has. His youth as he thinks it was, as everyone thinks it was, is a pure creation of his later years. And now he is beginning to erase the Gallic and the Civil Wars. I once reviewed five pages of the *Commentaries* in minute detail with my brother, Quintus, who was in closest association with Caesar during the events he is describing. There is not a single untruth, no—but after ten lines Truth shrieks, she runs distraught and disheveled through her temple's corridors; she does not know herself. 'I can endure lies,' she cries. 'I cannot survive this stifling verisimilitude.' "

       [Here follows the passage in which Cicero discusses the possibility that Marcus Junius Brutus

". . . Never forget that throughout the twenty most critical years of his life Caesar was penniless. Caesar and
money! Caesar and money! Who will ever write that
story? In all the myths of the Greeks there is no story to
equal it, however fantastic—spendthrift without income
and lavish with another's gold. There is no time to go into
that now, but to put it in a word: Caesar could never
conceive of money as money when it was *at rest*. He
could never think of it as a safeguard against the future,
or as a thing of ostentation, as an evidence of one's dignity, or power, or influence. For Caesar, money is only
money at the moment of its doing something. Caesar felt
that money is for those who know what to do with it.
Now it is obvious that multimillionaires do not know what
to do with their money except to hug it or to brandish it;
Caesar, indifferent to money—an attitude which is of
course most impressive and bewildering and even frightening to the rich—could always find plenty to do with
money. He could always activate another's gold. He could
sing gold out of the strongboxes of his friends.

"But doesn't his attitude go deeper than indifference?
Doesn't it mean that he is not afraid, not afraid of this
world about us, not afraid of the future, not afraid of that
Potential Predicament in the shadow of which so many
people live? Now isn't a large part of fear the memory of
past fright and of past predicament? To a young child
who has never seen his guardian frightened by thunder
and lightning, it does not occur to be frightened by them.
Caesar's mother and aunt were very remarkable women.
Greater terrors than thunder and lightning could not dis-
compose their features. I can imagine that through all the
terrors of the proscriptions and massacres—with flights by
night through a burning countryside, hiding in caves—they
never allowed the boy to see anything in them but a confi-
dent serenity. Could that be it, or does it go farther and
deeper still? Does he believe himself to be a God, descendant of the Julian clan, born of Venus?—and hence
beyond the reach of this world's evil as he is beyond receiving any satisfaction from this world's gifts?

"At all events, he lived all those years without money of
his own, in that little house down among the working people, with Cornelia and his little daughter; and yet the pa-

trician of all patricians, wearing as wide a purple band as Lucullus's, contradicting Crassus, contradicting me—oh, there's no end to him!

"But—and there is a subtle point here—Caesar is delighted to enrich others. The chief charge laid against him now by his enemies is that he permits his intimates to amass unconscionable fortunes, and the majority of his intimates are scoundrels. Yet isn't that a sign that he despises them, for he identifies the possession and accumulation of money with weakness—what am I saying?—with *fright?*"

¶ Asinius Pollio to dinner. He talked of Catullus and the poet's bitter epigrams against the Dictator. "Strangest thing in the world. In conversation the poet defends Caesar against the constant contempt of his fellow club members; yet in his work releases that unbounded virulence. To observe: Catullus, most licentious in his verses, is astonishingly strict in his life and in his judgments on the lives of others. He apparently regards his relations with Clodia Pulcher—relations which he never mentions in conversation—as a pure and lofty love which no one could confuse with the ephemeral loves in which his friends are continuously involved. His epigrams against the Dictator though superficially political are uniformly couched in terms of obscenity. His hatred of Caesar seems to spring from two sources—his disapproval of the Dictator's notorious immortality and his disapproval of the type of men with whom the Dictator surrounds himself and whom he permits to enrich themselves at the public expense. Again it is possible that he fears the Dictator as a rival for the affection of Clodia Pulcher or feels for him a jealousy, as it were retrospectively.

XIII   Catullus to Clodia.
        [September 14.]
        [Catullus on the 11th and 13th wrote two
        drafts for this letter. They were never sent to
        Clodia, but were read by Caesar among papers
        found in Catullus's room and transcribed for the
        Dictator by his secret police. These drafts can be
        found in Book II as Document XXVIII.]

I do not wish to be spared any knowledge that this world is a place of night and horror.

The door you closed on me at Capua had that to say.

You and your Caesar came into it to teach us this: You, that love and beauty of form are a deception; he, that in the farthest reaches of the mind one finds only the lust of the self.

I have always know that you were drowning. You have told me so. Your arms and your face still struggle above the surface of the water. I cannot drown with you. The very door you closed upon me was a last appeal, for cruelty is the only cry that is left you to utter.

I cannot drown with you, because I have one thing left to do. I can still insult this universe which insults us. I can insult it by making a beautiful thing. That I shall do; and then put an end to the long crucifixion of the mind.

Claudilla, Claudilla, you are drowning. Oh that I were deaf; oh that I were not here to know that struggle, to hear those cries.

XIII-A Clodia to Catullus.
        [*By return messenger, the same day.*]
        [*In Greek.*]

Little-Stag—true, all true—how can I do other than be cruel to you?—Endure it, suffer it, but do not leave me.

I will tell you all—it is my last resource—Prepare yourself for this horror: my uncle violated me at the age of twelve—on what, on whom can I avenge that? *That?* In an orchard, at noon. Under a blazing sun. Now I have told you all.

Nothing can help me. I do not ask help. I ask companionship in hatred. I could not endure it in you that you did not hate *enough*.

Come to me. Come to me, Little-Stag.

But what is there to say?

Come.

XIII-B Catullus.

    Odi et amo. Quare id faciam, fortasse requiris.
      Nescio, sed fieri sentio et excrucior.
    "I hate and I love. Perhaps you ask how that is possible.

I do not know; but that is what I feel and I hang upon a cross."

XIV Asinius Pollio, at Naples, to Caesar in Rome.
[*September 18*].
[*Asinius Pollio, traveling as Caesar's confidential agent, answers twenty questions forwarded to him by the Dictator*.]

My General:
[*Here follow several thousand words concerning certain highly technical procedures employed by the great banking houses situated near Naples; an equally long reply concerning some administrative problems in Mauretania; then some information about the wild beasts that were being shipped from Africa to take part in the festival games at Rome*.]

Question 20: The reason for Gaius Valerius Catullus's ill-will against the Dictator and an account of the poet's love affair with the Lady Clodia Pulcher.

I have attempted many times, my General, to obtain from the poet a clear statement of his antagonism against you. My General should know that Valerius is an extremely complicated and contradictory nature. For the most part he is judicious, patient, and even-tempered. Although he is only slightly older than the majority of the members of our [Aemilian Draughts and Swimming] Club, he has long held the position there of being councilor and peace maker. He is, as we say, "head of the table." Nevertheless, there are three subjects which he cannot discuss or hear discussed without being thrown into a violent rage. He changes color; his voice alters, and his eyes flash. I have frequently observed him to be trembling. These subjects are bad poets, loose behavior in women, and yourself and certain of your associates. I have had occasion to tell my General already that the majority of the members of that Club affect the Republicans. This is even more true of the two other clubs whose membership is restricted to the young patricians, the Tiburtine Rowing Club, and the Red Sails. It is not true of the Forty Steps which remains exceedingly proud of having been founded by my General. The Republican opinions held by the former clubs, however, do not pass beyond the degree of table talk. The young men are extremely ill-informed on affairs of state, and they are not sufficiently interested to listen to an extended discussion of them; nor will Valerius. His objections veer from position to position; at one moment he is inveighing against the private character of certain officials, the next he is invoking certain principles of political theory, the next he is rendering you responsible for some burglaries that were reported in the suburbs.

I cannot help feeling that his irrational irritability on these three subjects is a reflection of the unhappy situation he is in respecting Clodia Pulcher. It is extremely unfortunate that of all the women in Rome he should have fallen in love with her. When he first came to the city eight years ago she was already the laughingstock of the Club, though at that time her husband was still living. She was the laughingstock not because of the number of her lovers, but because of the unvarying course followed by any amatory relationship with her. She exerts her fascination over a man in order to learn his weaknesses and in order finally to insult him with the greatest possible thoroughness and precision. Unfortunately for her, she does not do this very well. She is in such haste to arrive at the phase wherein she is to humiliate her lover that the fascination is quickly dispelled. Certain Club members who had promised themselves at least six months of enchantment have returned to the Club in the middle of the first night and without their cloaks.

That Valerius should love this woman with such intensity and for so long a time has caused consternation in all who know him. My brother—who is a much closer friend of the poet than I can claim to be—says that when he talks of her he seems to be talking of someone we have never known. It is generally conceded that, next to Volumnia, she is the handsomest woman on the Hill, that she is easily the wittiest and the most intelligent, and that the diversions, country parties, and dinners which she gives are not equaled by any others in Rome; but Valerius tells my brother of her wisdom, her kindness to the unfortunate, the delicacy of her sympathy, her greatness of soul. I have known her for many years; I enjoy her company; but I am never unaware that she hates the air she breathes and everything and everyone about her. It is generally thought that there is one exception, her brother Publius. Cornelius Nepos laid before me his theory that her campaign of ven-

geance against men is possibly a consequence of the inces-
tuous relations she may have had with her brother. It may
be, though I do not think so. Her attitude to him is that of
an exasperated and relatively indifferent mother. Passion
or the revulsion from passion would have rendered it
more exasperated and more possessive.

My admiration—indeed, my love—for the poet is very
great. Few things could make me happier than to see him
recover from the infatuation which is torturing him and to
see him shed the childish and incoherent prejudices which
he holds against my General.

The Lady Clodia Pulcher has invited me to a dinner to
which she tells me she has invited both my General and
that poet. At first the prospect seemed to me unpleasing,
but on second thought it seems to offer a peculiarly fitting
occasion for dispelling certain misunderstandings. I could
well understand that my General would not wish to attend
that dinner, however; in that case, I hope that I may be
permitted to arrange a meeting with the poet at a later
time.

XIV-A   Cornelius Nepos: Commonplace Book

¶ Met Asinius Pollio in the Baths. As we sat in the
steam we discussed again the reasons for Catullus's hatred
of our master.

"There is no doubt about it," he said. "It has to do with
Clodia Pulcher. Now to my knowledge Caesar has never
shown any interest in her. Do you know of any?"

I replied that I knew of none, but was not likely to
know.

"I think there has been none. She was a mere child in
the years when he was fluttering the boudoirs. There has
certainly been nothing between them; but for some reason,
Catullus [I feel certain of it] associates them. The epigrams against the Dictator are violent, are savage, but
they are very little point. Have you remarked that they
are all, without exception, couched in obscene terms? To
denounce Caesar for immorality and for enriching a few
high officials, believe me, that is like—throwing sand
against a strong wind. There is something childish about
them; the only thing that is not childish about them is that
they are unforgettable."

Here he brought his mouth close to my ear: "You
know my admiration for our master. Nevertheless, I say
to you: a man who cannot formulate a more pointed, a

more piquant case against him has not yet begun to reflect. . . . No, no, I think there is no doubt about it: Catullus has conjured up some grounds for sexual jealousy."

Here he waved his hands in the air: "Catullus is both a man and a child. It must be seen to be believed. You heard what Cicero said when he first read the love poems? No? 'This Catullus is the only man in Rome who takes passion seriously; he will probably be the last.' "

XV   Catullus to Clodia.
      [*September 20.*]

My soul, soul of my soul, life of my life, I have slept all day.

Oh, to be able to sleep until [*Friday*]. It is torture to be awake and not beside you; it is starvation to be asleep and not beside you. At dark I went out with Attius—another torture, to be thinking only of you and yet not to talk of you. It is midnight. I have written and written and torn up what I have written. Oh, the sweetness, the wildness of love, what tongue can tell it? Why must I attempt it; why was I born to be hunted by demons to tell of it?

Forget, oh forget the cutting things we have said to one another. The passion which is our joy is also our furious enemy. It is the vengeance of the Gods that we cannot be forever *one* and totally *one*. It is the rage of the soul that there is a body and the rage of the body that there is a soul. But oh! let us succeed where so few have succeeded. Let us burn the two into one; and oh, Claudillina, let us efface whatever the past held; let us stamp it out. Believe me, it no longer exists. Be proud; refuse to remember it; it is within your power to ignore it. Resolve every morning to be each morning's new Claudilla.

I kiss you to hide my eyes from you. I hold you. I kiss you. I kiss you. I kiss you.

XVI   Pompeia to Clodia.
       [*September 21.*]

Here's a letter from him to you. It's a perfectly horrible letter and I'm ashamed to forward it.

57

Anyway! So you see I *can* come. But don't thank *me*. Why didn't you tell him from the beginning that that poet would be there? Sometimes I think that all my husband thinks about is poetry. Almost every night he reads it aloud to me in bed. Last night it was Lucretius. All about atoms, atoms, atoms. He doesn't read it; he knows it by heart. Oh, dear, he's such a strange man. This week I simply adore him, but he's such a strange man. Clodiola, I've just heard Cicero's nickname for him. Isn't that simply *death-defying!* I've never laughed so in my life. [*It is hard to know which of Cicero's soubriquets for Caesar so convulsed the Dictator's wife. It may have been simply* The Dominie, *or it may have been one of several complicated compound Greek epithets*: The Autophidias, *or* The Man who lived as though he were shaping his own honorific sepulchral monument; the Benevolent Strangler—*which reflects his contemporaries' bewilderment at Caesar's wholesale pardon of his enemies and his deeply disturbing failure to display the least resentment against them; or* "Nobody-here-but-smoke" *a phrase from Aristophanes's* The Wasps, *where a man imprisoned in his house by his son gives this answer when he is discovered trying to escape by the chimney.*]

I tried on the dress. It's marvelous. I'm going to wear the Etruscan tiara and I'm having gold beads sewn on the skirt, very thick at the bottom and gradually thinning out until there are none at the waist. I don't know whether the sumptuary laws permit it and I'm not going to ask.

Did you see me give you the sign during the Foundation Day *ballet?* When I pull the lobe of my right ear that's a message to you. Of course, I don't dare turn my head to right or left. Even though he's two miles away, doing all that marching up and down and shouting gibberish I know that he's got his eyes glued on me.

I'm learning my piece for the you-know-what [*the Mysteries of the Good Goddess*]. Darling, I have simply no memory. All that old-fashioned language. *He* helps me with it. Madam President said that since he's Supreme Pontiff he's allowed to know *certain parts* of it. The awful parts, of course not; do you suppose any wife has ever told her husband about *them?* I suppose not.

I hear that Aunt Julia's coming to your dinner, too. She's going to stay with us. This time I'll make her tell me about the days of those earlier civil wars when they had to eat snakes and toads and when she and my grandmother

58

killed lots of men. It must be a very *odd* feeling to *kill* a man!

Hugs.

XVI-A   [*Enclosure*] Caesar to Clodia.

The Dictator's respects to the Most Noble Lady. The Dictator has deferred the engagement that prevented his presence and accepts the invitation of the Most Noble Publius Claudius Pulcher and the Most Noble Lady. He also requests their permission to invite the Spanish Commissioner and the Deputation of Twelve to her house following the dinner.

The Dictator understands that the Greek mime Eros is performing before the Most Noble Lady's guests. The performance of this mime is of the highest artistry. It is reported, however, that it is accompanied by a considerable degree of obscenity, particularly in the composition called "Aphrodite and Hephaestus." It is unsuitable that the generals and administrators from Spain and the remoter districts of the Republic carry back to their posts the impression that the diversions of the capital are of such a character. The Dictator requests that the Most Noble Lady call the attention of the artist to this observation of the Dictator.

The Dictator sends his thanks to the Most Noble Lady and requests that during the earlier part of the evening she waive the protocol which it is customary to observe in his presence.

XVII   Cicero from his villa at Tusculum to Atticus in Greece.
   [*September 26.*]

Only the Muses, my Pomponius, can console us for the loss of all the things we have valued. We have become slaves, but even a slave can sing. I have reversed the procedure of Odysseus: to save himself and his associates from destruction he deafened his ears to the sirens; I, however, have given all my attention to the Muses in order to drown out the death rattle of the Republic and the expiring groans of liberty.

59

I do not agree with you: I lay the general suffocation to the charge of one man.

The patient at the point of death called in this doctor who restored in him every faculty but the will and promptly bound him to himself as his personal slave. I entertained for a time the hope that the doctor would rejoice in his patient's restoration and release him to the full exercise of his independence. That hope has dwindled.

So let us cultivate the muses; that is one freedom no man can take from us.

The doctor himself takes an interest in the melodies that arise from this universal jail. He has sent me a sheaf of verses by this Catullus you speak of. I have known the young man for some time and am even addressed in one of the poems. I have known this poem for a year, but by the Gods, I am not certain as to whether it is addressed to me in admiration or in derision. I am sufficiently grateful that he does not call me pander nor pickpocket—playful attributions which few of his friends escape.

I do not share Caesar's unbounded enthusiasm. For some of these poems I have not so much admiration as a weakness. Those which are based upon Greek models we may call the most brilliant translations we have yet seen; when they depart from Greek prototypes we are confronted with some strange matter.

These poems are in Latin but they are not Roman. Catullus comes from over the border and prepares us for that adulteration of our language and our forms of thought which must inevitably overwhelm us. The poems to Clodia, and particularly those commemorating the death of her sparrow, are not without grace, but they have their comical side. I am told that they are already scrawled across the walls of the Baths and that there is no Syrian sausage vendor who has not committed them to memory. The sparrow! We are told that it often perched in Clodia's bosom—a much-traveled thoroughfare, only occasionally available to birds. Well, let us have Anacreontic threnodies on this bird and impassioned exhortations to kisses beyond counting—but what do I find? A rapid transition, or rather no transition, and we are talking about death; and by Hercules, the commonplaces of stoic philosophy are richly marshaled.

> Soles occidere et redire possunt;
> Nobis cum semel occidit brevis lux
> Nox est perpetua et una dormienda.

[*A translation is given in II-B.*]

That is high and mournful music. I am having it cut into the wall of the pergola that looks toward the setting sun;—but where is the sparrow and where are the kisses? An indefensible disproportion joins the beginnings and the ends of those poems. That is neither Greek nor Roman. A secret train of thought, an association of ideas beneath the surface of the lines, is operating in the poet's mind. It is Clodia's death, it is his own, that is figured in that of the sparrow.

If we are to be condemned to a poetry based on buried trains of thought, my dear Pomponius, we shall soon be at the mercy of the unintelligible parading about among us as a superior mode of sensibility. It is true that our minds are a market place in which the slave brushes against the sage, or an untended garden where the weed springs beside the rose. At any moment a trivial thought may leap and associate itself with the sublime which in turn may be illustrated or interrupted by the homeliest detail of daily life. This is incoherence; this is the barbarian within us all and from which Homer and the great writers of six hundred years have worked to free us.

I am to meet this poet at a dinner which Clodia is giving in a few days. Caesar will be there. I intend so to direct the conversation that this truth will be made clear to them. The maintenance of categories is the health not only of literature, but of the State.

XVIII Report from the Dictator's Secret Police: concerning Gaius Valerius Catullus.

[*September 22.*]

[*These reports were submitted daily. They included intercepted letters, conversation engaged in or overheard, and accounts of persons or the activities of persons whose names were often forwarded to the police by the Dictator.*]

Subject 642: Gaius Valerius Catullus, son of Gaius, grandson of Titus; gentleman from the region of Verona. Age: 29. Resides at the Aemilian Draughts and Swimming Club. Frequents: Ficinius Mela; the brothers Pollio; Cornelius Nepos; Lucius Calco; Mamilius Torquatus; Horbatius Cinna; the Lady Clodia Pulcher.

The papers in this subject's rooms have been examined. They include family and personal letters and in large quantity material of poetry.

Subject shows no political interests and it is assumed that inquiries in regard to him may be dropped.

> [*Notation by the Dictator:* "Reports on subject 642 will be continued. A transcript of all documents found in Subject's lodgings will be forwarded as soon as possible."
>
> *The following papers were then placed before the Dictator.*]

XVIII-A Catullus's Mother to Catullus.

Your father has taken on many new duties in the town. He is busy from morning to night. The crops have not been what was expected. This is due to the many storms. Ipsitha had a very bad cold but is better. Your dogs are well. Victor is pretty old now. He sleeps by the fire most of the time now at my feet.

We heard from Cecinnius's agent that you had not been well. You do not tell us such things in your letters. Your father is distressed. You know what a good doctor we have here and what care would be devoted to you. We beg you to come to us.

All Verona knows your poems by heart. Why do you never send them to us? Cecinnius's wife brought over twenty of them to us. It is strange that we must receive from a neighbor's hand the one you wrote about your dear brother's death. Your father carries it with him wherever he goes. It is hard to speak of it. It is very beautiful.

I pray daily that the Immortal Gods may protect you. I am well. Write us when you can. August 12.

XVIII-B Clodia to Catullus.
[*The preceding spring.*]

It is too boring to have to deal with a hysterical child.

Never try to see me again.

I will not be spoken to in such a fashion. I have broken no promises, for I made none.

I shall live as I choose.

XVIII-C Allius to Catullus.

Here's the key. No one will disturb you. My uncle uses

the rooms sometime, but he has gone to Ravenna. "Oh, Love, ruler of Gods and men."

XIX Anonymous Letter [written by Clodius Pulcher, but in a woman's hand] to Caesar's wife.

It has been reported to me, great and noble lady, that you have accepted an invitation to dine at the house of Clodius Pulcher tomorrow night. I would not take up the time of one who fills with such distinction so lofty a place did I not have information to impart to you which you could not obtain elsewhere.

This is a letter of warning for which I think you will not be ungrateful. I know to my great sorrow that Clodius Pulcher bears toward you a sentiment which has long passed the bounds of admiration. He who hitherto has never known what it is to love, who—alas!—has caused more suffering than joy to our sex has at last been humbled by that God who spares no one. It is not likely that he will ever declare his passion to you; the respect he bears to your immortal husband will and must prevent that; but it may be that what he feels may break even the restraints of duty and honor.

Do not attempt to ascertain who I am. One of my motives in writing to you I cannot hope to conceal: it is jealousy—jealousy that you hold undisputed sway in a heart where once I thought myself beloved. Soon after writing this letter I shall put an end to an existence which has lost its reason for being. Let my dying words warn you that even your noble nature would not be able to reform one who has dissipated his golden promise in thoughtless disorder; even you cannot recall him from the influence of that most wicked woman, his sister; even you cannot avenge the wrongs he has done to our sex. He believes that you could reclaim him to virtue and to public usefulness. He is deceived; even you, great lady, could not do that.

XX Abra, Caesar's wife's Maid, to Clodia.
[*September 30.*]

Our party will start for your dinner at three. My mistress and the Old Lady in litters, himself walking.

Himself cheerful. Herself in tears. He made me take all the gold beads off the gown. Sumptuary laws.

Heard an important conversation. Forgive me, my lady. Old Lady had long talk with her. Said that maybe you will be forbidden [*underneath, half-erased*: disbarred] from ceremonies. My mistress very angry, shouted that himself would prevent. Old Lady said maybe yes, maybe no. My mistress tears; begs that Old Lady will prevent it. My mistress goes to himself, begs that that will not happen. Himself calm and cheerful, says he knows nothing about it and unnecessary to get alarmed.

Am about to do my mistress's hair. Will take an hour.

My mistress asks questions about your brother.

My respectful obedience to your ladyship.

XX-A   Caesar's wife to Clodia.

TERRIBLE THING HAS HAPPENED. ON THE WAY TO YOUR DINNER THREE MEN JUMPED OVER WALL AND TRIED TO KILL MY HUSBAND. DO NOT KNOW HOW BADLY HE IS WOUNDED. WE HAVE ALL GONE HOME. DO NOT KNOW WHAT WE ARE GOING TO DO. WRETCHED AT MISSING YOUR DINNER. HUGS.

XX-B   Head of the Official Police to Head of the Secret Police.

We have rounded up two hundred and twenty-four persons found near the scene of the attack. Have begun the questioning. Six men highly suspect. We have begun the torture. One killed himself before questioning.

Crowds have collected before the house of Publius Clodius Pulcher. The rumor has spread that the Dictator was on his way to dine there and the attempted assassination is imputed to Clodius's agents. The crowd has begun throwing stones at the house and is talking of setting fire to it.

A number of the house servants attempted to leave by a gate on the Trivulcian Lane and were beaten by the crowd.

Later.

Crowds before the house increasingly threatening.

Marcus Tullius Cicero was in the house, wearing insignia as former consul. Was escort to his home by military detachment. Crowds spat at him and some stones were thrown.

In the house remain Clodia Pulcher, a young man who gave his name as Gaius Valerius Catullus and one servant.

Asinius Pollio was also a guest, but left immediately on hearing of the attempt and went to the Dictator's house. As he was in uniform he was allowed to pass by the crowd and was applauded.

Publius Clodius Pulcher escaped before we could detain him.

Later.

The Dictator suddenly arrived at the door of the house accompanied by Asinius Pollio and six guards.

He received loud acclamation. He addressed the crowd; bade them return to their homes and give thanks to the Gods for his safety. He assured them that he knew no reason why the residents of this house should be suspected of participation in the attempt on his life.

In the hearing of all, he directed that none of the suspects be tortured until he had seen and questioned them.

He directed me to make every effort to put my hand on Clodius Pulcher, but to treat him respectfully.

XXI   Asinius Pollio to Vergil and Horace.
        [*This letter was written some fifteen years after the preceding.*]

Gout and a bad conscience, my friends, are enemies of sleep; both held me long awake last night.

Some ten days ago, at our master's table. [*i.e., that of the Emperor Caesar Augustus*] I was abruptly called upon to recount the curious events connected with the interrupted dinner given by Clodia Pulcher to Catullus the poet, to Cicero, and to the Divine Caesar during the last year of his life. Fortunately for me, the Emperor was called away soon after I had begun my narration. Even in the brief portion which I had recounted, you must have been aware that I was stumbling. Our Emperor is a large-minded man, but he is master of the world, a God, and the nephew of a God. As his divine uncle used to say: Dictators must know the truth, but must never permit themselves to be told it. Unprepared, I was hastily trimming my story to fit an Emperor's ears. You two should know the truth, however, and tonight I shall hope, in dictating the story, to forget and to appease my two discomforts.

We had been awaiting for some time the arrival of the Dictator and his party. Outside the house, Clodia had lined the streets with priests and musicians and a large crowd had gathered to watch him pass. We were the last to learn that an attempt had been made upon his life. From the first [and to this day] the people of Rome have believed that it was Clodius Pulcher's hired bullies who attempted to assassinate his guest. As we waited stones began falling in the court and bundles of burning straw were flung over the walls and fell at our feet. Finally some terrified servants told us the news. I received permission from Clodia to go to Caesar's house. As I was in uniform I passed through the crowd without difficulty. I learned later that Cicero had addressed the mob from the door of the house, reminding them of his services to the Republic and bidding them return to their homes; that the crowd had been unimpressed and even insolent, and that he had hurried home barely escaping with his life; and that a number of servants, attempting to leave by the garden gate, had been clubbed to death.

On my way across the Palatine Hill I picked up the trail of Caesar's blood. I found him sitting in the courtyard of his house being treated for his wounds. The faces of his servants were white; his wife was distraught; only he and his aunt were calm. The assassins' knives had made two deep cuts in his right side, reaching from his throat to his waist. The physician was washing and binding these with sea moss. Caesar sat jesting impatiently. As I approached him I saw in his eyes an expression which I had only seen there during the moments of greatest danger in the wars, a look of expectant happiness. He called me to him and asked me in a whisper how things were at Clodia's house. I told him.

"Good physician," he said. "Make haste, make haste, make haste."

From time to time members of his secret police entered bringing reports of the search for his attackers.

Finally the surgeon drew back and said: "Sire, I now resign the healing to nature herself. She asks of you immobility and sleep. Will the Dictator graciously drink this opiate."

Caesar rose and took several turns about the court, attentive to his condition, his eyes resting smilingly on me. "Good physician," he said at last, "I shall obey you in two hours; but first I have an errand I must perform."

"Sire! Sire!" cried the physician.

His wife flung herself at his knees, wailing like Cytheris in a tragedy. He raised her up, embraced her, and beckoned me sharply to the door. There he collected a few guards, bade his litter follow him, and we sped across the Palatine. At one point he was forced to stop by pain or weakness. He leaned against the wall in silence; his hand directed me to be silent. For a few moments he breathed deeply; then we continued on our way. As we drew near to Clodia's house we could see that the police were having difficulty in their attempt to disperse the crowds. All Rome was streaming up the hill. When the people recognized the Dictator a great cry went up and space was cleared for him to pass. He walked slowly, smiling from right to left and touching the shoulders of those beside him. Before Clodia's door he turned, raised his hand, and waited for silence.

"Romans," he said, "may the Gods bless Rome and all who love her. May the Gods preserve Rome and all who love her. Your enemies have attempted to take my life—"

Here he opened his dress and showed the bindings on his side. There was a horror-struck silence followed by a roar of grief and rage. He continued calmly:

"—but I am still among you, capable, and earnest to serve your welfare. Those who attacked me have been caught. When we have examined the matter to the bottom a report will be made to you of all that has happened. Return to your homes; draw your wives and your children about you and give thanks to the Gods; then sleep well. A measure of wheat shall be given to every father of a family that he and his may rejoice with me and mine over this happy issue. Go quietly to your homes, my friends, without lingering; for the rejoicing of a child is noisy, but the rejoicing of a man is silent and contained."

He stayed a moment while many came forward to press their foreheads on his hands.

We went into the house. In the courtyard Clodia stood ready to receive him, at the point where her brother should have been standing. A few steps behind her Catullus was holding himself, erect and sullen. Caesar greeted them formally and apologized for the absence of his wife and aunt. In a low voice Clodia apologized for the absence of her brother.

"We will make the tour of the altars," he said. This he did with that incomparable mixture of serenity and gravity which he brought to the performance of all ritual. After giving a smiling glance toward Catullus he added the Collect for the Setting Sun which is customary in households north of the Po. He then suddenly became extraordinarily lighthearted. He had found one servant crouching behind an altar. He took her playfully by one ear and led her to the kitchen. "Surely, the dinner is not all spoiled. You can make us one dish; and while you are making it we will begin with our drinking. Asinius, you will fill our cups. I see, Clodia, that you have prepared a dinner in the Greek manner. We shall have a feast of talk, for the company is well chosen and there is no lack of subjects for our discussion." Here he put the garland on his head saying: "I shall be [*in Greek*] *King of the Banquet*. I shall select the subject, reward the discreet, and impose the penalties upon the stupid."

I attempted to fall in with his mood, but Clodia could not find her tongue and for a time remained pale and shaken. Catullus reclined with lowered eyes until he had drunk several cups of wine. Caesar continued talking, however, with animation; to Clodia about the sumptuary laws, and to Catullus about his plans for controlling the floods on the Po. Finally, when the tables were withdrawn, Caesar rose, poured the libation, and announced the subject of our symposium: whether great poetry is the work of men's minds only, or whether it is, as many have claimed, the prompting of the Gods. "Before we begin," he said, "let us each recite some verses that we may be reminded of the matter before us." He nodded toward me. I recited the "Oh, love, ruler of Gods and men" [*from Euripides' play, now lost, the* Andromeda]; Clodia spoke Sappho's "Invocation to the Morning Star" [*also lost*]; Catullus spoke very slowly the opening of Lucretius's poem. There was a prolonged silence while we waited for Caesar to take his turn and I knew that he was struggling against the tears which so frequently overcame him. After he had drunk deep he recited, as though negligently, some verses of Anacreon.

The first speech fell to me. As you know, I am more at home in the countinghouse and in the councils of war than in these academies. I was glad to remember the lessons of my pedagogue and I repeated the commonplaces of the schools, that poetry, like love, indeed proceeded from the Gods and that both were accompanied by a state of possession that had universally been conceded to be more than human; that the perdurance of great verses was itself a sign of a more than human source, for all the works that a man makes are destroyed by overwhelming time but that the verses of Homer outlive the monuments they describe and like the Gods who inspired them are eternal. I said many foolish things, but none which had not already been said many thousand times.

When I had finished, Clodia rose, drew the folds of her gown about her and saluted the *King*. My opinion of Clodia had never been as harsh as that held by the majority of our community. I had known her for many years, though I had never been among those of whom Cicero had said that "only her dearest friends are in a position truly to detest her." Never, however, did I have occasion to admire her more than on that evening. Her house was in disorder; she had good reason to believe that her brother had been killed and that she herself lay under suspicion of having planned or at least foreknown, the attempt on the Dictator's life. At that moment the behavior of Caesar must have seemed inexplicable to her. She was pale, but composed; her famous beauty seemed to have been enhanced by the dangers through which she had passed; and the speech that she made was so ordered and of such cogency that at its termination I was more than half-swayed to her opinion. She began by saying that she accepted in advance whatever penalties the *King* would impose upon her, for she knew that the things she had to say would be unfavorably received in this company.

"If it be true, Oh King," she began, "that poetry comes among us at the prompting of the Gods, then indeed we are twice miserable—once because we are men, and twice because we would know this much of the Gods, that they wish us to remain as children ignorant and as slaves deceived. For it is poetry that puts a fairer face on life than life can claim to; it is the most seductive of lies and the most treacherous of counselors.

"Neither the sun nor the situation of man permit themselves to be gazed at fixedly; the first we must view through gems, the second through poetry. Without poetry men would go into battle, brides would enter into marriage, wives would become mothers, men would bury their dead and themselves die; but drunk on poetry, all these men and women rush toward these occasions with I know not what unbounded expectations. The soldiers acquire glory, the brides call themselves Penelope, the mothers bear heroes to the state, and the dead sink into the arms of their mother the Earth that bore them, living forever in the memory of those they leave behind. It is by poets that all men are told that we press forward to a Golden Age and they endure the ills they know in the hope that a happier world will arrive to rejoice their descendants. Now it is very certain that there will be no Golden Age and that no government can ever be created which will give to every man that which makes him happy, for discord is at the heart of the world and is present in each of its parts. It is very certain that every man hates those who have been placed over him; that men will as easily relinquish the property they have as lions will permit their food to be torn away from between their teeth; that all that a man wishes to accomplish he must complete in this life, for there is no other; and that this love—of which poets make so fine a show—is nothing but the desire to be loved and the necessity in the wastes of life to be the fixed center of another's attention; and that justice is the restraint of conflicting greeds. But these are things which no man says. Our very state is goverened in the language of poetry. Among themselves our leaders rightly call the citizens a dangerous beast and a many-headed monster; but from the hustings, well surrounded by armed guards, in what terms do they address the turbulent voters? Are the voters then not 'lovers of the Republic,' 'worthy descendants of their noble fathers'? Office in Rome is won by bribes in one hand, threats in the other; and in the mouth, quotations from Ennius.

"Many will say that this is the great virtue of poetry that it civilizes men and sets the patterns by which they may aspire to live, and that thereby the Gods are handing down laws to Their children. It is most evident, however, that this is not so, for poetry has upon men the action which all flattery has: it puts to sleep the springs of action; it robs men of the desire to deserve such commendation. At first glance it seems to be merely a childishness, an aid to weakness and a consolation to misery, but no! it is an evil. It weakens weakness and redoubles misery.

"Who are the poets who have added these new discontents to the eternal discontents of men? It is a small company, renewed generation after generation. Popular observation has long since made portrait of a poet: they are inept in all practical matters; their absentmindedness renders them frequently ridiculous; they are impatient, easily exasperated, subject to excessive passions of all sorts. Pericles's sneer on Sophocles as a governor of the city is but the other half of the story of Menander passing through the market with one foot sandaled and one foot bare. These traits, which are known to all, are interpreted by some as indicating that poets are occupied with truths that lie behind appearance and that their contemplation of these truths is like a madness or a God-given wisdom. For me, however, there is another explanation. I believe that all poets in childhood have received some deep wound or mortification from life which renders them forever fearful of all the situations of our human existence. In their hatred and distrust they are driven to build in imagination another world. The world of poets is the creation not of deeper insights but of more urgent longings. Poetry is a separate language within the language contrived for describing an existence that never has been and never will be, and so seductive are their images that all men are led to share them and to see themselves other than they are. I take it to be confirmation of this that even when the poets write verses which pour scorn on life, describing it in all its evident absurdity, they do it in such a way that their readers are uplifted by it, for the terms of the poets' condemnation presuppose a nobler and fairer order by which we are judged and to which it is possible to attain.

"These then are the men who some say are the mouthpieces of the Gods. I say that if the Gods exist I can imagine them to be cruel or indifferent or incomprehensible, to be inattentive to men or beneficent; but I cannot imagine them to be occupied in the childish game of deluding men as to their state through the agency of poets. Poets are men like ourselves, but they are ill and suffering. They are in possession of one consolation which is their feverish dreams. But it is not from a dreaming life but from a waking life that we must learn to live in a waking world."

When Clodia had finished, she again saluted *The King* and passing the garland to Catullus sat down. Caesar praised her speech in large terms and without the irony which Socrates employed in similar occasions. His sense of delight at the occasion seemed to have increased; he bade me fill the cups again and when we had drunk he called on Catullus. Throughout the earlier part of Clodia's speech, the poet had continued sitting with lowered eyes, but gradually his aspect had changed and from the mo-

71

ment he arose and placed the garland on his head all were
aware that he was deeply engaged, either through anger or
through interest in the matter discussed.

> [*There are many versions extant of the so-called*
> "*Alcestiad of Catullus." That which Caesar sent
> as Entry 996 of his journal-letter to Lucius Ma-
> milius Turrinus is substituted here for Asinius
> Pollio's briefer account.*]

Every child knows, Oh King, that Alcestis, the wife of
Admetus, King of Thessaly, was the golden pattern of all
wives. As a girl, however, marriage was the last thing she
wanted. She was tormented by such a question as has been
placed before us today. She wished before her life ended
to have acquired some certain answers to the most important questions which can be asked. She wished complete
assurance that the Gods existed and that They were attentive to her; that the promptings of her heart were guided
by Them and that the good things and the ill that might
befall her were known to Them and, as it were, designed
by Them for purposes of Their own. She looked about her
and saw that there was little likelihood of her learning
these things if she were to pass her life as Queen, wife,
and mother. Her heart was filled with one ambition: to
become a priestess of Apollo at Delphi. There she had
heard one lived in the very presence of the God; there
messages were received from Him daily; there one could
be certain. It is reported of her that she said of wives and
mothers that there were many; that to them there was
nothing more important than the good or ill-will of their
husbands; that the sun rose only for their children to
whom they were bound by that furious love that tigresses
feel for their cubs; that their years passed, filled with the
innumerable duties of ordering a household, as their minds
were filled with the fears and prides and joys of their pos-
sessions; and that finally they were laid to rest, knowing
no more of why they lived and suffered than the animals
of the hills. She felt that there was more to be obtained
from life than being the instrument of its forces and that
that *more* could be obtained at Delphi. The priestesses of
Apollo, however, are called by the God; and for her, in
spite of all her prayers and sacrifices, no call came. Her
days were spent in waiting for a message and in trying to
read the will of the God in signs and portents.

Now Alcestis was the wisest and the most beautiful of
the daughters of King Pelias. All the heroes of Greece

sought her hand in marriage; but the King, wishing to keep her beside him, imposed upon these suitors an all but impossible task. He declared that Alcestis would be given as a bride only to that man who, harnessing together a lion and a boar, could drive them once around his city's walls. Year followed year and suitor after suitor failed in the attempt. Peleus, who was to be the father of Achilles, failed and the sagacious Nestor; Laërtes, the father of Ulysses, failed and Jason the mighty leader of the Argonauts. Lions and boars fell upon one another in fury and the drivers barely escaped with their lives. And the King laughed and was well pleased and the Princess interpreted their failures as a sign from the God that she was destined to remain a virgin and to serve Him at Delphi.

Finally, as is well known, Admetus, King of Thessaly, came down from his mountains. He drove the lion and boar like mild oxen about the city and won the hand of the Princess Alcestis. With love and rejoicing he carried her off to his palace at Pherai and great were the preparations for the wedding.

Alcestis was not ready, however, to become wife and mother. Daily, with a sort of fear, she felt herself coming to love Admetus more and more, but she continued to await the call of Apollo and with one pretext after another she deferred the day of the wedding.

Admetus for a time was patient throughout these delays, but finally he could contain his ardor no longer. He besought her to give him an explanation of this reluctance and in reply she told him all that was in her mind. Now Admetus was a pious and devout man, but he had long ceased to look outside himself for any aid or consolation from the Gods. On one occasion in his life, however, he had felt Their closeness to his interests and this he now reported to her eagerly:

"Aclestis," he said, "look no further for a sign from Apollo concerning your marriage, for that sign has clearly come. It is He alone who has brought you here, as you will see from my story.

"Before I returned to Iolcos to attempt the trial, I fell ill, as well I might, for my great love was at war with my despair lest I fail to harness the lion and the boar. For three days and nights I lay at the point of death. I was tended by Aglaia who had been my nurse and my father's before me. It is she who tells me that in my delirium during the third night she was aware that Apollo was present in my mind and was teaching me how to yoke together a lion and a boar. Aglaia is here now; you have but to ask her."

"Admetus," said Alcestis, "there is no lack of reports about the Gods from the delirium of young men and the tales of old nurses. It is just such stories which have increased the confusion in which all men live. No! Admetus, let me go to Delphi! Even though I have not been chosen to be priestess there, I can be a servant. I can serve His servants and clean the steps and pavements of His house."

Admetus did not understand her difficulty, but he was sadly giving her his permission when their conversation was interrupted. Word was brought them that a visitor had arrived at the palace, an old blind man who turned out to be Tiresias the priest of Apollo at Delphi. In amazement, Admetus and Alcestis went to the courtyard to receive him. When they drew near he called out in a loud voice:

"I bring a message to the house of Admetus, King of Thessaly. I am in haste to deliver it and to return whence I came. It is the will of Jupiter that Apollo live on earth as a man among men for the space of a year. And Apollo has chosen to live here as a herdsman of Admetus. I have given my message."

Admetus took a step forward and asked: "Do you mean, noble Tiresias, that Apollo will be here, daily, daily,—?"

"Outside the gate," shouted Tiresias, "are five herdsmen. One of them is Apollo. Do not seek to know which one is He. Assign them their duties; do justly; and ask me no more questions, for I have no answers."

With these words and without any sign of reverence, he called the herdsmen to come into the court and himself went on his way. The five herdsmen that slowly came into the courtyard were like any herdsmen; they were covered with dust after their long journey and greatly abashed by the intense gaze that was fixed upon them. King Admetus could scarcely find his voice, but finally he welcomed them and directed they be given their lodging and their dinner. For the rest of the day a silence fell upon all the people in Pherai. They knew that some great honor had come to their country, but it is difficult to be at once happy and puzzled.

Toward the end of that day, when the first stars were appearing, Alcestis slipped out of the palace and went to where the herdsmen were sitting about a fire. She stood at the edge of the firelight and besought Apollo to speak to her in His own person, to emerge from that hiding in which the Gods delight, and to give her an answer to the questions that were her very life. Her prayer was not short. The bewildered shepherds were at first quiet and respectful; then they began passing the wineskin from hand to hand, grunting; one fell asleep and snored. Finally, the shortest one dried his mouth with the back of his hand and said:

"Princess, if there be a God here, I do not know which it is. For thirty days we have walked across Greece. We have drunk from the same wineskin, have put our hand in the same dish, and slept by the same fire. If there were a God among us, would I not know it? Yet, lady, this I shall say: those are no ordinary herdsmen. That fellow that's asleep—there's no illness he can't cure, snake bite or broken bones. When I fell into a quarry five days ago I was most certainly a dead one, but that fellow leaned over me and said some abracadabra and look at me now. Yet I know well that he's no God, Princess. Why, in one town, Princess, there was a child with a stopped-up throat, Princess; she'd turned purple and it would have cut your heart to see her. This fellow wanted to sleep. He wouldn't cross the road to see her. Is that a God? And that fellow beside him, that one—can't you stop drinking while the Princess is looking at you?—he never loses his way. In the darkest night he knows his north from his south. But I know well that he's not the God of the Sun. Now the redhaired one, he's no ordinary herdsman, either. He performs miracles and wonders. He reverses the order of nature. He is an inventor."

With these words the herdsman walked over to his redhaired companion and began kicking him awake. "Wake up. Wake up. Show the Princess some wonders." The sleeping man stirred ond groaned. Suddenly from the upper air and from the distant hills voices could be heard calling "Alcestis! Alcestis!" Whereupon the man turned over and fell asleep. Again he was kicked awake. "Do some more. Do the waterfall from the treetops. Do the balls of fire." The man swore gruffly. Balls of fire began racing across the ground. They slid up the trees and burst; they climbed onto his companions' heads; they played with one another drolly like animals. Finally the glade fell into darkness. "Those are indeed things which no other man can do, but I would take my oath, Princess, that he is no God. One of the reasons is that none of his wonders mean anything. We are astonished and after astonishment comes disappointment. During the first days of our journey we asked for more and more wonders, for they diverted us; but finally we were tired of them and to tell the truth, we were ashamed of them and he was ashamed of them, for his tricks had no relation to anything outside themselves. Would a God be ashamed of his wonders? Would He ask Himself what they meant?

"So, you see, Princess!" he concluded, stretching out his arms as though he had finished his reply to her prayer. But Alcestis would not be put off so easily. She pointed to the fourth herdsman.

"That man? He is no ordinary herdsman, either. He is our singer. Believe me, when he plays his lyre and sings, lions hang suspended in their leap. It is true that at times I have said to myself, 'Sure, this is a God.' He can fill us to the brim with joy or sorrow at times when we have no reason to rejoice or grieve. He can make the memory of love more tender than love itself. His wonders are greater than those of our healer, our nightwalker, and our miracle worker; but I have watched him,—Princess, his wonders have more effect upon us than upon him. He soon rejects the song he has made. Us it can transport each time, but not him. He loses joy in the thing he has made and is in labor to fashion another. That is enough to assure me that he is not a God, not even a messenger of the Gods, for the Gods cannot be thought of as despising their handiwork.

"And I? What do I do? What I am doing now. My interest is to inquire into the nature of the Gods—whether they exist and in what ways we may find Them. You may well imagine—"

[Here the narrative was interrupted, and we return to Asinius Pollio's letter.]

At this moment the Dictator arose and murmuring, "Continue, my friend," began to cross the room. Catullus repeated, "You may well imagine," but had scarcely said the words when Caesar fell to the floor in a convulsion of the Sacred Malady. In his writhing he tore the bandages from his side and the floor was soon streaked with his blood. I had been present before at these seizures. I made a ball of the folds of his robe and placed it between his teeth. I directed Catullus to help me straighten his body and Clodia to bring all the robes she could find to warm him. Soon his babbling ceased and he fell into a deep sleep. We watched beside him for a time, then placed him in his litter and the poet and I accompanied him to his home.

Such were the events of Clodia's twice-interrupted dinner. Both my friends were to die within the year. The poet who had seen that greatness humbled in insanity wrote no more stinging epigrams against him. My master never alluded to his illness, but on several occasions he reminded me of the "happy occasion" when we dined with Clodia and Catullus.

Dawn has come as I have dictated these words. My pain has been forgotten or has abated, and I have acquitted myself of a debt which I have been owing my friends.

✦ BOOK TWO ✦

The reader is reminded that the documents in each Book begin at an earlier date than those in the preceding Book, traverse the time already covered, and continue on to a later date.

XXII   Anonymous Letter [*written by Servilia, mother of M. Junius Brutus*] to Caesar's wife.
        [*August 17.*]

Madam, it is not likely that the Dictator has yet informed you that the Queen of Egypt will soon arrive in Rome for an extended visit. Should you wish confirmation of this fact you have only to visit your villa on the Janiculan Hill. On the farther slope you will find workmen engaged in constructing an Egyptian temple and in elevating obelisks.

It is important that your attention be called to this visit and to its political dangers, for it is the subject of laughter around the world that you are completely inadequate to the high place you occupy and that your understanding of the political situation of Rome is no better than that of a child.

Cleopatra, madam, is the mother of a son by your husband. The boy's name is Caesarion. The Queen has kept him hidden from the eyes of her court, but continually spreads about the rumor that he is of divine intelligence and great beauty. The truth on very good authority, however, is that he is an idiot and that although he has passed his third birthday he is unable to talk and is scarcely able to walk.

The Queen's sole aim in coming to Rome is to legitimize her son to establish his succession to the mastery of the world. The plan is preposterous, but there are no limits to the ambition of Cleopatra. Her skill at intrigue and her ruthlessness—which did not stop short of the assassination of her uncle and of her brother-husband—and her ascendancy over your husband's lust are sufficient to bring confusion to the world even though she cannot dominate it.

This is not the first time that you have been publicly insulted by your husband's ostentatious adulteries. That his infatuation should blind him to the danger this woman brings to the public order is but another evidence of the senility which has begun to be apparent in his administration.

There is little you can do, madam, either to safeguard the State or to defend the dignity of your position. You should be informed, however, that the women of the aristocracy of Rome will refuse to be presented to this Egyptian criminal and will make no appearance at her court. Should you show a similar firmness you will be making some first steps in regaining the respect of the City which you have lost through your selection of friends and through the thoughtlessness of your conversation—a thoughtlessness which even your extreme youth cannot excuse.

XXIII Caesar's Journal—Letter to Lucius Mamilius Turrinus on the Island of Capri.
   [*About August 18.*]

942.   [*On Cleopatra and her visit to Rome.*]

Last year the Queen of Egypt began requesting permission to pay a visit to Rome. I finally granted it and have offered her for residence my villa across the river. She will stay at least a year in Italy. The whole matter is still a secret and will not be announced to the City until the very eve of her arrival. She is now approaching Carthage and should be here in about a month.

I confess that I look forward to this visit with much pleasure and not only for the reason which first leaps to the mind. She was a remarkable girl. Even at twenty she knew the loading capacity of each of the major wharves of the Nile; she could receive a deputation from Ethiopia and refuse all of its requests and make the refusals appear to be benefits. I have heard her scream at her ministers' stupidity during a discussion of the royal tax on ivory and she was not only right, but right with a wealth of detailed and ordered information. Indeed, she is one of the few persons I have known who have a genius for administration. She will have become a still more remarkable woman. Conversation, conversation will be a pleasure again. I shall be flattered, understood and flattered, in a realm where few are capable of understanding my achievements. What questions she asks! There are few pleasures equal to that of imparting to a voracious learner the knowledge that one has grown old and weary in acquiring. Conversation will be a pleasure again. Oh, oh, oh, I have sat holding that catlike bundle on my lap, drumming my fingers on ten brown toes and heard a soft voice from my shoulder asking me how to prevent banking houses from discouraging the industry of the people and what are the just wages of a chief of police relative to those of the governor of a city. Everyone in our world, my Lucius, everyone is lazy in mind except you, Cleopatra, this Catullus, and myself.

And yet she is lying, intriguing, intemperate, indifferent to the essential well-being of her people, and a lighthearted murderess. I have been receiving a series of anonymous letters warning me of her propensity to murder. I have no doubt that the lady is not long separated from a beautifully wrought cabinet of poisons; but I know also that at her table I need no taster. The prime object of her every thought is Egypt and I am its first security. If I should die, her country would fall a pray to my successors—patriots without practical judgment or administrators without imagination—and this she knows well. Egypt will never recover its greatness; but Egypt, for what it is, lives by me. I am a better ruler over Egypt than Cleopatra; but she shall learn much. During her stay in Rome I shall open her eyes to things that no Egyptian ruler has ever conceived of.

946. [*Again, on Cleopatra and her visit to Rome.*]
Cleopatra can never do a thing without pomp. She asked to be permitted to bring a court of two hundred and a household of a thousand, including a large royal guard. I have cut down these numbers to a court of thirty and a retinue of two hundred, and have told her that the Republic will undertake the responsibility of guarding her person and her party. I have directed, also, that outside of her palace grounds—my villa has already been renamed the Palace of Amenhotep—she may not employ the insignia of royalty except on the two occasions of her official welcome on the Capitoline Hill and of her official leave-taking.

She informed me that I was to appoint twenty ladies of the highest birth, headed by my wife and my aunt, to constitute for her a company of honor for the illustration of her court. I replied that the women of Rome are free to enter into whatever engagements of this kind they may wish to and I sent her a form of invitation which she might forward to them.

This did not please her. She replied that the extent of her domains, which are more than six times as large as Italy, her divine descent—which she now traces back, in the greatest detail through two thousand years to the Sun—entitle her to such a court and that it is unbecoming that she *request* the ladies of Rome to attend her receptions and routs. The matter rests there.

I have had a part in the formation of these swelling claims. When I first met her, she was proud to state that there was not one drop of Egyptian blood in her veins. This was obviously untrue; descent in the royal house to which she belongs had always been confused by substitutions and adoptions; the effects of consanguineous marriage having been fortunately mitigated by impotence on the part of the Kings and gallantry on the part of the Queens, and by the fact that the beauty of Egyptian women far surpassed that of the descendants of the Macedonian mountain brigands. Moreover, Cleopatra at that time, apart from participation in a limited number of traditional functions, had not deigned to interest herself in the customs of the ancient country over which she ruled. She had never seen the pyramids, nor such temples on the Nile as were farther removed than an afternoon's journey from her palace at Alexandria. I advised her to make public the fact that her mother's mother was not only an Egyptian but the true heir of the Pharaohs. I persuaded her to wear Egyptian costume at least half of the time and I took her on a journey to view the monuments of a civilization that dwarfed, by Hercules, the woven huts of her Macedonian ancestors. My instructions succeeded beyond my reckoning. She is now the true Pharaoh and the living incorporation of the Goddess Isis. All the documents of her court are in hieroglyphs to which she appends, in condescension, a Greek or Latin translation.

All this is as it should be. The adherence of a people is not acquired merely by governing them to their best interests. We rulers must spend a large part of our time capturing their imaginations. In the minds of the people, Fate is an ever-watching force, operating by magic and always malevolent. To counter its action we rulers must be not only wise but supernatural, for in their eyes human wis-

dom is helpless before magic. We must be at once the father they knew in their infancy who guarded them against
evil men and the priest who guarded them against evil
spirits.

Perhaps I have forgotten to tell you also that I directed
that she may bring in her train no child under five years,
neither hers nor one belonging to any member of her
company.

XXIV   Cleopatra, in Alexandia, to her Ambasador in
Rome.

[*August 20.*]

Cleopatra, the Everliving Isis, Child of the Sun, Chosen
of Ptah, Queen of Egypt, Cyrenaica, and Arabia, Empress
of the Upper and Lower Nile, Queen of Ethiopia, etc.,
etc., to her Faithful Minister.

Benediction and Favor

The Queen departs from Alexandria on the morrow for
Carthage.

On this journey she will present herself to her subjects
at Parastonium and Cyrene. She will rest at Carthage
awaiting your word as to the most suitable time for her
arrival in Rome.

You are directed to send to her at Carthage the following information:

A list of the Lay Directresses of the Mysteries of the
Good Goddess, and

A list of the votaries of Hestia—both lists with notes as
to their family relationships, earlier marriages, etc.

A list of the personal associates of the Dictator, men
and women, particularly those whom he visits or who are
visitors to his house for other than official reasons.

A list of the confidential servants in the Dictator's
house, with their length of service, previous employment,
and such details concerning their private lives as you can
discover. This study is to be continued by you at all times
and the Queen wishes to see further information when she
arrives in Italy.

A list of the children, living or dead, who at any time
have been attributed to the Dictator, together with their
supposed mothers and all relevant information.

An account of the previous visits of all Queens to

Rome, together with precedents of etiquette, ceremonial,
official receptions, gifts, etc.

The Queen trusts that you have not been negligent in in-
suring that her apartments will be sufficiently warmed.

XXV   Pompeia to Clodia at Baiae.
       [*August 24.*]

Dearest Mousie:
The invitation to dinner has just arrived and I'm saving
it until my husband comes home at dark. I am writing this
letter in haste to return by your messenger.

What I have to say is very *very confidential* and I hope
you'll destroy it the minute you've read it.

This is the secret: a *person* from the banks of the Nile
is going to spend a long visit in the City. There are certain
aspects of that visit that I do not *deign* to consider or discuss, particularly as the *political* aspects are of far greater
importance and danger than the personal ones. I hope it
will never be said of me that I regarded my *personal* life
as of the slightest importance compared to the world-wide
considerations which are inextricably bound up with the
situation I occupy. I am not sure whether you know that
this person has a son whom she *claims* to be of very high
Roman blood indeed. On that claim she bases hopes and
ambitions for the future greatness of her country which
are, of course, preposterous.

A Certain Person is, for *reasons,* completely blind to
these dangers, and I have no choice but to be doubly
clear-sighted. It may be that on two official occasions I
must permit this Egyptian criminal to be presented to me.
I shall indicate by my manner that I consider her presence
an impertinence and I shall be watchful for an opportunity
to humiliate her publicly and if possibly to force her to return to her own country. I shall, of course, refuse to put
my foot into the residence which has been loaned to her.

Do write me your thoughts on this matter. My cousin
will be returning here from Naples soon after you receive
this. Please send word by him.

Postscript: Everybody knows that she killed her uncle
and her husband, and that her brother was her husband
which is an Egyptian custom and is an example of what we
may expect.

Many thanks, my good, good friend, for entrusting the secret to me.

Your letter is very like you. How wise you are to look at the matter from all sides, and to see all the dangers that lie concealed behind the event you foretell. And how right and noble of you it is not to fly off into passionate indignation as so many other women would do.

May I make one small suggestion, however, and one which I would only make to you because only you *could* put it into effect? You might consider approaching this annoying visitor in another way. It occurs to me that if you conducted yourself—as only you can—with all the graciousness compatible with your dignity, how surprised she would be! In that way you could insinuate yourself into this visitor's circle; you could keep your eye on what is going on; and you could prevent the Other Person in the Case from completely forgetting himself.

I would not recommend this course to anyone but you, for it requires great skill. You could do it. Do think this over.

I long to talk to you about it—which will be very soon. In the meantime I send you my admiration and affection and this bottle of Sicilian perfume.

XXVI   Clodia, at Baiae, to Catullus in Rome.
       [*August 25.*]

My sister tells me I should write you a letter. A number of other people have appointed themselves to be your advocate and have told me that I should write you a letter.

Here, then is a letter. You and I long since agreed that letters are nothing. Yours tell me what I knew already or could well imagine, and they frequently depart from the rule which we had laid down that a letter should consist principally of facts.

Here are my facts:

The weather has been incomparable. There have been many parties on sea and on land. I leave all reunions which have been abandoned to conversation only and for which the host has made no plans for entertainment. It is not necessary to say that conversation is more than usually insupportable in the environment of Baiae.

I studied astronomy with Sosigenes and am henceforth the enemy of all poets who enlarge upon their own idiotic sentiments in the presence of the stars. I took up the study of the Egyptian language. When I discovered that it sounded like the babbling of infants and that its grammatical structures were at a level with its sounds I gave it up. We did a great deal of amateur theatricals in Greek and Latin. I worked many days with Cytheris. She refused all payment and returned a present I had sent to her. When I insisted that she receive some mark of my indebtedness she asked for a poem of yours in your handwriting. I gave her "The Wedding of Peleus and Thetis." She refused to take part in any plays, but she declaimed that poem most remarkably, and during my lessons with her she frequently rendered portions of the tragedies. My style is very different from hers but she is absolute mistress of her style. Marc Antony often joined us at the end of my lessons. There is only one pleasing thing about him, his laughter; he laughs all the time and yet it is not tiresome. When she is not talking about her art Cytheris is tiresome. She has the apathy of happy women. I discovered, though not from her, that she is one of the few persons who are permitted to visit Lucius Mamilius Turrinus on Capri. [*Clodia wrote to Turrinus, asking permission to visit him; she was courteously denied.*] I know a number of men whom I could love very much, if they were mutilated and blind. I went over Verus's new book of verses with him.

I made a number of new enemies. You know that I never lie and that I do not permit people to lie in my presence. I was, as you call it, "unfaithful to you" on a number of occasions. As I am unable to sleep at night, I sometimes arrange companionship for those hours.

Those are the facts concerning my life this summer and those are the answers to the questions contained in your extremely monotonous letters. On rereading them I find that you have given me very few facts. You have not been writing to me but to that image of me lodged in your head whom I have no wish to confront. The facts about you I have learned from my sister and your other advocates. You have paid visits to my sister and to Manilius and Livia [*Torquatus.*] You have taught their children how to swim and how to sail. You have taught their children how to train dogs. You have written reams of verses

88

for children, and another poem for a wedding. I tell you again you will lose your poetic gift, if you abuse it. Such verses can only increase the blemish that already mars so much of your work, that resort to colloquial terms and provincial expressions. Many people are already denying that you are even a Roman poet. You and I are agreed that Verus has not the basic talent which you have, but both in his manners and in his verses he has a uniform elegance and taste; while you continue to cultivate a *northern* uncouthness.

This letter, like all letters, is totally unnecessary. However, I have two more things to say: on the last day of September, my brother and I are giving a dinner and I hope you will be present. I have asked the Dictator and his wife. (Incidentally, I am told that you have been spitting some more epigrams; why do you not acknowledge that you know nothing and care nothing about politics? What possible satisfaction can you derive from making vulgar little noises in the shadow of that great man?) I have also asked his aunt, Cicero, and Asinius Pollio.

I am starting north on the eighth. I am bringing a number of friends with me, including Mela and Verus. We shall stop a number of days with Quintus Lentulus Spinther and Cassia at Capua. I suggest that you join us there on the ninth and return with us to the city a few days later.

Should you decide to come to Capua I beg of you to entertain no expectation of sharing my insomnia. For the tenth time I ask you to consider the nature of friendship, to learn its advantages and to abide within its limits. It makes no claims; it establishes no possession; it is not competitive. I have made some plans for my life during the coming year. I will differ widly from that of the year just passed. The dinner to which I have invited you will give you an idea of its character.

XXVI-A Catullus:

Miser Catulle, desinas ineptire
Et quod vides perisse perditum ducas.
Fulsere quondam candidi tibi soles,
Cum ventitabas quo puella ducebat,
Amata nobis quantum amabitur nulla.
Ibi illa multa tum iocosa fiebant;

Quae tu volebas nec puella nolebat.
Fulsere vere candidi tibi soles.
Nunc iam illa non volt; tu quoque inpotens, noli,
Nec quae fugit sectare, nec miser vive;
Sed obstinata mente perfer, obdura

At tu, Catulle, destinatus obdura

"Wretched Catullus, put an end to your raving
And that which you see to be lost, count it truly lost.
Radiant were the days that formerly shone upon you
When you hastened whither the girl led the way—
She who was loved by you and me as no woman will ever be loved.
Many then were the delights;
What you wished for she wished no differently.
Radiant indeed were the days that shone upon you.
Now she is of a different mind; you, being helpless, give up your longing;
Cease to pursue the fleeing and to live in wretchedness;
But endure with affirmed heart; hold fast.

You, Catullus, since these things are so, hold fast."

XXVI-B   The Commonplace Book of Cornelius Nepos.
[*This entry is of a later date.*]

"Do you not find it extraordinary," I asked, "that Catullus should let these poems pass from hand to hand? I can think of no precedent for so candid a revelation."

"Everything there is extraordinary," replied Cicero, raising his eyebrows and lowering his voice as though we were being overhead. "Have you remarked that he is constantly holding a dialogue with himself? Whose is this other voice that is so often addressing him—this voice that urges him to 'bear up' and to 'pull himself together'? Is that his genius? Is that some other-self? Oh, my friend, I resist this poetry as long as I can. There is something indecorous about it. Either it is the raw experience of life which has not yet sufficiently made its transmutation into poetry or it is a new kind of sensibility. His grandmother, I am told, was from the North Country; perhaps these are the first airs blowing on our literature from the Alps. They are not Roman. Before these verses a Roman does not know where to rest his glance; a Roman blushes. Nor is it Greek. Poets before now have told us of their sufferings, but their sufferings are already half-healed by song. But these!—there is no mitigation. This man is not afraid to acknowledge that he suffers. Perhaps that is because he shares it in dialogue with his genius. But what is this other-self? Have you one? Have I one?"

XXVII   Caesar in Rome to Cleopatra in Carthage.
         [*The following letter, in the Dictator's hand, ac-
         companied a formal greeting on the Queen's ap-
         proach to Rome.*]
         [*September 3.*]

August Queen, it gives me no pleasure to add to this most sincere message of welcome the following injunctions: I must remind you that I place much importance on the conditions you agreed to when this visit to Rome was planned. I refer to the number of persons in your retinue, the regulations concerning the arboring of royal insignia, and to the requirement that there shall be no child under five years of age in your company. Should you fail to observe this agreement I shall be obliged to distress myself and to distress you by taking action derogatory to your dignity and inconsonant with the esteem I bear you. Should there be any children now in your company you will either leave them at Carthage or return them to Egypt.

Do not allow the severity of my words, however, to mislead you as to the great satisfaction with which I look forward to your stay in Rome. Rome gains heightened interest for me when I think that I shall be soon showing it to the Queen of Egypt, the Rome that is here now and the Rome that I am planning. The world holds but a few rulers, and among them but a small number who have any inkling of what it is to direct the fortunes of nations. The Queen of Egypt is great in genius as she is great in position.

The condition of leadership adds new degrees of solitariness to the basic solitude of mankind. Every order that we issue increases the extent to which we are alone, and every show of deference which is extended to us separates us from our fellows. In looking forward to the Queen's

91

visit I promise myself a mitigation of the solitude in which I live and work.

I have this morning made a visit to the palace which is being prepared for the Queen. Nothing is being left undone which would minister to her comfort.

XXVII-A   First Reply to the Above Letter. Cleopatra to Caesar.

> [*In hieroglyphs, preceded by the Queen's titles, descent, etc., on an enormous sheet of papyrus, followed by the Latin translation; sent through the Roman administration's messenger service in advance of the royal progress.*]
> [*September 2.*]

The Queen of Egypt has directed me, her unworthy chamberlain, to acknowledge the reception of the Dictator's letter and presents.

The Queen of Egypt thanks the Dictator for the presents she has received.

XXVII-B   Second Reply. Cleopatra to Caesar.

> [*Sent from the royal ship on its arrival at Ostia, October 1.*]

The Dictator has sent the Queen of Egypt a letter on the difficulties of being a monarch.

There are others.

A Queen, great Caesar, may be a mother. Her royal position renders her more, not less, subject to those loving anxieties which all mothers feel, particularly if their children are of delicate health and affectionate disposition. You have told me that you were, in your time, a loving parent. I believed you. You defended yourself to me against the charge that you permitted reasons of state to force you to deal unfeelingly with your daughter. [*Apparently at the instigation of her father, Julia broke her engagement to one man in order to marry Pompey. She died before the Civil War arose between Caesar and Pompey, but the marriage was a completely happy one.*]

Unfeelingly you have dealt with me, and not only with me but with a child who is no ordinary child, being the son of the greatest man in the world. He has returned to Egypt.

You have described to me the solitude of a ruler. A ruler has reason to feel that most of the approaches made to him are colored with self-interest. It is not the danger of rulers to increase this solitude by ascribing to others that motivation alone? I can imagine a ruler turned to stone by such a view of his fellow men and turning to stone all those who approach him.

As I approach the city I wish to say to its master that I am the Queen and the servant of Egypt and that my country's fortunes are never absent from my mind, but that I would feel myself less than royal did I not recognize also that I am a mother and a woman.

To return to you your own words: *Do not allow the severity of my tone, in the words I have just written, to mislead you as to the satisfaction with which I look forward to my stay in Rome.*

I ascribed the ungentleness of your conduct to the fact that you have, indeed, created for yourself a solitude that is excessive even for the ruler of a world. You have said that it may be possible that I might lighten that burden.

XXVII   Catullus to Clodia, in Rome.
         [*The following two letters, probably written on Sept. 11 or 12, were never sent. They are the drafts for the letter already given as Document XIII. Catullus did not destroy them at once, for two weeks later they were discovered in the poet's rooms by Caesar's secret police and copies of them were forwarded to the Dictator.*]

Kill me outright—since that is what you desire—I cannot kill myself—it is as though my eyes were bound on some play, as though I were watching breathlessly—to see what new horror you would devise. I cannot kill myself until I have seen the last terrifying exposure of what you are—what are you?—murderess—torturer—mountain of lies—laughter—mask—traitor—traitor of our whole human race.

Must I hang on this cross and not die—watching you for eternities?

To whom can I turn? To whom can I cry? Do the Gods exist? Have you shrieked them from the skies?

Immortal Gods, did you then send this monster to the

earth to teach us something? That beauty of form is but a sack of evils? That love is a hatred in disguise?

No—no—that lesson I will not take from you—the opposite is true—I shall never know love; but by you I know that love exists.

You came into the world—a monster and an assassin—to kill the Loving—you laid a treacherous ambush and with laughter and a howl you raised the ax to kill the part in me that lives and loves—the Immortal Gods will aid me to recover from my horror—that you in the disguise of the Lovable are moving about among men, waiting for occasion to inspire love and to slay it—it was me you selected for this assassination—me who have one life to live and one love to love and who shall never love again.

But know—exhalation of Hell—that though you have killed the one love I have to give, you have not killed my belief in love. By that belief I know you for what you are.

There is no need for me to curse you—the murderer survives the victim only to learn that it was himself that he longed to be rid of. Hatred is self-hatred. Clodia is locked with Clodia in eternal loathing.

XXVIII-A   Catullus to Clodia.

I know, I know that you never promised to be constant.

How often—with the ostentatious honesty of the dishonest—you broke a kiss to affirm your independence of all engagement. You swore you loved me, and laughed and warned me that you would not love me forever.

I did not hear you. You were speaking in a language I did not understand. Never, never, can I conceive of a love which is able to foresee its own termination. Love *is* its own eternity. Love is in every moment of its being: all time. It is the only glimpse we are permitted of what eternity is. So I did not hear you. The words were nonsense. You laughed and I laughed too. We were pretending that we were not to love forever. We were laughing at all those millions in the world who are Pretenders to Love, who know well that their love will have a termination.

But I put you forever out of my mind I think of you once more:

What will become of you?

What woman in the world walked in such love as I gave to you?

Insane one, do you know what you have thrown away?

While the God of Love gazed at you through my eyes age could not touch your beauty. While we spoke to you, your ears could not hear the tongues of the world, envy and detraction and all the gusts that are blown about in the malignant air of our human state: while we loved you you could not know the solitude of the soul—does that mean nothing to you? Insane one, do you know what you have thrown away?

But that is not all. Your state is a thousand times worse. Now you are revealed; your secret is out. Since I know it, you can no longer hide it from yourself: you are the eternal assassin of life and love. But how terrifying to you must be the knowledge of your failure, for you have made clear the greatness and the majesty of your enemy, love.

All, all that Plato said was true.

It was not I, I in myself, who loved you. When I looked at you the God Eros descended upon me. I was more than myself. The God lived in me, looked through my eyes and spoke through my lips. I was more than myself and when your soul was aware that the God was in me, gazing at you, for a time you too were filled with the God. Have you not told me so? In what hours, in what whispers have you not told me so.

But you could not long endure this presence, for you came into the world, a monster and an assassin, to kill all the lives and loves. You wear the disguise of the Lovable and you live only to prepare one treacherous ambush after another; you live only for the moment when with laughter and a shriek you may lift the ax and slay the promise of life and the promise of love.

I am no longer breathless with horror. I have ceased trembling. I can muse with wonder, asking myself where you obtained the passionate hatred of life and why the Gods permit this enemy of the world to move about among us. I will never feel pity for you, this horror has no room for pity. Some great intention for the world's enlightenment stirred in you and was poisoned at the source.

I loved you and I shall never be the same again, but what is my state compared to yours?

XXVIII-B   Catullus.

O di, si vestrum est misereri, aut si quibus unquam
Extremam iam ipsa in morte tulistis opem,

95

Me miserum aspicite et, si vitam puriter egi
    Eripite hanc pestem perniciemque mihi,
Quae mihi subrepens imos ut torpor in artus
    Expulit ex omni pectore laetitias.
Non iam illud quaero, contra ut me diligat illa,
    Aut, quod non potis est, esse pudica velit;
Ipse valere opto et taetrum hunc deponere morbum.
    O di, reddite mi hoc pro pietate mea.

"Oh, immortal Gods, if pity be among your attributes,
Or if ever you have brought supreme aid to one already at
  the point of death,
Turn your eyes upon me, a most wretched man, and if I
  have lived a pure life,
Tear out from my heart this plague, this pestilence
Which, stealing like a lethargy throughout my deepest fi-
bers
Has driven all joy from my breast.
I no longer ask that this woman return my love
Nor—for that is impossible—that she be chaste;
All I aspire to is that I be healed and that this black
  malady be removed.
Oh, immortal Gods—grant this in return for my devo-
tion."

XXIX   Caesar to Cornelius Nepos.
      [September 23.]

This letter is confidential.

I have been informed that you are a friend of the poet
Gaius Valerius Catullus.

Word has reached me in a very direct way that the poet
has been ill or at least in extreme distress of mind.

I have been a friend of his father for many years and
although I have had few occasions of meeting the poet
himself I follow his work with much interest and admiration. I wish that you would call upon him and send me
word as to his condition. In addition, I should feel very indebted to you if you would report to me, at any time and
at any hour, that you find him ill or in any kind of distress.

The esteem in which I hold you and your work leads
me to add that I should feel it to be an unkindness did

you or your family not keep me informed of any ill-fortune (which the immortal Gods avert) that might befall you or yours. At a very early age I was convinced that the true poets and historians are the highest ornaments of a country; this conviction has only increased with time.

XXIX-A   Cornelius Nepos to Caesar.

It is a satisfaction to know that the great leader of the Roman people feels concern for the health of my friend and fellow countryman Catullus and has expressed himself in friendly terms toward me and my household.

It is true that some ten days ago a member of the Aemilian Draughts and Swimming Club, where the poet resides, called on me in the middle of the night saying that Catullus's condition was causing alarm to his friends. I hurried to his rooms and found him in pain and in delirium. A doctor Sosthenes, the Greek, was administering emetics and then calmatives. My friend did not recognize me. We sat with him through the night. In the morning he was much improved. Gathering himself together with resolution he thanked us for our attentions and assured us that his illness was at an end and requested us to leave him. I returned later in the afternoon and found him in untroubled sleep. He was awakened soon after by a clumsy messenger bringing a letter from that woman who plays no small part in the troubles we had been witnessing—as his delirium had attested. In my presence he read the letter and remained a long time silent in deep thought. He made no reference to what he had read but against all persuasion dressed in formal attire and left the Club.

I have given the Dictator these details in order that he may make his own observations.

XXX   Caesar's Journal—Letter to Lucius Mamilius Turrinus on the Island of Capri.

991.   [*On Cleopatra and her visit to Rome.*]
The Queen of Egypt is approaching. Missy Crocodile is being fanned across the straits.

My correspondence with Majesty has been as spirited as could be expected. Her Latin is broken, but I notice that she manages to achieve precision when an occasion requires it.

I do not expect a literal obedience to the regulations that I have laid down governing her visit here. The Queen is incapable of complying precisely with any direction that may be given her. Even when she believes herself to be obeying implicitly, she manages to admit a deviation or two. I must expect this. I confess that I am charmed by this invariable variation, though I have been obliged before now to show her a stern face on it. It is prompted by her unfathomable pride and by the independence of a woman who is herself accustomed to punish any slightest disobedience by death.

Her letters—even in one conjuncture, her silence—have delighted me. She is indeed a woman now and a most queenly one. At moments I find myself dreaming that she is more woman than queen and must arrest my thoughts.

Cleopatra is Egypt. No word she lets fall and no caress she dispenses is without a political implication. Each conversation is a treaty and every kiss a pact. I could wish that association with her did not require so constant a vigilance and that her favors had more abandon and less art.

It is many years, many years, however, since I have known a disinterested friendship on the part of anyone except yourself, my aunt, and my soldiers. Even in my home I seem to be playing a perpetual game of draughts. I lose a "man"; I am menaced from the flank; I rally to a sortie; I capture a "horseman." My good wife seems to derive some pleasure from this skirmishing, though it is not conducted without tears.

Nay more, it is many years since I have felt directed toward me a disinterested hatred. Day by day I scan my enemies looking with eager hope for the man who hates me "for myself" or even "for Rome." I am much condemned for surrounding myself with unscrupulous adventurers who enrich themselves from the appointments I accord them. Yes, I sometimes think that it is the candor of their greed that pleases me; they do not pretend to love me for myself. I shall go so far as to say that I have occasionally been moved to pleasure when one or other of them lets fall an expression of his contempt for me—in that ocean of flattery in which I live and move.

It is difficult, my dear Lucius, to escape becoming the person which others believe one to be. A slave is twice enslaved, once by his chains and once again by the glances that fall upon him and say "thou slave." A dictator is believed to be niggardly of benefits, incalculable in displeasure, jealous of capable men, athirst for flattery, and not ten but twenty times a day I feel myself drifting toward those qualities and must draw back sharply. And ten times a day, as I await the arrival of the Queen of Egypt, I find myself dreaming of the possibility that she, now grown a woman, can see that all that I can give to her and to her country I give outright; that she need not contrive to obtain it; that all the devices within her power cannot obtain what it is unsuitable to accord her; and that these things being understood, we may move in a realm that is ... but am drifting beyond the possible.

XXXI   Cicero, in Rome, to Atticus in Greece.

[This letter aroused much merriment and derision in antiquity and in the Middle Ages. It is perhaps apocryphal. We know that Cicero wrote Atticus a letter concerning marriage and that in the two succeeding letters he implored his friend to destroy it—which Atticus would certainly have done. On the other hand, there have come down to us over a dozen versions of what might well have been the letter in question. All these differ widely among themselves and all are larded with obviously burlesque interpolations. We here select the passages which the majority of the versions have in common, our theory being that a secretary of Atticus probably made a copy of the original letter before its destruction and that this copy began circulating surreptitiously throughout the Roman world.

[It should be remembered that Cicero not only divorced his universally respected wife Terentia after many years of increasingly contentious marriage, but that he promptly married and divorced his rich young ward Publilia; that Cicero's brother Quintus had long been stormily married to Atticus's sister Pomponia whom he had recently divorced; and that Cicero's beloved daughter Tullia had been none too happily married to Dolabella, an ambitious and dissolute friend of Caesar whom her mother had selected for her.]

One marriage in a hundred is happy, my friend. This is one of those things which everyone knows and which no one says. No wonder that the exceptional marriage is widely celebrated for it is the exceptional which makes news. But it is a part of the folly of our human race that we are forever tempted to elevate the exception into the norm. We are attracted to the exception, for every man thinks himself exceptional and destined for the exceptional; and our young men and women advance into marriage under the assumption that ninety-nine are happy and one unhappy, or that they are marked for the exceptional happiness.

Given the nature of women and the nature of the passion which draws men and women together, what chance has marriage of being happier than the combined torments of Sisyphus and Tantalus?

By marriage we place into the hands of women the governance of our household which they promptly extend, as far as they are able, to an interest over all our goods. They rear our children and thereby acquire a share in the disposition of the children's affairs when they have reached maturity. In all these matters they pursue ends totally opposed to those a man envisages. Women wish only the warmth of a hearth and the shelter of a roof. They live in fear of catastrophe and no security is sufficiently secure for them and in their eyes the future is not only unknown but catastrophic. To forfend those unknown evils there is no deception to which they will not resort, no rapacity they will not exert, and no other pleasure or enlightenment they will not combat. Had civilization been left in the hands of women we should still be housed in the caves of mountains and man's invention would have ceased with the domestication of fire. All they ask of a cave beyond its shelter is that it be a degree more ostentatious than that of a neighbor's wife; and all they ask for their children's happiness is that they be secure in a cave similiar to their own.

Marriage inevitably commits us to extended examples of our wives' conversation. Now the conversation of women within the married relationship—I do not now speak of that other crucifixion, their conversation at social gatherings—behind all the disguises of guile and incoherence treats of only these two subjects: conservation and ostentation.

It shares a characteristic of the conversation of slaves,

and logically so, for the position of women in our world has much in common with that of slaves. This may be regrettable but I would not be among those who would apply themselves to altering it. The conversation of slaves and women is directed by ruse. Guile and violence are the sole resorts available to the dispossessed; and violence on the part of slaves can only be resorted to through close consolidation with their fellow unfortunates. Against such consolidation the state rightly maintains a constant vigilance and the slave is driven to seek his ends by guile. The recourse to violence is likewise closed to women because they are incapable of consolidation; they distrust one another like Greeks and with good reason. Hence, they, too, resort to ruse. How often in visiting my villas and conferring all day with my foremen and laborers I have retired to bed as exhausted as though I had wrestled with each, body and mind at the alert lest I be crippled or robbed. The slave introduces the aims he has in mind from every direction and by every indirection; there is no trap for concession that he does not employ, no flattery, no show of logic, no pressure on fear or avarice; and all this to avoid building a pergola, to eliminate an inferior, to enlarge his cottage, or to obtain a new coat.

Such too is the conversation of woman; but how much more diverse her aims, how much wider her resources of attack, and how much more deeply rooted her passion to attain her ends.

For the most part, a slave merely desires conveniences; but behind a woman's wishes lie forces which are for her the very nature of life itself: the conservation of property; the esteem in which she is held by those matrons of her acquaintance whom she despises and dreads; the claustration of a daughter, whom she wishes to be ignorant, joyless, and brutified. So deeply rooted are a woman's aims that they have to her the character of self-evident truth and unshakable wisdom. Hence, she can feel only contempt for any opinion that opposes her own. Reason is unnecessary and trifling to one so endowed; she is deaf in advance. A man may have saved the State, directed the affairs of a world, and acquired an undying fame for wisdom, but to his wife he is a witless fool.

> [*Here follows a paragraph about the sexual relationship. It has been so distorted by the glee and invention of copyists and transmitters that it is impossible to determine the original text.*]

These things are not often said, though occasionally the poets reveal them—those same poets who are primarily responsible for the delusion that marriage is a heaven and who betray us into seeking the Perilous Exception. Euripides left no word of it untold in the *Medea*. Little wonder that the Athenians drove him from Athens with imprecations for telling such truths. The mob was led by Aristophanes who has shown that he knew these things—though with less candor; he stifled his knowledge in order to hound from the city a greater poet. And Sophocles! What husband has not smiled grimly to himself before the scene where Jocasta heaps lies on lies, putting a fair face on a calamitous situation. Notable example of that so-called conjugal love that will conceal any fact from a husband in order to maintain an ostensible contentment; bold illustration that for mentality a wife can barely distinguish a husband from a son.

Oh, my friend, let us console ourselves with philosophy. There is a realm where they have never entered; indeed, in which they never have taken the faintest interest. Let us welcome that old age which frees us from that desire for their embraces—embraces which must be paid for at the cost of all order in our lives and any tranquility in our minds.

XXXII. Abra, Pompeia's Maid, to Clodia.
        [*October 1.*]

I have been in great anxiety, honored Madam, concerning yourself and your house and concerning our Master after the attempt on his life. Madam, all has been in great dismay here; the house always full of visitors and police and my mistress at her wits' end. Himself, praise the Immortal Gods, woke up at noon and seemed none the worse; in fact, very merry which made my mistress most angry. He was very hungry and ate and ate and the doctor protested and my mistress got down on her knees and begged him not to eat. But he made such jokes that we had all we could do to keep straight faces.

I heard him say to everybody standing around, Madam, that he never enjoyed a dinner more than the one he enjoyed at your house. The General Marc Antony said why and he said because the company was so good. And, begging your pardon, Marc Antony said you mean Claudilla and himself said Claudilla is an extraordinary woman. I hope I am correct in telling things like this to Madam.

Now I should tell Madam that he announced to all who came in during the day that Cleopatra, she that is queen of Egypt, will arrive today or tomorrow.

[*October 6.*]

The Master was not home last night, the first time in a very long time and everybody has their ideas.

The Queen has sent my mistress the most wonderful presents, especially one the most wonderful thing ever seen. Some workmen came yesterday in great secrecy and set it up and put it in motion. It is an Egyptian palace, Madam, no higher than one's knee. And when you take off the front wall you can see all the people inside and there is a barnyard and a royal procession and in the most beautiful clothes and colors. But that is not all. When you start water running, this is hard to explain, Madam, the little people all move, the Queen and all her court walk into the house, *up the stairs, yes,* and through the house and the animals go and drink in the Nile and a crocodile swims *against the water,* and the women weave and fishers fish and, Immortal Gods, I cannot tell all that they do. One could look at it forever. My mistress was very delighted and had lights brought and we thought she would never go to bed. Everybody says how clever it was of the Queen, because my mistress forgot everything when she was watching this palace and she forgot that her husband was not at home.

[*October 8.*]

Yesterday the Queen came to visit my mistress. We thought she would wear very fine clothes, but she just wore a blue dress and not a single jewel, so she must know the law about them. Her hair was not dressed at all, madam, just anyhow and I had taken two hours with mistress's. My mistress thanked her for the toy palace and then the whole time was taken up in explaining it. The Queen is very simple. She even knew my name and explained things to me. But as my mistress's secretary said you can see that she's thinking all the time. When the Master he came home, he asked how did it go and my mistress very dignified said why very well, what did you think? Oh, Madam, you should see my Master these days. It is like having ten boys in the house. He is always teasing my mistress and pinching her.

103

XXXIII   Cornelius Nepos: Commonplace Book.
       [*October 3.*]

The Queen of Egypt has arrived. She was received at Ostia by a deputation from the City and the Senate but refused to disembark because the Dictator's insigne was not present among the welcoming guidons. This was reported to Caesar who hastily dispatched Asinius Pollio to the port bearing his trophies. She then came to Rome, traveling by night.

The Queen has received no one and is reported to be indisposed. She has, however, sent magnificent presents to some thirty persons of note.

       [*October 5.*]

The Queen was received at the Capitoline today. The magnificence of her train exceeded anything ever seen in the City. To me at a distance she seemed very beautiful; Alina [*his wife*], having a view of better advantage [*probably sitting among the votaresses of Hestia*] and being a woman, reports that she is decidedly plain, having cheeks so plump that they are condemned as "jowls." Gossips report that there was a fierce struggle with the Dictator in regard to her costume. The Queens of Egypt, in dress of ceremony, apparently through identification with the Goddess Isis, wear no garments above the girdle. Caesar insisted that she cover her bosom according to the Roman usage, and it was done though lightly. She made a short speech in broken Latin, a longer one in Egyptian. The Dictator replied in Egyptian and Latin. The omens at the sacrifice were extremely favorable.

XXXIII-A   Cicero in Rome to his Brother.
       [*October 8.*]

The words "Queen of Egypt" cast a deep spell, my friend, but not upon me.

I have corresponded for a number of years with this Queen; I have done innumerable services for her chancellery. It can be presumed that she knows my interests and my disposition and my services to this Republic. Arriving in this city she distributes presents to every clerk in the backstairs of government, gifts of a splendor that are suitable only from one royalty to another. To me she sent another such gift. It could feed Sicily for a year; but what have I to do with jeweled headdresses and emerald cats. By the Immortal Gods, I let her steward, the blockhead Hammonios, know that I am not a drunken actor and that I am a man who more values a gift by its appropriateness than by its expense. "Has the library at Alexandria no manuscripts?" I asked him.

The spell cast by this Queen is greatly diminished by the closer view. I indulge a theory that each of us has one age in life toward which we are directed as iron filings are directed toward the north. Marc Antony is forever sixteen and the discrepancy between that age and his present years makes for an increasingly sorry view. My good friend Brutus has been a deliberative and judicious fifty since the age of twelve. Caesar is at forty—a Janus looking toward youth and age, irresolute. By this law, young though she is, Cleopatra is a woman of forty-five, which renders what youthful charms she possesses embarrassing. Her plumpness is the plumpness of a woman who has had eight children. Her walk and port is much admired but not by me. She is twenty-four; her walk is the walk of a woman trying to give the impression that she is twenty-four.

One must be on the alert to recognize these things, however. The prestige of her title; the magnificence of her dress; the effect of her two signal advantages—namely, her fine eyes and the beauty of her speaking voice—subdue the unwary.

XXXIV   Letter and Questionnaire: Cleopatra to Caesar.
         [*October 9.*]

My *Deedja, Deedja, Deedja—Crocodeedja* is very unhappy-happy, very happy-unhappy. Happy that she is to see her *Deedja* on the night of the twelfth, all the night of the twelfth, and unhappy that the night of the twelfth is a thousand years away. When I am not with my *Deedja* I sit weeping. I tear my robe to pieces, I wonder why I am here, why I am not in Egypt, what I am doing in Rome. Everybody hates me; everybody sends me letters wishing me dead. Cannot my *Deedja* come before the twelfth? Oh, *Deedja,* life is short, love is short; why cannot we see one another? All day and night other people are seeing my *Deedja*. Do they love him more than I do? Does he love them more than he loves me? No, no, there is nothing in the world that I love more than my *Deedja*, my *Deedja* in my arms, my *Deedja* happy, happy, happy in my arms. Separation is cruel, separation is waste, separation is meaningless.

But if my *Deedja* wishes it so I weep; I do not understand, but I weep and wait for the twelfth. But I must write a letter every day. And on my *Deedja*, write me a letter every day. I cannot sleep when night comes after a day when I have had no real letter from you. Every day there are your presents with five words. I kiss them; I hold them long; but when there is no real letter with the presents I cannot love them.

I must write a letter every day to tell my *Deedja* that I love only him, and think only of him. But there are other tiresome little things I must ask him, too. Things I must know so that I will be a dignified guest worthy of his protection. Forgive *Crocodeedja* these little tiresome questions.

1. At my party, at my rout, I go to the lowest step of my throne to welcome my *Deedja's* wife. Do I also go to the lowest step to meet my *Deedja's* aunt? What do I do to welcome the consuls and the consuls' wives?

> [*Caesar's answer:* Hitherto all queens have come to the lowest step. I am changing all that. My wife and my aunt will be with me. You will meet us at the arch. Your throne will not be raised by eight steps, but by one. All other guests you will greet standing before your throne. This arrangement may seem to rob you of the dignity of eight steps, but eight steps are not a dignity for those who must descend them and you would have to descend them to welcome the consuls who are or have been sovereigns. Think this over and you will see that *Deedja* is right.]

2. The Lady Servilia has not replied to my invitation. *Deedja*, you understand that I cannot suffer that. I know ways to enforce her attendance and I must use them.

> [*Caesar's answer:* I do not understand you. The Lady Servilia will be present.]

3. If it's a cold night, I shall not move an inch from my

braziers or I shall perish. But where can I get enough braziers for my guests at the water-ballet?

> [*Caesar's answer:* Furnish the ladies of your court with braziers. We Italians are accustomed to the cold and we dress to warm ourselves.]

4. In Egypt royalty does not receive dancers and theater people. I am told I should invite the actress Cytheris, that she is received by many patricians, and that your nephew or cousin Marc Antony goes nowhere without her. Must I invite her? Indeed, must I invite *him?*—he comes every day to my court; he has very impudent eyes; I am not accustomed to being laughed at.

> [*Caesar's answer:* Yes, and more than invite her: learn to know her. She is the daughter of a carter but there is no woman of the highest aristocracy who could not learn from her what dignity, charm, and deportment are.
>
> You will soon discover all the reasons for my admiration of her. In addition I am indebted to her for a personal reason: her long association with my relative Marc Antony has given me, in him, a friend. We men are for the most part what you woman make us—and women too; for men cannot remake a woman who is herself ill-made. Marc Antony was and always will be the best athlete and the best-liked athlete in a provincial school. Ten years ago a few moments of sober conversation exhausted him and he would be fretting to balance three tables on his chin. Wars themselves employed but a fraction of his thoughtless energy. Rome lived under the menace of practical jokes which did not stop short of setting fires to entire blocks, to loosing all the boats on the riverside, and to stealing the garments of a Senate. He had no malice; but he had no judgment. All this Cytheris has remade; she has taken nothing away, but has rearranged the elements in a different order. I am surrounded by and hate those reformers who can only establish an order by laws which repress the subject and drain him of his joy and aggression. The Cato and the Brutus envision a state of industrious mice; and in the poverty of their imaginations they charge me with the same thing. Happy would I be if it could be said of me that

like Cytheris I could train the unbroken horse without robbing him of the fire in his eye and the delight in his speed. And has not Cytheris had a fair reward? He will go no place without her, and with reason, for he will find no better company.

But I must close. A deputation from Lusitania has been waiting this half hour to protest against my cruelty and injustice. Tell Charmian to put all in readiness for a visitor tonight. He will enter, dressed as a night guard, through the Alexandrian port. Tell Charmian that it will be nearer sunrise than sunset; but as soon as ardor at war with prudence can effect it. Let the great Queen of Egypt, the phoenix of women, sleep; she will be awakened by no ungentle hand. Yes, life is short; separation is insane.]

XXXIV-A Cytheris, the actress, at Baiae, to Cicero, at his villa near Tusculum.
[*This letter, written the previous year, is append-ed here to illustrate further the subject treated in Question 4 of the preceding questionnaire.*]

The Lady Cytheris presents her profound respects to the greatest advocate and orator which the world has seen and to the savior of the Roman republic.

As you know, honored sir, the Dictator has directed that a collection of your witticisms be prepared for publi-cation. Word has reached me that the collection contains an account of the table conversation carried on at the din-ner which Marc Antony gave in your honor some three years ago and includes some remarks of mine which now appear to be disrespectful of the Dictator.

I implore you, encouraged by the generous words which you have so frequently and graciously bestowed on me, to remove any such expressions as may be ascribed to me at that time.

It is true that during the Civil Wars I felt differently toward the Dictator. My two brothers and my husband fought against him and my husband lost his life. Since then the Dictator, however, has pardoned my brothers, with the clemency that distinguishes him; he has given them lands, he has introduced reforms into our troubled state; he has won our hearts and our loyalties.

Next year I am retiring from the stage. My retirement and my old age would be rendered a misery by the thought that these impatient words of mine were in circulation, and in the wide circulation destined for any work that bears your illustrious name.

This misery you alone could spare me. As a token of my gratitude and my admiration, kindly accept the manuscript which I enclose. It is the prologue which Menander wrote for his "The Shipwrecked Girl" and is in his own hand.

XXXV   Caesar to Clodia.
        [*October 10*.]

It is with regret that I see that appeals will be lodged with me urging that you be excluded from a reunion which includes all the respected women in Rome. No reports have yet reached my attention that would justify your exclusion.

There is, however, another matter I must lay before you. I read many letters which were never intended for my eyes and whose writers and recipients are not aware of my knowledge.

No blame attaches to a woman who being loved is unable to love in return. In such a situation, however, a woman knows well the ways in which she may intensify or mitigate the sufferings of her suitor. I am referring to the poet Catullus, whose gifts to Rome are not of less consequence than those of her rulers and whose composure of mind I feel to be among my responsibilities.

Threats constitute a weapon all too easily placed at the hand of a man in power. I employ them seldom. Yet there arise cases when those in authority are aware that neither the persuasion of reason nor the appeal to mercy can alter the mistaken conduct of a child or of a wrong doer. When threats are of no avail, punishment must follow.

You may judge that the right action requires your retiring from the City for a time.

XXXV-A   Clodia to Caesar.

The Lady Clodia Pulcher has received the letter of the Dictator, not without surprise. The Lady Clodia Pulcher requests permission of the Dictator to remain in Rome until the day following the reception of Cleopatra, Queen of Egypt; thereafter she will retire to her villa in the country until December.

XXXVI. Caesar to Cleopatra: From the daily letters.
[*Second half of October.*]

> [*In Egyptian. Many of the words of this letter are unknown today and are here supplied by conjecture. They are probably in the* argot *of the Alexandrian waterfront taverns and were acquired by Caesar during the riotous excursions made into that underworld during Caesar's stay there a few years before.*]

Tell Charmian to open this package carefully.

I stole it. I haven't stolen anything since the age of nine and have been experiencing all the sensations of the housebreaker and the snatcher of purses. I see that I am now setting out upon that road of prevarication and play acting which is the criminal's part. [*It has been suggested that Caesar may have robbed his wife's dressing table of a bottle of perfume.*]

But what would I not do for the great Queen of Egypt? I have not only become a thief; I have become an idiot. I can think only of her. I blunder in my work. I forget names; I mislay papers. My secretaries are in a consternation; I can hear them whispering behind my back. I make visitors wait; I postpone tasks—all this that I may hold long conversations with the everliving Isis, with the Goddess, with the witch who has stolen my mind away. There is no drunkenness equal to that of remembering whispered words in the night. There is nothing in the world that can compare with the great Queen of Egypt.

[*In Latin.*]

Where is my wise *Deedja,* my good *Deedja,* my most intelligent *Deedja?*—Why is she so unwise, so obstinate, so cruel to herself and to me?

My pearl, my lotus, if our Roman wheat paste disagrees with you *why will you eat it?*

It disagrees with all Easterners. It disagreed with your

110

father. It disagreed with Queen Anes'ta. We Romans are brutish. We can eat anything. I pray of you, I implore you: be wise. I pray that you are not suffering; but I am, I am. My messenger will wait until Charmian sends me back some report about you. Oh, star and phoenix, take good care of yourself; be wise.

You turned my doctor away from your door. Could you not let him see you? Could you not talk to him for *one moment?* You tell me your Egyptian medical knowledge is ten thousand years old and that we Romans are children. Yes, yes, but—I must speak severely with you—your doctors are ten thousand years old in nonsense. Think, think for a moment about medicine. Doctors are mostly impostors. The older a doctor is and the more venerated he is, the more he must pretend to know everything. Of course, they grow worse with time. Always look for a doctor who is hated by the best doctors. Always seek out a bright young doctor before he comes down with nonsense. *Deedja*, tell me you will see my Sosthenes.

I am helpless. Take care of yourself. I love you.

Oh, yes. I obey the Queen of Egypt. I do everything she tells me to do.

The top of my head has been purple all day.

Visitor after visitor has looked at me with horror, but no one has asked me what was the matter with me. That is what it is to be a Dictator: no one asks him a question about himself. I could hop on one foot from here to Ostia and back and no one would mention it—*to me*.

At last a cleaning woman came in to wash the floor. *She* said: "Oh, divine Caesar, what is the matter with your head?"

"Little mother," I said, "the greatest woman in the world, the most beautiful woman in the world, the wisest woman in the world said that baldness is cured by rubbing the head with a salve made of honey, juniper berries, and wormwood. She ordered me to apply it and I obey her in everything."

"Divine Caesar," she replied, "I am not great nor beautiful nor wise, but this one thing I know: a man can have either hair or brains, but he can't have both. You're quite beautiful enough as you are, sir; and since the Immortal Gods gave you good sense, I think they didn't mean for you to have curls."

111

I am thinking of making that woman a Senator.

Never have I felt so helpless, great Queen. I would resign all my other powers in exchange for this one, but I cannot; I cannot control the weather. I rage at these cold rains as I have not raged at anything for many years. I am become a sort of farmer: my clerks glance at one another with raised eyebrows; they see me continually going to the door to examine the sky. During the night I rise and go to my balcony; I estimate the wind; I look for the stars. I send you herewith another blanket of fur; wrap yourself well. I am told that these cruel rains will last two days more. All through the winter we shall have occasional days of sunlight. A friend of mine has a villa at Salerno, shielded from the north. You will go there in January and I shall join you. Be patient; occupy yourself. Send me word.

XXXVII   Catullus to Clodia.
        [*October 20.*]

Soul of my soul, when your word came this morning I wept.

You have forgiven us. You understand that we meant no offense, no offense, Caudilla. I ask myself what I said that could have made you so angry. But we will think of it no longer. You have forgiven us and it is forgotten.

But oh, great Claudilla, incomparable Claudilla, be ready to forgive us again. We do not know when we are about to stumble into your displeasure. Be assured now and forever that we never, oh NEVER, intend to cause you pain. Let this declaration stand for all time. What meaning or offense could you have found in—but there! it is forgotten.

But Claudilla, I must add that you also must try not to wound me. When you said in front of *him:* "Valerius has never quite made a poem which is equally successful throughout." Claudilla, don't you know that just that is the terror of a poet? A few verses come right; the rest he must contrive. What, have I never made an entire poem? And in front of *him!*

In the matter of the Queen's reception, I shall, of course, obey you. I had no particular interest in going.

Many members of our Club are going in a body and they have been urging me to write an Ode for it. I have a few strophes down; but it is not going very well and I shall be glad to give it up. All that I hear about her leads me to believe that she is insupportable—particularly, the immodesty of her dress.

No, I have not been ill.

Later.

I was about to send this letter off when I heard by chance that *you are going to the country for several months*. Why? WHY? Is it true? Immortal Gods, it cannot be true. You would have told me WHY? You have never been away in the winter. What does it mean? I do not know what to think. You have never been away in the winter.

If it is true, Claudilla, Claudilla, you will send for me. We shall read. We shall walk by the sea. You will point out the stars to me. No one has ever talked about the stars as you talk about them. I worship you always, but then you are all Goddess. Yes, go to the country, my brightest star, my treasure, and let me join you there.

But the more I think of it, the more unhappy I become.

What does it mean?

I know that I must ask for nothing. I must make no claim. But a love like mine must speak; it must cry out a little. Great and terrible Claudia, listen to me this once. Do not go into the country—I mean: if you must go into the country, GO ALONE. I dare not ask again that it be with me; but, at least, alone.

Yes, I will say it: I have been ill. Since love first came among men, despised lovers have pretended they were ill; but this was no pretense. Do you wish to kill me? Is that your aim? I do not wish to die. I swear to you I shall fight it to my last breath. I do not know how much longer I can endure. Something that is stronger than I is lying in wait for me. It is in the corner of my room all night, watching me while I sleep. I awake suddenly and seem to feel it above my bed.

I tell you now that if you go into the country with him I shall surely die. You call me a weakling. I am not. I could hold your friend in the air for an hour and then hurl him against a wall, and remain untired. You know that I am not a weakling and that only a powerful force could kill me.

I do not mean these words to sound angry. If it is true

113

that you are going to your villa, promise me that you will be alone. And then if you do not wish me to join you there, I will do what you have so often urged: I shall go to my home in the north until you return to the city.

Send me word about this. And oh, Claudia, Claudilla, ask me to do something—something that I can do. Do not ask me to forget you or to be indifferent to you. Do not ask me to have no interest in how you pass your time. But if we are separated, set me a task, something that will be a daily link with you. Great queen, greater than all the queens of Egypt, wise and good, learned and gracious, with one word you can make me well. With one smile, you can make me, make us, the happiest poet that ever praised the Immortal Gods.

XXXVII-A   Clodia to Catullus.
[By return messenger.]

Yes, it is true, dear Gaius. I am going into the country and alone, entirely alone. That is, only with Sosigenes the astronomer. The life of the city has become tiresome. I shall write you frequently. I shall think of you with affection. I am unhappy to hear that you have been ill. I think it would be wise for you to go to your home. I am sending presents for you to give to your mother and your sisters.

You ask me to assign you a task. What task could I assign you that your genius has not already whispered in your ear? Forget all that I have ever said about your verses and remember only this: you and Lucretius alone have made Rome a new Greece. You once said that the writing of tragedies was not your work. At another time you said that you might be able to write a "Helena." Any verses you write would give me happiness; if you also wrote a "Helena," we could play it when I return from the country. I shall leave on the morning after the Queen's reception and shall return a few days before the festival [*of the Good Goddess*].

Take every care of your health. Do not forget your "Ox-eyed."

XXXVIII   Caesar's Journal—Letter to Lucius Mamilius Turrinus on the Island of Capri.

1008. [*Of Cleopatra's admiration for the wine of Capri.*]

1009. [*Apology for tardiness in sending off the packet.*]

1010. [*Of love poetry.*] We are all vulnerable to the songs of the country people and of the market place. There have been tiems when I have gone about tormented for days by some song heard over the garden wall or sung by my soldiers around their campfires. *"Don't say no, no, no, little Belgian,"* or *"Tell me, moon, where is Chloe now?"* But when the verses are of a sovereign hand, it is no torment, but—Hercules!—an enlargement. My stride is doubled and I am twice my height.

Today I can hardly refrain from blurting out to the faces of all my callers some lines—no need to cite the verses of Greece for, by the Immortal Gods, we now fashion our own songs in Rome.

> Ille mi par esse deo videtur,
> Ille, si fas est, superare divos,
> Qui sedens adversus identidem te
> Spectat et audit
> Dulce ridentem. . . .
>
> [*That man to me seems equal to a God,*
> *That man surpasses the Gods—if such*
> *a thought be allowed—*
> *Who sitting before you*
> *Gazes and hears you*
> *Sweetly laughing. . . .*]

Those are the words of Catullus, written in what were for him happier times. I have reason to suspect that he is now the unhappiest of men. He captured his noontime in song; I am now at high noon and he has heightened its blaze for me.

XXXIX   Notes from Clodia to Marc Antony.
         [*Toward the end of October.*]

Court was very brilliant today. The oldest portions of the Roman wall have fallen before the invader: Servilia; Fulvia Manso; Sempronia Metella.

Your absence was noted. Majesty deigned to speak graciously of you, but I know her now and that pinched expression about her mouth.

Tell my dear Incomparable [*Cytheris*] that the Queen

has been inquiring about her. She said that the Dictator has spoken of her, the Incomparable, with great admiration.

After you left the Nile was overflowing its banks with ill-contained rage. She muttered to me that there was an Egyptian proverb that said: "All the braggart's wounds are on his back." I protested and was taken into the boudoir and given some pastries. I told of your bravery at Pharsalia; your bravery against Aristobulus. I have no doubt you were very brave in Spain, too, but I knew no details so I invented a towering exploit for you before Cordova. It is now history. She abruptly, too abruptly, changed the subject.

[*October 27.*]

All is ready.

Egypt is certainly yours, if you do exactly what I tell you. And when I tell you. All depends on the when.

Arrive early at the reception and pay little attention to her.

The Master of the Citadel will certainly be going home early with his wife and aunt.

I shall arrive late. I shall tell her that you are going to propose to show her the greatest feat of daring ever exhibited in Rome and I shall urge her not, oh not, not to consent to see it. And is not that what it will be?—the greatest feat of daring ever seen in Rome?

Do not forget your promise, however. You are not to fall in love with her. If there is any danger of that, I refuse to help you and all wagers are off.

Destroy this note, or rather give it to my messenger so that I may destroy it.

XL   The Lady Julia Marcia to Lucius Mamilius Turrinus on the Island of Capri.

[*October 28.*]

With what joy, my dear boy, I received your letter and learned that I may write to you. And that I may visit you. Let me come soon after the new year. All my thoughts are bent now on the Ceremonies [*of the Good Goddess*]; then I must return to my farm, put the year's accounts in

116

order, and surpervise the Saturnalia in our hill village. That done I shall come to the South—with what joy!

You say that you have time to read long letters and I generally have all too much time to write them. This will not be a long letter, I trust; it is just a word to acknowledge yours and to tell you of the events of last night which I think will interest you. You assure me that you have channels whereby you learn the externals of what passes in Rome and I shall try to restrict my account to such matters as I observe personally and as are not likely to have reached you by other hands.

Last night took place the reception at which the Queen of Egypt opened her palace to Rome. You will be told by others, no doubt, of the magnificence of the appointments, the lakes, the shows, the games, the tumult, the food, and the music.

I have made a new friend where least I expected to acquire one. There are perhaps reasons why the Queen should go to considerable lengths to ingratiate herself with me, but I think I am not easily deceived and I can say that the interest we took in one another was not feigned. Each was an object of curiosity to the other, each of an extreme difference; such contrasts with a touch of distrust may turn to contempt and ridicule, with a touch of good will to delighted friendship.

I arrived by boat with my nephew and his wife; we were greeted by the Queen at the gate which had been built as a reproduction of the Temple of Philae on the Nile. Our Tiber was all Egyptian and of new beauty; and such was the Queen. There are those who deny it; surely their eyes are askew with prejudice. Her skin is the color of the finest Greek marble and as smooth; her eyes are brown, large and most living. From them and from her low but ever-varying voice proceeds an unbroken message of happiness, well-being, amusement, intelligence, and assurance. Our Roman beauties were there in number and I became aware that Volumnia and Livia Dolabella and Clodia Pulcher were stiff, ill at ease, and as it were haunted by an imminent irritability.

The Queen was dressed, I am told, as the Goddess Isis. The jewels she wore and the embroidery on her gown were of blue and green. She led us first through the gardens, directing her remarks chiefly to Pompeia who seemed struck with fright and could find no answers, I am sorry to say. The Queen's manner is completely simple and should be

117

able to banish constraint from all who address her; so it did with me. She led us to her throne and presented to us the nobles and ladies of her court. She then turned to greet the long lines of guests who had been waiting while her attention was given to the Dictator.

I had intended to return early to bed, but lingered viewing the countless diversions with friends of my generation and tasting the extraordinary dainties (much to the fright of Sempronia Metella who assured me that they had been poisoned). Suddenly I felt a hand brush my arm. It was the Queen asking me if I would sit down with her. She led me to a sort of bower, warmed by braziers, and seating me beside her on a couch smiled at me for a moment in silence.

"Noble Lady," she said, "it is the custom in my country when one woman meets another to ask certain questions . . ."

"I am delighted, great Queen," I said, "to find myself in Egypt, and to observe the customs of that country."

"We ask one another," she replied, "how many children we have had and whether the confinements were difficult."

At this we both burst out laughing. "That is not a Roman custom," I said, thinking of Sempronia Metella, "but I think it very sensible." And I told her my history as a mother and she told me hers. She drew from a cabinet beside her some admirable paintings of her two children and showed them to me. "All else," she whispered, "is like a mirage of our deserts. I adore my children. I could wish to have a hundred. What is there in the world to equal one of those darling heads, those darling fragrant heads? But I am a Queen," she said, looking at me with tears in her eyes, "I must go on journeys. I must be busy with a hundred other things. Have you grandchildren?" she asked.

"No," I said. "None."

"Do you understand what I mean?" she asked.

"Yes, Majesty, I do."

And we sat silent. My dear boy, that is not the conversation I expected to have with the Witch of the Nile.

We were interrupted by my nephew bringing forward Marc Antony and the actress Cytheris. They were indeed taken aback to see the two of us sitting in tears amid the loud orchestras and the high torches.

"We were talking of life and death," said the Queen, rising and passing her hand across her cheeks. "My party is the happier for it."

She appeared to ignore my great-nephew, but she addressed Cytheris: "Gracious lady," she said, "I have been told—and by no mean judge—that no one speaks the Latin language, nor the Greek, more beautifully than you do."

This letter is already too long. I shall be writing you again before I see you. Your last request I shall indeed comply with explicitly. Your letter and the prospect of my visit have made me very happy.

XLI Cytheris, the Actress, to Lucius Mamilius Turrinus on the Island of Capri.
[*October 28.*]

I have been looking forward with happy expectation, my dear friend, to my visit to you in December. We shall talk and we shall read and again I shall climb all the heights and descend to all the coves. No cold and no storm will discourage me.

Something took place last night which renders this voyage doubly grateful. A long and dear association of my life came to an end; a bell rang; a music ceased. You are the only person who will ever hear any word of it from me. You, who have heard so much of its progress, will hear its ending. The life that I have lived with Marc Antony for fifteen years has come to an end.

Since long before the arrival of the Queen of Egypt, Marc Antony had been engaged in mocking her reputation for fascination and astuteness. He boasted to me of how he had been able to irritate the Dictator by representing himself as superior to any meretricious charms that Cleopatra might cast over natures less firmly rooted than his own. Few can have been in the position that I have been to observe the unbelievable patience with which the Dictator has supported the thoughtlessness of his nephew, a patience which has borne provocations of greater consequence than the one I am describing—though they could scarcely have been more exasperating.

Since the Queen's arrival, Marc Antony has attended her court frequently, and reports have reached me that there he has harassed her with an ironic gallantry. The Queen, apparently, did not counter this impertinence with playful superiority as she could well have done; but on several occasions in full presence she rebuffed him with undisguised anger. Rome began talking.

Last night we attended together her great reception. My friend was in the highest spirits. On the way I noticed for the first time that his remarks about her betrayed true admiration and a sort of amazed delight. I knew then that, still unknown to himself, he was the victim of passion.

When I see you I shall describe to you the magnificence of the palace and of the entertainment offered to us. I do not know how such receptions are conducted in Alexandria, but I suspect that the Queen was amazed to see how ill we Romans behave at large gatherings.

As usual the women withdrew into constrained groups, standing or sitting by themselves. In other portions of the grounds the younger men, drinking heavily, became boisterous and engaged in those inevitable contests of daring and strength which are their only pastime. You may well imagine that Marc Antony was in the forefront. They built first one and then another bonfire and forming in long lines raced across the gardens to jump them. I have learned to turn my back to these hazards; but I was soon aware that my friend was climbing trees and leaping from bough to roof followed by those whom he had challenged. Accidents occurred; heads and limbs were broken, but the tumultuous drunken singing only rose the higher. The exquisite pageants which the Queen had prepared were left to be viewed by a few women and a few grandfathers.

By midnight the men began to tire of these sports; many lay in drunken sleep among the bushes; the bonfires died down. A ballet was staged amid many-colored torches on an island and the artificial lake was filled with swimming girls.

The Dictator came upon me watching this show and did me the honor of sitting beside me. His wife had not enjoyed the evening and was pressing him to take his leave. I am now convinced that what then took place had been contrived by Clodia Pulcher, though she had worked with material all too ready to her hand. Clodia, like Marc Antony, had been attending the Queen's court almost daily. Rightly or wrongly, she had come to regard herself as the Queen's intimate and principal confidante in Rome. I had had occasion to witness Clodia's arrival at the party. She came late, accompanied by her brother and and a sprinkling of gallants from the Aemilian Draughts and Swimming Club. The Queen had long since left her station before the throne and was mingling with the guests. Throughout the greater part of the evening the Dictator had remained by his wife's side and had merely paid the Queen the most objective deference; but at this moment they were advancing side by side toward the avenue, returning from a fight between lions and tigers which had taken place in the stockade for wild beasts. Clodia saw before her a situation in which she could never participate: a woman who envied no one in the world; a Dictator twenty years younger; and a happiness that was then expressing itself in a laughter that meant ill-will to no one. I have known Clodia for many years; I could divine the pain that this spectacle cost her.

When the water-ballet was ended, Caesar's party rose to go in search of the Queen in order to take our leave. She was not at the lake. She was not in the palace. At the left of the avenue a stage had been constructed. Earlier in the evening it had served as the scene for a musical drama based on Egyptian history, but it now lay deserted and fitfully lighted by the torches from the court of honor near by. I cannot now remember what guided our steps in that direction. The scene represented a glade by the banks of the Nile, a grove of palm trees, bushes, and a thicket of reeds. To be brief, we surprised the Queen struggling and protesting in the embrace of a very drunken and ardent Marc Antony. There is no doubt that she was protesting, but there are degrees of protest and one could gather that this protest had been continuing for some time in a situation where escape was not difficult. In the half-dark we could not be sure what we saw.

Appearances were saved. Charmian, the Queen's attendant, appeared at that moment from behind the scene, bearing the brazier without which Cleopatra cannot support our cold weather. The Queen berated Marc Antony for clumsiness. The Dictator berated him for drunkenness. The moment was apparently passed off in laughter. No explanation was made, however, of why they had found themselves in so deserted a spot. I, from whom Marc Antony can keep no secret, knew that he was experiencing what he had experienced for me fifteen years before and had not known elsewhere in all his vagaries. What it meant for the Queen I could not know save as it was reflected in the great man beside me; no actor can equal Caesar and only an actor could divine that he was struck to the heart. No one else, I think, observed this. Pompeia had lingered behind us on the path.

We took our leave. In the litter, Marc Antony laid his head against my ear sobbing and repeating my name a hundred times. There could be no clearer farewall.

I knew that sooner or later this hour would come. The lover had become a son. I shall not pretend to a lightheartedness I do not feel; but I shall not exaggerate a suffering which, without my realizing it, had already been half-transmuted into resignation. I come to Capri with a higher recognition of friendship—that friendship which I could never know with Marc Antony, for friendship flowers from minds which are akin. Wonderful are its resources; but I am a woman. Only to you, whose wisdom and patience have no end, can I cry out for the last time that friendship—even yours—is and must be second to the love I have lost. It filled my days with radiance as it filled my nights with unbearable sweetness. For fifteen years I have found no reason to ask myself why one lives or why one suffers. I must now learn to live without the loving glances from those eyes on which I have dreamed my life away.

XLI-A   Cleopatra to Caesar.
          [*Midnight, October 27.*]

Deedja, Deedja, believe me, believe me, *what could I do?* He led me there, pretending that he and his companions were to show me the greatest feat of strength ever seen in Rome. He was both drunk and very sly. I am in a maze. I do not know how that could have taken place. I am certain that creature Clodia Pulcher was somehow a part of it. She had goaded or challenged him to it. She had shown him the plan first. I am sure of it.

Deedja, I am innocent. I shall not sleep until you send me word that you understand it all; that you trust me and love me. I am mad with horror and grief.

Send me, I pray you, word by this messenger.

XLI-B   Caesar to Cleopatra.
          [*From the house of Cornelius Nepos, whither Cleopatra's messenger had traced Caesar and where he found him sitting beside the sick bed of G. Valerius Catullus.*]

Sleep, sleep well.

Now it is you who are doubting me. I know my nephew well. I understood what had taken place at once. Do not doubt your *Deedja's* understanding.

Sleep well, great Queen.

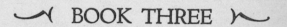

BOOK THREE

XLII   Caesar, Supreme Pontiff, to Madam, the President
of the College of the Vestal Virgins.
        [*August 9.*]

Reverend Maid:
    This letter is for your eyes alone.
    Last spring the Lady Julia Marcia repeated to me some
admirable words which you had let fall in a conversation
with her. She is unaware of the importance your words
were to have for me and she knows nothing of the letter I
am now writing you.
    She remembered your saying that you regretted that
there were occasional elements of grossness in the sublime
rituals of our Roman religion. Those words recalled a similar expression of my mother, the Lady Aurelia Julia. You
may remember that when I was previously elected to the
office of Supreme Pontiff in the year [*61*] the ceremonies
of the Good Goddess, being held in my house, my mother
was Lay Directress. The Lady Aurelia was a woman of
exemplary piety and deeply versed in the religious tradi-
tions of Rome. As Supreme Pontiff I gave her every assistance in the celebration of the rites at that time, but you
may be assured that I was told no more of what takes
place during them than was fitting for a man holding that
high office to hear. She did tell me, however, that she en-
ergetically deplored certain passages of ancient and barbarous coarseness that inhered in the ritual and which, she
said, were not essential to the greatness of the action arising from it. You may also remember that in that year (this
much I was permitted to know) she took upon herself the
responsibility of substituting serpents of clay for living serpents—an innovation which was adopted without opposition and which, if I am not mistaken, has persisted to this
day.
    I am aware, revered Madam, that it is the custom that
the Vestal Virgins retire from the ceremonies at midnight,
that is prior to the concluding ceremonial. I think I am

not wrong in concluding from this that certain symbolic actions take place after that hour which might be repugnant to the sensibilities of the dedicated and the chaste. A reflection of such a repugnance I have not failed to notice throughout my life in the attitude of the women of my household. To a far greater extent I have been aware, however, of their joy in those rites, and of the deep devotion they brought to them. The great Marius said of them, "They are like a column upholding Rome." I could wish that it be said of them and of the body of our Roman ceremonies what Pindar said of the Eleusinian mysteries: *that they held the world together from falling into chaos.*

Permit me to urge you, noble maid, to meditate upon the subject I have brought to your attention. Should you think it advisable you may send this letter to the Lady Julia Marcia. I feel it to be within the power of you two, mutually aiding one another, to perform a signal service in the highest interests of our people. It is not without fear and awe that one would venture to alter one word or gesture in such ancient and hallowed exercises. It is my opinion, however, that it is the law of life that all things grow and change, casting aside the husks that protected their origins and emerging into fairer and nobler forms. It is so that the Immortal Gods have ordained it.

XLII-A Caesar to the Lady Julia Marcia on her farm in the Alban Hills.
[*August 11.*]

I enclose the copy of a letter which I have just written to the President of the College of the Vestal Virgins. I hope I have expressed correctly the idea which you had in mind.

A great deal of resistance to any innovations in these matters is to be expected. Women, for good and for ill, are impassioned conservators. Men have long since eliminated the grosser elements in their rituals—the rites of the Arval Brethren and others. Perhaps I should say, they have dethroned them and set them to one side; they remain as vestiges, marginal to the ceremonies, some harmless clowning which takes place before and after the principal rites.

It is with mortification that I survey the roster of our first families, seeking several women of good sense who would be of assistance and support to you in this neces-

128

sary work. In the preceding generation it would not have been difficult to have named a score. Now I see only those who will attempt to place obstacles in your way: Sempronia Metella and Fulvia Manso, from unthinking conservatism; Servilia, from resentment that she was not the initiator of the project; Clodia Pulcher, from the spirit of contradiction. I would not be surprised if Pompeia also attempted to voice an opinion contrary to our intentions.

My dear aunt, I gave myself yesterday some not inconsiderable pleasure. As you know I am founding some colonies on the Black Sea. My map shows me an admirable location whose conformity suggests that it furnish the site of two adjacent towns. I am naming them after your great husband and yourself; they will be called Marius City and Julimarcia. I am told that the place is salubrious and of great beauty, and I am sending to it the most highly recommended of the families who have applied for transportation.

XLII-B   Caesar's Journal—Letter to Lucius Mamilius Turrinus on the Island of Capri.
[*About September 6.*]

973.   [*Concerning reforms introduced into the Mysteries of the Good Goddess.*] As an anonymous letter has recently informed me, a dictatorship is a powerful incitement to the composition of anonymous letters. I have never known a time when so many were in circulation. They are continually arriving at my door. Inspired by passion and enjoying the irresponsibility of their orphaned condition, they nevertheless have one great advantage over legitimate correspondence: they expose their ideas to their ultimate conclusion; they empty the sack.

I have stirred up a hornet's nest of them by attempting to remove certain primitive crudities which I know—though none too clearly—are incorporated in the celebration of the Mysteries of the Good Goddess. My shrouded correspondents are, of course, women. They do not suspect that I am at the bottom of this effort at reform; they merely appeal to me as Supreme Pontiff and ultimate arbiter.

What takes place during those twenty hours must make a powerful impression on the votaries, an effect so great that the majority of the celebrants, elevated to a pitch of ecstasy and supplication, are scarcely aware of the obscenity. The obscenity is for them an intensification of the truth and of the magic efficacy of the rites.

The Mysteries, I take it, avert sterility and prevent monstrous or catastrophic births. They harmonize and, as it were, sanctify that woman's life about which even the most skilled doctors tell me they know very little. In doing this I can well understand that it does not stop there; it affirms life itself, all mankind, and the creation. Little wonder that our women return to us like beings from another world and move about us for a time like radiant strangers. They have been told that they keep the stars in their courses and that they maintain in place the very paving stones of Rome. When after a time they give themselves to us it is with a pride not unmixed with contempt, as though we men were but the accidental instruments of their mighty task.

Now far be it from me to rob these ceremonies of one jot of their power and consolation. I ask only to increase their influence. I have observed, however, that these good effects do not endure beyond a few days. Were our women able to remain for a longer time in their elevated state I would willingly concede that they rule the stars in the sky and support the pavements of Rome. I am beyond any man I have ever met the admirer of the essential feminine; beyond any man I have ever met I am least censorious of their failings and least exasperated by their vagaries. But then!—what advantages I have had! I ask myself in amazement: "What opinion must that man hold of womankind who has not had the advantage of living in the proximity of great women?" What arrogance he must acquire from the mere fact that he is a man! What easy honors he must obtain from brutalizing over the women of his association! My eye travels over many men every day; it is not difficult to single out those who are what they are because of their proximity at some time to an exceptional woman. I have done more for the status and independence of women than any ruler that has ever lived. In these matters Pericles was obtuse and Alexander a stripling. I have been widely charged with light behavior toward them. That is nonsense. Among the women whom I have frequented I have left but one enemy behind me, and she, before I met her, had chosen to become the enemy of all men. Her I almost won from her self-hatred and almost saved from her damnation, but that only a God could do.

I have no hesitation in ascribing the brevity of that festival's good effects to the fact that it is overstrained; the celebrants are stretched to a pitch of excitement that obliterates the mind, and this degree of excess is a result of the obscene elements. I have grounds for believing that these aspects are more in evidence in the concluding session which begins at midnight. At that hour it is the custom thet the Vestal Virgins, unmarried women, and pregnant mothers retire to their homes; and I now understand why my loved Cornelia and Aurelia used to feign illness at midnight and withdraw to their apartments, even when they had responsibilities in the ceremonial, leaving the governance to Servilia who must indeed have conducted herself like a maenad.

You may well say that I am working in the darkness of ignorance in attempting to alter the balance of good and evil in this matter. But when have I ever done anything else but work in darkness? Particularly these last months, each step I take seems to me like that of a man blindfolded. He hopes that there is no precipice before him. I write my will and make Octavius my heir—is that a step into the darkness? I appoint Marcus Brutus to be Praetor of the City and close to me—is that a sure step?

—I have just reread these lines, two days after having written them. I am astonished to see that I have not drawn from them the consequence that is uppermost.

Who is this Good Goddess?

No man has ever been told her name; no woman is permitted to utter it; perhaps themselves do not know it.

Where is she? In Rome? Present at the confinements of our wives? Prefenting the births of wolf-children? Presumably she was present at my birth, ripped by the doctor from my mother's side.

Why, it is very certain she does not exist, apart from the imaginations of these votaries. That is also an existence and, as we have seen, a useful one.

But if our minds can make such Gods and if from the Gods we have made there flows such power, which is no more than a power resident within us, why cannot we employ that power directly? These women are employing but a small part of their strength, because they are ignorant that that strength is their own. They regard themselves as helpless, as victims of malevolent forces and as beneficiaries of this Goddess whom they must implore and propi-

131

tiate. Little wonder that their exaltation soon subsides, that they again descend into that incessant occupation with details where every detail is of equal power to enthrall or to distress them, that unremitting activity which so resembles a despair—a despair which does not know it is despairing, or an application to duties so intense that it can drown out despair.

Let each woman find out in herself her own Goddess—that should be the meaning of these rites.

At least, the first steps toward that end shall be the elimination of obscenity. Let us at least say of religion that it means that every part of the body is infused with mind, not that the mind is overwhelmed and drowned in body. For the principal attribute of the Gods, without or within us, is mind.

XLIII   Cleopatra, in Egypt, to Caesar.
        [*August 17.*]

Cleopatra, the Everliving Isis, Child of the Sun, Chosen of Ptah, Queen of Egypt, Cyrenaica, and Arabia, Empress of the Upper and Lower Nile, Queen of Ethiopia, etc., etc. To Caius Julius Caesar, Dictator of the Roman Republic and Supreme Pontiff.

Herewith the Queen of Egypt submits her application for inclusion among those in Rome who are permitted to attend the Rites in Celebration of the Good Goddess.

XLIII-A   Caesar's Journal—Letter to Lucius Mamilius Turrinus on the Island of Capri.

975.   It was from you that I obtained an idea which is now so self-evident to me that I am in danger of forgetting that you gave it to me: the importance for administration of encouraging an identification of the Gods of other countries with those of our own. In some regions this has been difficult; in others, astonishingly easy. In most northern Gaul the God of the oak tree and the storms (no Roman has ever been able to pronounce his name—Hodan, Quotan) has long since coalesced with Jupiter; He smiles daily on the marriages of our soldiers and clerks with the golden-haired daughters of those forests. The Temples of my ancestress [*Venus; the Julian*

132

family traced its descent from Julus, son of Aeneas, son of Aphrodite] in the East are one with those of Astarte and Ashtoreth. If I live long enough, or if my successors also see the importance of this unity among the cults, all the men and women in the world will call themselves brother and sisters, children of Jupiter.

This world-wide unification has recently produced a slightly ridiculous consequence, some illustrations of which I am enclosing in this packet. Her Pyramidal Majesty, the Queen of Egypt, has applied for admission to the mysteries of our very Roman Good Goddess: You have always had a taste for both genealogy and theology, but even you would not wish to explore the immense documentation with which she supports her claims. Cleopatra does nothing by halves; my anteroom is filled with the bales of this documentation.

Her application rests on two counts: her descent from the Goddess Qu'eb and her descent from the Goddess Cybele.

A little of this makes one dizzy, but I shall digest for you some three hundred pages as though they were in her own words, though I have not the texts before me:

"The Greek theologians authorized the identification of Qu'eb and Cybele over two hundred years ago (see attached two hundred pages). On the occasion of the visit of Queen Dicoris of Littoral Armenia to Rome in [89] the Master of Rites ruled an 'identity of emanation' between Cybele and the Good Goddess (see attached bundles X and XI).

"The Supreme Pontiff will remember that when the Queen of Egypt laid the charts of her ancestry before him in Alexandria [fiddlesticks]—although at that time she had not made public her Egyptian lineage (indeed, she hadn't)—she was preparing to announce her claim to Tyre and Sidon by reason of her great-grandfather's marriage (her great-grandfather was no stronger lying down than standing up) to Queen Aholibah. I am therefore through Queens Jezebel and Athaliah, descendant and hereditary archpriestess of Ashtoreth. Through this relationship, Queen Jezebel having been cousin-german to Dido, Queen of Carthage (notice the threat—my grandfather wronged her great-aunt) and so on and so on." It is all quite true. The Eastern potentates are each ones their own cousin many times. I have written her that after suitable instruction she will be admitted to the earlier portion of the rites; that the permission is not accorded to her through any claim on her part to be descended from the Good Goddess or from any other divinity, but merely that the Goddess rejoices receiving—during the earlier part of the evening—all women who wish to bow before her.

I wish to add that the above rigmarole tends to present an unjust picture of the Queen of Egypt. It happens to refect the only aspect of her mind on which she is not exceptionally sensible.

I should add that the Queen failed to include an extremely curious fact among the arguments supporting her request. Perhaps she does not know of it. The votaries of the Good Goddess during the rites wear a headdress which is certainly neither Greek nor Roman and which is known among them as the "Egyptian Turban." How it came to be there no one has ever explained. But who can explain the symbols, the influences, and the expressions of that universal mixture of joy and terror which is religion?

XLIV The Lady Julia Marcia from Caesar's House in Rome, to Clodia.
     [*September 29.*]

This letter is confidential.

Julia Marcia sends regard to Clodia Pulcher, daughter and granddaughter of her most dear friends.

I am looking forward to being present at your dinner tomorrow night, to meeting there for the first time your brother, to renewing an old friendship with Marcus Tullius Cicero, and to seeing you.

I returned to the City three days ago in order to attend a meeting of the Directresses of a religious festival venerated for its antiquity and held in grateful awe by its votaries. At this meeting eight petitions were laid before me that you be excluded from this year's festival. I have read these petitions with regret, even with great sorrow, but I do not find the charges sufficiently grave or definite to justify the measure they request. That these petitions exist, however, is a matter which myself and the other women responsible for the devotion and harmony of the rites cannot ignore.

The procedure I am about to propose is one of compromise. I feel certain that I can insure its acceptance, always granting that no further petitions are submitted which contain incontrovertible evidence that your disbarment be advisable. In proposing this compromise I do not wish to be understood as taking lightly the many protests which rightly or wrongly your actions have aroused. My motive is to avoid unjustifiable scandal in an institution which was so greatly loved by those who greatly loved you.

I inform you in great confidence that Cleopatra, Queen of Egypt, will be in Rome before long and that she has submitted a petition that she be admitted to the ceremonies we are discussing. This application, accompanied by much argumentation and many precedents and analogies, has been laid before the Directresses and before the Supreme Pontiff. The decision will probably be that the Queen will be permitted to attend the rites before midnight when it is customary that the Vestal Virgins, unmarried women, pregnant women, and [here follows a technical term meaning not belonging to the tribes into which citizens of Rome were divided] withdraw. I am going to propose that you be appointed Instructress of the Queen of Egypt and that therefore you will be obliged to accompany her to her palace at midnight. Your enemies will be satisfied, I feel sure, by the knowledge that you will not return to the rites after you have retired from them with your guest.

You will think my proposal over, Clodia, and I hope that tomorrow night you will find occasion to convey to me your compliance. The only alternative is that you challenge the petitions brought against you and face your accusers in a plenary session of our committees. If we were dealing with secular matters I should certainly advise you to do so; these charges and their defense are, however, matters of decorum, dignity, and reputation. To discuss them openly is to admit that these attributes are damaged.

The Supreme Pontiff is not aware of these discussions and I need hardly say that I shall make every effort to prevent their reaching his attention save in the final disposition which I have proposed for your decision.

XLIV-A   Caesar's Journal—Letter to Lucius Mamilius Turrinus on the Island of Capri.
      [About October 8.]

1002.   [On Clodia and a mime of Pactinus] I am

more frequently discomfited by little things than by big. I have just found myself obliged to forbid the performance of a play on the stage. I enclose a copy of the play in question, a mime by Pactinus called *The Prize of Virtue*. You are probably aware, though I forgot to tell you, that I instituted the practice of giving twenty prizes of varying amounts of money to girls of the working class who receive the highest commendation from their neighbors for good manners, faithful attendance on their parents and masters, and so on. I think this has had some good effect. It has incidentally provoked as great a plague of witticisms and satire as any action in which I have ever engaged. It has added enormously to the merriment of Rome; every street cleaner discovers himself to be a wit and you may well imagine that I am not spared.

One result has been the overwhelming success of the attached farce. You will observe that the fourth episode treats of Clodia and her brother. The audience was not slow to perceive the application. It was reported to me that at the close of that scene, on each occasion, the audience rose in a tumult of applause, derision, and savage glee. Strangers embraced one another, shouting; they leaped up and down and on two occasions tore down the handrails of the aisles.

After eight representations I ordered that the play be withdrawn. After the second Clodius Pulcher appeared in my offices to protest. I sent word that I was busy on African matters and could not see him. I wished the famous couple to drink for a time the bitter brew of their own concocting. Finally, he reappeared in sufficiently humble suppliance and I complied with his request.

It vexed me to close it. It is without literary merit, but hitherto I have never curbed the freedom of expression of the citizens nor punished opinion however outrageous. Moreover, I wince to think that many will suppose that I suppressed it because it contained many shafts directed at myself.

The audience at a theater is the most moral of congregations. The fact that all those Romans are seated shoulder to shoulder seems to instill into them an elevation of judgment which they are not found to exercise anywhere else. They have no hesitation in deciding whether the behavior of the characters in a play is good or bad and they demand of them an ethical standard which they are far from requiring of themselves. Pandarus in an audience

136

trembles with virtuous indignation before the pander on the stage. Twelve prostitutes side by side at a play are more prudish than one Vestal Virgin. I have often remarked that the moral and ethical attitudes of a theater audience are some thirty years out of date; in a mass, men reflect the views they received as children from their parents and guardians. And so at this farce the audience was whipped up into an ecstasy of denunciation of our Clodia. Each spectator felt himself or herself to be irreproachably virtuous.

That lofty emotion may well have lasted an hour. Oh, that we had an Aristophanes among us. He could both pillory Clodia and Caesar, and then turn the laughter on the audience's laughter. Oh, Aristophanes!

XLIV-B—From *The Prize of Virtue*, a mime by Pactinus.
> [*A judge of the contest, obviously intended to be Caesar, sits in his office interviewing applicants for the prize. He is represented as a sly and lecherous old man. He is attended by a clerk.*
> *The play is in verse.*
> *This is the fourth episode.*

Clerk: There is a pretty girl waiting to see Your Honor.
> [*Latin* pulcher: *pretty.*]
Judge: What? Is there to be no pretty boy? [*This is one of those innumerable imputations to Caesar of pederasty with which the literature abounds.*]
Clerk: This is his sister, Your Honor.
Judge: Well, get on with it. You know I'm not particular.
Clerk: She's weeping, Your Honor.
Judge: Of course, she's weeping, if she's virtuous, blockhead. Virtuous women weep the first half of their lives, and women without virtue weep the second half of their lives, and so the Tiber never runs dry. Show her in.
> (Enter a Young Girl, dressed in rags.)
Come nearer, little girl. I don't seem to see anything clearly any more—except villas at Tivoli. [*Where Caesar had confiscated the estates of two noblemen of Pompey's party who had been particular favorites of the Roman populace.*] So you want a prize for virtue, do you—you little darling?
The Young Girl: Yes, Your Honor. You won't find a more virtuous girl in the whole city.

137

Judge: (caressing her): Are you sure you haven't come to the wrong office, my little pigeon? Hm . . . let me see, let me see. This is, ahem, not your first youth, is it?

The Young Girl: Oh, no, sir. The first youth was under the consulship of Cornelius and Mummius [*i.e. 146* B.C.].

The Judge: I can well believe it. Tell me, little rose, is your father living?

The Young Girl: (weeping): Oh, sir, it's not kind to bring that up against me now.

The Judge: Then, perhaps you'll tell me if your husband's living?

The Young Girl: Your Honor, I didn't come here to be accused of this and that in the most insulting way.

The Judge: Sh. Sh. I just thought I saw a snowflake in your hand. [*Murderers were popularly believed to suffer from a scrofulous flaking of the skin in the palm of the hand.*] Tell me, my dear, did you always take tender care of your father and mother?

The Young Girl: Oh, I did, I did. I helped them to their last breath.

The Judge: A loving daughter. And have you been kind to your pretty brothers?

The Young Girl: Your honor, I've refused them nothing.

The Judge: You haven't gone beyond the bounds of modesty, I hope. [*Modesty was a village and temple ten miles north of Rome.*]

The Young Girl: Oh, no, sir! Not beyond the city gates. We kept it all in the home.

The Judge: A paragon! A paragon! Now tell me, little sweetness, why are you dressed in rags?

The Young Girl: You may well ask, kind gentleman. There's no more money circulating in Rome. I think Mammurra has taken it all up to Lower Gaul. [*In a previous episode, Mammurra, dressed as a wise woman of Gaul, received a prize of virtue for "sweeping the house clean."*] My older brother brings no money in, of course, because he's a pensioner of the Veined Nose [*i.e. Caesar. The frugality of Caesar's domestic life had long led to the charge that he was parsimonious*]. My second brother brings in no money, because all his holdings were beetled into The Tiber. [*Caesar had recently straightened the course of the Tiber by digging away portions of its banks under the Vatican and Janiculan hills. The Roman populace had been particularly fascinated by this opera-*

tion, because of a new excavating device or machine which had been employed. This machine, invented by Caesar during his military campaigns, was promptly labeled a "beetle." The region sacrificed to the river had contained the lowest resorts of the city.]

The Judge: And you, little butterfly? Haven't I heard that you pick up many a fourpenny bit?

[*And so on.*]

XLV   Abra, Pompeia's maid, to the Headwaiter at the Taverns of Cossutius (an agent of Cleopatra's Information Service).

[*October 17.*]

Like you say first I will answer your questions by number.

I.   I worked for the lady Clodia Pulcher for five years. During the war we left Rome and lived in her house in Baiae. I will be free in two years. I have worked here two years. I am thirty-eight years old. I have no children.

II.   This month I am not allowed to leave the house. None of the servants are. They have found that somebody is stealing things. That's what they say, but I do not think it is that. We all think that it is the secretary, the one from Crete, that they are watching.

III.   My husband is allowed to visit me every five days. He is searched when he goes out. No peddlers can come in. They come to the garden door and we buy there.

IV.   Yes, I send letters to the Lady Clodia Pulcher every time that Hagia, the midwife, comes. [*It is presumed that the midwife was attending a servant in Caesar's household.*] She is not searched. The things I write the Lady Clodia Pulcher are like this: how the Queen of Egypt came to call on my Mistress; when my Master is away from the house all night; sometimes things that the wine butler says they are talking about at table; when the Master has the falling sickness. The Lady Clodia Pulcher does not pay me money. She has made a tavern for my husband on the Appian Way by the Tomb of Mops. If my letters are satisfactory to you, my husband and I would like a cow.

V.   No, I am sure, nothing definite. But I think my Master does not like me. Six months ago they had a big quarrel about me, and a bigger quarrel two days ago. But my Mistress would never let him send me away she would cry so. She is never tired of talking about jewels, clothes, hair, et cetera, and there is nobody but me to talk to. That's how it is.

VI. About my Mistress's letters. Last year my Master told the Porter that all letters for my Mistress should be put with his. When they arrived during the day they were kept in the Porter's room until they were sent to the Master's offices. But several times a day my mistress went to the Porter and said are there any letters for me and he would give them to her. She made a big quarrel and cried and now all letters come to her. Only he said all anonymous letters must be destroyed without being read. Most are. There are many. Some are exciting. Some not.

Here begins my letter:

My Master is very kind to my mistress. From the time he comes home from the offices he spends almost all the time with her. When he has visitors on business he talks to them in the next room and keeps the door open and makes the visits as short as possible. When she goes to bed, he has friends come to see him for an hour or two because he does not like to sleep much, I mean does not need to sleep much. As these friends, like Hirtius, Mammurra, Oppius, drink much and laugh loud, they go to the Master's workroom on the cliff over the river. As it takes my Mistress almost two hours to get ready to go to bed, she is often still awake when he comes back. Often while she is getting ready, he leaves his friends and sits by us and talks to her while I am combing her hair, etc. Now what I mean to say is this: she almost always finds something to quarrel about. She almost always cries. Many times he sends me from the room while they talk about something. She quarrels about the sumptuary laws, about the leopard cub which the Queen of Egypt gave her, about the Lady Clodia Pulcher not being invited to come to the house, about what days we go to the villa at Lake Nemi, about going to the theater.

Now there has been a great quarrel two days ago. When my Mistress left the room for a moment I think my Master quickly pushed his hand around among all the jars and bottles on her toilet table and he found an anonymous letter that came to her many weeks ago. I think he read it and put it back where it was. When she came back he pretended to find it all over again. That's what I think hap-

140

pened. It was a letter saying that Clodius Pulcher, the man that burned Cicero's house and that threatened to kill all the Senators, that man, that he loved my mistress like madness, and that she must be warned against him because maybe he could not control his love. My Master was very calm, but I know him he was also white with rage. He said that the letter was obviously written by Clodius Pulcher himself and that only a man who really despised a woman and wished to make a fool of her would write a letter like that. My Mistress said she hated Clodius Pulcher, but that it was obvious that he did not write that letter. Then I was made to leave the room. When I came back she had cried and she began to cry again and she kept saying that life was impossible, simply not to be endured.

My Master sent for me and said that I had brought the letter in. I swore by a terrible oath that he gave me that I had known nothing about the letter; but I think he knows. I do not think, however, that he will send me away.

Do you want me to write to you what nights my Master stays away from the house all night?

The wine butler says that he heard the Master talking to Balbus and Brutus—Decimus Brutus, that is, not the good-looking one—about moving Rome to Troy. Troy is in Egypt, I think.

The secretary, the one from Sicily, says that he has changed his mind, there will be no war against the Parthians. The Cretan secretary said you fool, of course, there will. That's all I know about that.

There's going to be an edict about no carts coming into the center of town after ten o'clock and they can only stay an hour.

I forgot to say that Clodius Pulcher rode up on his horse while my Mistress was in her litter going to Lake Nemi and began talking to her until Affius came up and said he had orders no one was to speak to our party. Affius is head of the farm and in charge of our journeys. He was with the Master in the wars and has only one arm.

Now I will stop.

I wish to say this that I do not like it here, I am uncomfortable. I have asked the Lady Clodia Pulcher to take me back, but she says I must stay here. I know a way that I could leave here. If this letter to you is what you want I will stay and write a few more.

The cow we would like is a tawny spotted one.

[*About October 13.*]

1012. The Queen of Egypt and I have been quarreling. It is not the quarrel habitual in boudoirs, though it frequently arrives at a termination which cannot be said to be new.

Cleopatra declares that I am a God. She is shocked to discover that I have not long since come to acknowledge that I am a God. Cleopatra is very certain that she is a Goddess and the worship of her people confirms her daily in this belief. She assures me that the divinity which lives in her has endowed her with unusual perspicuity in recognizing divinity. Through that endowment she is in a position to assure me that I am one also.

All this makes for conversation of a very flattering sort, interrupted by droll byplay. I pinch the Goddess and the Goddess squeals. I put my hand over the Goddess's eyes and, by the Immortal Gods, she is unable to see a thing. She has answers for all these sophistries. It is the one subject, however, on which the great Queen is not accessible to reason and on which I have learned not to permit our conversations to take a serious turn. On that subject alone she is, perhaps, oriental.

Nothing seems to me to be more dangerous—not only for us rulers, but for those who gaze upon us with varying degrees of adoration—than this ascription of divine attributes. It is not difficult to understand that many persons will feel at times as though they were inflated by unusual powers or caught up into currents of some inexplicable rightness. I had this feeling frequently when I was younger; I now shudder at it and with horror. How often I have had it thrown back at me, generally by flatterers, that I said to the timid boatman in the storm: "Have no fear; you bear Caesar." What nonsense! I have had no more exemption from the ills of life than any other man.

But that is not all. The history of nations shows how deeply rooted is our propensity to impute a more than human condition to those remarkable for gifts or to those merely situated in conspicuous position. I have little doubt that the demigods and even the Gods of antiquity are nothing more than ancestors about whom these venerations have been fostered. All this has been fruitful; it expands the imagination of the growing boy and it furnishes sanctions for good manners and public institutions. It must be outgrown, however—outgrown and discarded. Every man that has ever lived has been but a man and his achievements should be viewed as extensions of the human state, not interruptions in it.

There is no one but you with whom I can talk of this. Every year this discomfiting deification increases about me. I remember with shame that there was a time when I endeavored, for administrative reasons, to fan it: sufficient evidence that I am a man and a most fallible one, for there is no human weakness equal to that of trying to inculcate the notion that one is a God. I had a dream one night that Alexander appeared at the door of my tent with sword lifted, about to slay me. I said to him: "But you are no God," and he vanished.

The older I grow, dear Lucius, the more I rejoice in being a man—mortal, mistaken, and unabashed. Today my secretaries timidly brought me a succession of documents on which I had made various kinds of errors (to myself I call them Cleopatra-errors, so obsessive is that enchantress.) I corrected them one after one another, laughing. My secretaries frowned. They could not understand that Caesar would be delighted at his mistakes. Secretaries are not exhilarating companions.

The words "divinity" and "God'" have been in use among us for some time. They have a thousand meanings and for any one person a score.

The other night I found my wife under strong emotion imploring the Gods to send a sunny day for her trip to Lake Nemi. My aunt Julia is a farmer and she does not believe that they will alter the weather for her convenience, but she is certain that they are watching over Rome and have placed me here as governor. Cicero does not believe that they would hesitate to let Rome glide into ruin (he would not wish to share with them the honor of having saved the state from Catiline), but he has no doubt that they placed the conception of justice in men's hearts. Catullus probably believes that men have developed an idea of justice from quarreling with one another over property and over boundary lines, but he is certain that love is the only manifestation of the divine and that it is from love, even when it is traduced and insulted, that we can learn the nature of our existence. Cleopatra holds that love is the most agreeable of activities and that her attachment to her children is the most compelling emotion she

143

has ever experienced, but that these are certainly not divine—divinity for her resides in the force of one's will and the energy of one's personality. And none of these meanings are meanings for me, though at various times in my life I have held all of them. With the loss of each of them I have been filled with an increased strength. I feel that if I can rid myself of the wrong ones, I shall be coming closer to the right one.

But I am an aging man. Time presses.

XLVI-A   From the Commonplace Book of Cornelius Nepos.

The Dictator has issued an edict that no more towns may change their names to a form of his own. The reason for this is, I think, that he has discovered that he is being more literally worshipped than he cares to be. He has ceased sending presents to townships and regimental headquarters; they are invariably place in shrines and become centers of pilgrimage for healing and supplication.

There is no doubt that this is taking place, and not only in the barbarous outposts of the Republic and in the mountains of Italy, but here in the City.

It is said that his servants are continually being bribed to steal his garments, the parings of his nails, the refuse of his shaving, and his very urine—all of these are said to possess magical properties and are preserved for adoration.

Fanatics occasionally are able to penetrate into his house where they are mistaken for assassins. One of these prowlers, dagger in hand, was surprised one night near to where Caesar was sleeping. A summary trial was held on the spot and Caesar himself conducted the interrogation. The man was all but incoherent, but not with fear. As the interview proceeded he lay on the floor gazing ecstatically at the Dictator's face and babbling that all he wanted was "one drop of Caesar's blood with which to sanctify himself." Caesar, to the consternation of the guards and servants who had collected, asked him many questions and finally extracted from him the whole story of his life. This close interest, which many a consul has not been able to arouse, raised the poor man's veneration to a still more delirious state and at the end he was imploring Caesar to kill him with his own hand.

Turning to the bystanders, Caesar is reported to have

said with a smile: "It is often difficult to distinguish hate from love."

Caesar's physician Sosthenes to dinner.

He was talking about the effect of Caesar on others.

"Of what other men have such stories been told and believed?

"Until recently scores of ill persons were placed nightly by their families to sleep against the wall which surrounds his house. They have been driven away; now you will see them, row by row, lying under and around his statues. On his journeys farmers beseech him to plant his foot on their less productive fields.

"And the stories! You hear them in the soldiers' songs; you see them in verses and drawings scrawled in public places. It is said that he was conceived by his mother of a bolt of lightning; that he was born through her mouth or ear; that he came into the world without organs of generation and that those he ultimately possessed were grafted onto him from a mysterious stranger he met among the oak trees of the Temple of Zeus at Dodona whom he slew for that purpose; or that they came from a statue of Zeus by Phidias. There is no abnormality that has not been charged against him and it is believed that, like Jupiter, he has predilections within the animal kingdom. It is widely held that he is literally the father of his country and that he has left hundreds of children in Spain, Britain, Gaul, and Africa.

"And yet superstition and popular belief do not shrink from inconsistency. It is said, on the other hand, that he guards so austere a continence that the unchaste feel intolerable pain when he passes near them.

"What man, what mere man, has fired the imaginations of the people to so luxuriant a body of legend? And now that Cleopatra has come to town, what do we not hear?—Cleopatra, the rich mud of the Nile. Go to the taverns, go to the barracks—the heads of the Roman people are swimming at the thought of those embraces. We are celebrating the nupitals of the Unconquered Sun and the Fecund Earth.

"I am his physician. I have tended that body through convulsions and have bound its wounds. Yes, it is mortal; but we physicians learn to listen to our patients' bodies as musicians listen to the various lyres which are placed in their hands. His is bald, aging, and covered with the
145

wounds received from many wars; but every portion is informed by mind. Its powers of self-repair are extraordinary. Illness is discouragement. The illness from which Caesar suffers is the one illness which denotes over-reaching enthusiasm. It is related to the character of his mind.

"The mind of Caesar. It is the reverse of most men's. It rejoices in committing itself. To us arrive each day a sorce of challenges; we must say yes or no to decisions that will set off chains of consequences. Some of us deliberate; some of us refuse the decision, which is itself a decision; some of us leap giddily into the decision, setting our jaws and closing our eyes, which is a sort of decision of despair. Caesar embraces decision. It is as though he felt his mind to be operating only when it is interlocking itself with significant consequences. Caesar shrinks from no responsibility. He heaps more and more upon his shoulders.

"It may be that he lacks some forms of imagination. It is very certain that he gives little thought to the past and does not attempt to envisage the future clearly. He does not cultivate remorse and does not indulge in aspiration.

"From time to time he permits me to put him through certain tests. I ask him to exercise strenuously, then lie in repose while I engage in various observations, and so on. During one of these enforced immobilities he asked me, 'If I were to escape assassination and live into old age, of what organ's weakness, would I die?' 'Sire,' I said, 'of an apoplexy.' He seemed very pleased. I knew what was in his mind. There are two things he dreads: physical pain, to which he is most unusually sensitive, and indecorousness.

"At another time he asked me whether there were any pressure or action whereby a man might put an end to his life quickly and without bloodshed. I showed him three and I have no doubt that since that day he has regarded me with particular affection and gratitude.

"I, in turn, have learned much from him. I used to think that eating, sleeping, and the satisfaction of the sexual appetite were best regulated by the formation of habits. I now believe with him that they are best served by responding to them at the first prompting. I have thereby not only lengthened my day, but liberated my spirit.

"Oh, it is an extraordinary man. These legends have, in their way, a just base; but with one difference. Caesar does not love, nor does he inspire love. He diffuses an equable

146

glow of ordered good will, a passionless energy that creates without fever, and which expends itself without self-examination or self-doubt.

"Let me whisper to you: I could not love him and I never leave his presence without relief."

XLVI-B   From a Report of Caesar's Secret Police.

Subject 496: Artemisia Baccina, midwife, healer, and fortuneteller, resident in the suburb of the Goat. Under interrogation, Subject 496 confessed to having been present at rites celebrated by the Confraternity of the Buried Sun. Said there were ten or twelve chapters in Rome. (See Subjects 371 and 391.) Finally under intensive interrogation said the Confraternity was headed by Amasius Lenter (Subject 297, executed August 12.) Rites open with slow torture and death of a black pig, black cock, etcetera, and concluded with veneration of a vial of blood, said to be the blood of the Dictator. Subject is being deported to Sicily and placed under vigilance of the police there.

XLVI-C   From Notes left by Pliny the Younger.
         [*Written about a century later.*]

Curious. My gardener reported that the following belief is widely held by the common people. On my walks I have questioned vine dressers, hucksters, and others and find this report confirmed.

They believe that the body of Julius Caesar was not burned after his assassination (though we have no doubt of that), but that an organization or mystery cult seized it and dividing it into many pieces, buried each piece under one of the wards of Rome. They declare that Caesar knew of an old prophecy which affirmed that the survival and greatness of Rome was dependent on his murder and dismemberment.

XLVII   Announcement by the Queen of Egypt.
        [*October 26.*]

Cleopatra, Queen of Egypt, [*etcetera, etcetera*] regrets that the Reverend College of the Vestal Virgins will be unable to attend her reception tomorrow evening.

Arrangements have been made, however, to receive the Reverend College at three o'clock on that day.

With the concordance of the Supreme Pontiff and the Reverend President of the College a performance will be given at that time of

      The great Coming-Forth of Horus,
      The beauty of Osiris,
      The attack upon the Neshmet Boat,
      The Lord of Abydos comes to his Palace.

The portions of these ceremonies which are unsuitable for presentation in the evening will be rendered in all their solemnity before the dedicated guests in the afternoon.

The Queen of Egypt will graciously receive the Reverend Maids at that time.

XLVIII   Caesar to Cleopatra.
       [*October 29.*]

All Rome talks of the magnificence of the Queen's reception; the more discriminating return repeatedly to speak of her royal deportment, of her arts as a hostess, of her discretion, and of the spell of her beauty.

I am permitted to speak of my love and admiration which will never grow less.

My visits to the great Queen will be less frequent in the days that lie ahead, but I adjure her never to doubt my love nor my unceasing attention to the welfare of her country.

It would give me great pleasure to receive the Queen more frequently in my home. I am requesting the actress Cytheris to give lessons to my wife in the declamation and gestures that are required of her at the Mysteries of the Good Goddess. As you are to be present at that reunion also, I think you would derive much interest from these lessons—though far be it from me to imply that the Queen has anything to learn in beauty of speech or in dignity of port.

At the close of the lessons I feel certain that Cytheris will not refuse any wish you may express to hear her declaim passages from the Greek and Roman tragedies—a privilege which our descendants will envy us.

The Lady Clodia Pulcher is retiring to her villa in the country for a time. I think it is fitting that you should know that I indicated this move to her some time ago, though she asked permission to remain in the City until the day following your reception. The reason for this withdrawal springs from a matter which I shall recount to you at some time, if you wish to hear it.

The happiness which the Queen's visit has brought me has occasionally drawn my thoughts away from my work. Were I a younger man this happiness would become one with the work and would furnish new incentives to its prosecution. My lengthening days remind me, however, that I have not that apparently unlimited time for project and execution which I once possessed.

Allow me to combine my work with happiness by calling on the Queen on [Saturday] to show her the plans which I have drawn up for colonial settlements in North Africa. If the weather is favorable then, I should like to take the Queen to Ostia by boat, pointing out to her the measures we have taken for the control of flood and the deceleration of the current. At Ostia we shall be able to see the progress made on the harbor works, concerning which the Queen has already given me such invaluable advice.

There is one more thing I wish to say to the great Queen. I hope she will remain in Italy for an even longer visit than she had first planned. To encourage this decision, may I suggest that she send to Alexandria for her children? I shall place one of my newly finished galleys, which have already proved themselves to be the swiftest on the sea, at the Queen's disposal for this errand and shall look forward to sharing her joy at their arrival.

XLVIII-A   Cleopatra to Caesar.
     [By return messenger.]

A misunderstanding, great Caesar, has arisen between us.

I realize that no protests of mine can clear away the misapprehension under which you are laboring. In my suffering I can only hope that time and events will convince you of my devotion and loyalty.

Once more I must say, however, that the situation in which I found myself—with an astonishment no less than yours—was contrived by malicious persons.

Marc Antony had persuaded me to accompany him to that portion of the gardens to see what he called "the greatest feat of daring ever seen in Rome." He assured me that it would be undertaken by himself in association with some five or six of his companions. As the moment had come for me to make another tour of the grounds I acceded to his request, taking Charmian with me. The rest you know.

I shall not rest until I have obtained proofs of the complicity of others in what then took place. I know that proofs will not convince you of my innocence unless I can also furnish you evidence of my tireless concern with all that has to do with you and your interest and with your happiness. This ambition alone leads me to accept your invitation to prolong my stay in the City. I gratefully accept also your invitation to attend the sessions directed by Cytheris in your home.

I do not wish at this time, however, to send for my dear children, though I thank you for the opportunity you have extended.

Great friend, great Caesar, my lover, the thing which is uppermost in my mind is that you have unjustly been made to suffer. I cry out in anguish against those forces of destiny which by an infernal device that no mere humans could compound have made me an instrument for your disappointment. Oh, do not believe it. Do not permit yourself to be the victim of so transparent a mischance. Remember my love. Do not now begin to doubt the glance in my eyes and the joy in my surrender. I am still a young woman; I do not know what form a more experienced woman would give to the protestations of innocence. Should I be indignant that you distrust me? Should I be proud and angry? I do not know; I can only be candid, even at the expense of modesty. Never have I loved, never shall I love, as I have loved you. Who can have known what I have known—a delight that was not separable from gratitude, a passion that was none the less for being all homage? Such was the love suitable to the difference between our ages; it need fear no comparison with any other. Oh, remember, remember! Trust! Do not now separate me as by a curtain from that divinity within you. Blackest of curtains that is made up of a belief in my treachery. I treacherous! I unloving!

These words are not royal. They are sincere. I have expressed myself in this manner for the last time, until you premit me to resume it. I now adopt that of a visitor of state, for conformity with your wishes is the rule of my love.

XLIX   Alina, wife of Cornelius Nepos, to her sister Postumia, wife of Publius Ceccinius of Verona.
[*October 30.*]

You will have seen all the letters we sent concerning this matter by the Dictator's courier to you and to the poet's family. Here are a few details. I shall add for your eyes alone. My husband is grieving as though he had lost a son (avert the omen! our boys are very well, thanks be to the Gods). I loved Gaius [*Catullus*], also, and have loved him since we all played together as children. But affection should not blind our eyes—I can speak frankly to you—to the lessons of this deplorable mistaken life. I did not like his friends; of course, I did not like that wicked woman; I did not like the verses he wrote during these last years; and I shall never like nor praise the Dictator who has been in and out of our house these days as though he were an old family friend.

We had often asked Gaius to stay with us, but you know his brusque independence. So when he appeared at our door one morning, followed by old Fusco carrying his bedding, and asked to live in our garden house, then I knew he was really ill. My husband reported this move at once to the Dictator. The Dictator promptly sent over his physician, a Greek named Sosthenes, the most conceited pig-headed young man I have ever met. I have no hesitation in saying that I am an excellent physician myself. I think it's a gift which the Immortal Gods confer on all mothers, but this Sosthenes kept brushing away remedies which have *proved* their efficacy since time immemorial. But that's a long story.

Now, Postumia, there's not the slightest doubt that *that woman* killed him. After leading him through every avenue of hell for three years, she suddenly became all kindness and that's how she killed him. She never appeared herself, but every day came letters, gifts of food—and what food!—Greek manuscripts, and messages of inquiry twice a day. All this made Gaius very happy, but there are all kinds of happiness; this was that puzzled bodiless happiness which, I suppose, deceived husbands feel when their

151

wives are suddenly very kind to them. As the days went by and she did not appear herself we could see that he was resigning all hope of health and letting himself drift into death. At about three o'clock on the afternoon of the twenty-seventh his servant Fusco—you remember him; he used to tend boats on Lake Garda—came running to the house. He said that his master was delirious and was dressing himself to go to the Queen of Egypt's reception. I hurried out to the garden house and found him lying unconscious in a great pool of bile which he had vomited up. My husband sent at once for Sosthenes who came and sat with Gaius until his death an hour before dawn. I was not permitted entrance to the sickroom, but who should appear at about ten o'clock but the Dictator himself. He was splendidly dressed and must have slipped away from the Queen's reception which, after all, was less than a mile away. All night we could hear the orchestras and see the sky lit up by her bonfires. I overheard Fusco telling my husband that when the Dictator first came to the room, Gaius raised himself on one elbow and shouted to him wildly to go away. He called him "thief of liberty," "monster of greed," "murderer of the Republic" and many more names, all of which are, of course, *absolutely true*. My husband joined them at about that time—he had been away hunting for our old balsam-burner. He tells me that the Dictator was receiving all this in silence, but that he was as white as a ghost. It had probably been some time since Caesar had been ordered to leave a room, but he left.

He returned at about two hours after midnight, having changed from his fine clothes. Gaius was sleeping; when he awoke he seemed to be reconciled to his visitor. My husband said he even smiled and said, "What, no fringes, great Caesar?" Well, as you know, my husband worships the man. (For the most part we've arranged in our house simply not to discuss him.) Cornelius says that Caesar was quite wonderful from then on, wonderful in his silences and in his replies. He says that, of course, Caesar had been present at more deathbeds than anyone else. You know all those storeis about Gaul, of how the wounded soldiers used to refuse to die until their General had made his nightly rounds. Oh, I confess, Postumia, that—wicked ruler though he is—there is something very impressive and yet unforced about his presence. My husband says that he himself stayed in one corner of the room with Sosthenes and that he could hear very little of what the two were saying. Apparently at one point, Gaius, the tears streaming down his face, almost flung himself out of bed crying that he had wasted his life and his song for the favors of a harlot. I would not have known how to answer that, but it seems that the Dictator could. My husband says that he talked in even lower tones, but he gathered that Caesar was praising Clodia Pulcher as though she were some Goddess. Gaius was not in pain, but he was growing weaker. He lay with his eyes on the ceiling, listening to Caesar's words. From time to time Caesar fell silent, but when the silence had lasted too long for him, Gaius touched his wrist with his fingers, as though to say "go on, go on." And all Caesar was doing was talking about Sophocles! Gaius died to a chorus from *Oedipus at Colonus.* Caesar placed the coins on his eyes, embraced Cornelius and the wretched physician, and went home, without guards, through the first light of dawn.

You may wish to repeat some of this to his mother and father, though it seems to me that it would only distress them further. I should feel no small responsibility if either of my boys were to succumb to such an infatuation as we have witnessed here. I think I may say that their *upbringing* will have spared them that!

> [*The letter continues with the discussion of the sale of some real estate.*]

XLIX-A   Caesar's Journal—Letter to Lucius Mamilius Turrinus on the Island of Capri.
[*Night of October 27–28.*]

1013. [*On the death of Catullus.*] I am watching beside the bed of a dying friend, the poet Catullus. From time to time he falls asleep; I then take to my pen, as always, perhaps to avoid reflection. (Though I should have learned by now that to write to you is to invoke from the depths of my mind those questions which I have spent my life evading.)

He just opened his eyes, gave the names of six of the Pleiades, and asked me that of the seventh.

Even as a young man, Lucius, you possessed an unerring eye for the Inevitable Occasion and the Inevitable Consequence. You wasted no time in wishing that things were otherwise. From you I learned, but slowly, that there are large fields of experience which our longing cannot alter and which our fears cannot forfend. I clung for years to a host of self-delusions, to the belief that burning intensity in the mind can bring a message from an indifferent loved one and that sheer indignation can halt the triumphs of an enemy. The uinverse goes its mighty way and there is very little we can do to modify it. You remember how shocked I was when you let fall so lightly the words: "Hope has never changed tomorrow's weather." Adulation is continually assuring me that I have "accomplished the impossible" and "reversed the order of nature"; I receive these tributes with a grave inclination of the head, but not without a wish that the best of my friends were present to share with me the derision they deserve.

I not only bow to the inevitable; I am fortified by it. The achievements of men are more remarkable when one contemplates the limitations under which they labor.

The type of the Inevitable is death. I remember well that in my youth I believed that I was certainly exempt from its operation. First when my daughter died, next when you were wounded, I knew that I was mortal; and now I regard those years as wasted, as unproductive, in which I was not aware that my death was certain, nay, momently possible. I can now appraise at a glance those who have not yet foreseen their death. I know them for the children they are. They think that by evading its contemplation they are enhancing the savor of life. The reverse is true: only those who have grasped their non-being are capable of praising the sunlight. I will have no part in the doctrine of the stoics that the contemplation of death teaches us the vanity of human endeavor and the insubstantiality of life's joys. Each year I say farewell to the spring with a more intense passion and every day I am more bent on harnessing the course of the Tiber, even though my successors may permit it to expend itself senselessly in the sea.

He has opened his eyes again. We have had a paroxysm of grief. Clodia! Every moment as I watch this I understand more clearly her ruined greatness.

Oh, there are laws operating in the world whose import we can scarcely guess. How often we have seen a lofty greatness set off a train of evil, and virtue engendered by wickedness. Clodia is no ordinary woman and colliding with her Catullus has struck off poems which are not ordi-

154

nary. At the closer range we say *good* and *evil,* but what the world profits by is intensity. There is a law hidden in this, but we are not present long enough to glimpse more than two links in the chain. There lies the regret at the brevity of life.

He is sleeping.

Another hour has gone by. We talked. I am no stranger to deathbeds. To those in pain one talks about themselves; to those of clear mind one praises the world that they are quitting. There is no dignity in leaving a despicable world and the dying are often fearful lest life was not worth the efforts it had cost them. I am never short of subjects to praise.

During this last hour I have paid an old debt. Many times during the ten years of my campaigns I was visited by a recurrent waking dream. I have walked to and fro before my tent at night improvising a speech. I imagined that I had collected before me an audience of chosen men and women, particularly the young, to whom I wished to communicate all that I owed—boy and man, soldier and administrator, lover, father, son, sufferer and rejoicer—to Sophocles. Once before I died I wished to empty my heart—so promptly refilled—of that thanks and praise.

Oh, yes, he was a man and that was a man's work. An old question is answered. It is not that the Gods refused to help him, though it is certain They gave him no help. That is not Their way. If They were not hidden he would not so have peered to find Them. I too have journeyed through the highest Alps when I could not see a foot before me, but never with his composure. It was enough for him to live *as though the Alps were there*.

And now Catullus, too, is dead.

L   Caesar to Cytheris.
        [*November 1.*]

You may well imagine, gracious lady, that one in my position hesitates to submit requests to those for whom he holds the highest regard, lest the request seem to carry a weight that he does not intend to put upon it. Assume that I am in no other situation that that when I first had the pleasure of making your acquaintance and when you first aroused an admiration which has only increased with the passing of time.

My wife has been learning the responses which fall to her in certain ceremonies which will take place in December. I have been permitted to instruct her in these, but only to that limited extent which their secrecy admits. Could I request you to accord a few hours to instructing her in the delivery of these responses and in the deportment consonant with their solemnity?

As the Queen of Egypt is to be present at a portion of the ceremonial I should be particularly gratified if she were permitted to share whatever hours of instruction you felt able to give my wife.

It was with great happiness that I learned by accident a few days ago that you were a cherished friend of Lucius Mamilius Turrinus and that you occasionally visited him on the Island of Capri. It is his wish that as little reference be made to him as possible and even these lines confer upon this letter a character of secrecy. My happiness is not only that you enjoy his friendship and he yours, but that through you (and I hope, madam, through me) his genius may—if I may use the expression—operate in the world, even though we are not permitted to use his name. It would be remarkable enough that any man should have passed through the desperate situation that he did and be enduring its consequences and yet remain unshaken in soul; but that this should have befallen him who was already superior to all men in wisdom as he was superior to them in those attributes of soul which we call beauty is a subject of wonder, the limits of which I have never reached. The Island of Capri is surrounded for me by an air which I can only call awe. That I am not the sole reflector of that genius is not only a happiness to me, but a relief. Many things remain unspoken between my friend and myself. Among them is the regulation that I receive no letters from him and that I may visit him but once a year. I am occasionally saddened by these restrictions, but with the passing of time I come to see that they too are marked by that almost other-worldly wisdom that he never fails to impart.

Since we are talking of great men, I enclose transcripts of the last verses written by Gaius Valerius Catullus who died five nights ago.

156

LI The Queen of Egypt: Memorandum for her Secretary of State.

[*November 6.*]

The Queen of Egypt has received with satisfaction the imformation you have submitted to her. Her commendation has particular reference to your reports of October 29 and November 3, together with their attached documents.

The Queen has taken notice of your appraisal of the centers of discontent.

> [*Here follow Cleopatra's comments on twelve individuals or groups from among whom attempts to overturn the state or assassinate the Dictator might be expected. The potential conspirators do not include the Cascas, Cassius, or Brutus. Material from this section is reflected in our Book Four.*]

In addition, the Queen calls your attention to the following matters:

1. The reports from Source 14 [*Abra*] are worthless. Her simplicity is feigned. It should not be difficult to increase their value by threats of exposure and by other pressures.

2. Are you convinced that you have explored all the significance of the Dictator's disappearance during my reception on the 27th? His attendance at the sickbed of a scurrilious versifier does not appear to afford a sufficient explanation.

3. Every effort should be made to place an agent in the household of Marc Antony. The evidence you have collected of his disloyalty to the Dictator in [*46*] is herewith returned. It should be deposited among the documents which you are safeguarding against any possible theft or confiscation. I am retaining the other material you found in his home.

4. The dressmaker Mopsa. Obtain for me as soon as possible a complete account of her life, parentage, associates, and so on. Also a schedule of her engagements during this month. She is coming to me on the 17th to make my robe for the Ceremonies of the Good Goddess.

5. Your work for this week is to be an intensive study of the situation of the Lady Clodia Pulcher and her brother. What interpretations are being made of her retirement to the country? When is she returning to the City? The report of Sosigenes [*The Egyptian astronomer*]

157

was unsatisfactory. I wish you to instruct him in what to observe.

I agree with you that Clodius Pulcher is attempting to seduce the Dictator's wife. I wish you to follow this with the closest attention. There is little doubt that communications are passing between them through Source 14. Report to me any suggestions you have for taking advantage of this situation.

In acknowledgement of the diligence and skill you have shown in the difficult tasks laid before you, it is with pleasure that I assign to you and to your descendants forever the Oasis of Sesseben, together with its revenues and imposts, limited only by the regulations laid down under the 44th and 47th edicts of my reign [*limitations imposed on the levies which regional officials and landowners may assess against farmers, and limitation on the charge for the watering of camels at springs and waterways.*]

LII Pompeia to Clodia.
      [*November 12.*]

I miss you all the time, dearest Mousie. Nobody can understand why you have to go off into the country now when so much is going on in the city. I asked my husband what interest you could possibly take in mathematics and he said that you were very good at such things and that you knew all about the stars and what they did.

I give you ten guesses about who comes to our house all the time, at least every other day, and we have the most unusual times. Cleopatra! And not only Cleopatra, but Cytheris, the actress. And my husband arranged it all. Isn't that strange?

First Cytheris came to teach me you-know-what. Then Cleopatra started coming to learn some of that, too. At the end of the lesson the Queen asks Cytheris to recite, and oh, such things, my blood runs cold. Cassandra going mad and Medea planning to murder her babies, and everybody dying. And then my husband comes home early and it's jabber, jabber, jabber about Greek plays. And he gets up and he's Agamemnon and Cytheris is Clytemnestra and Cleopatra is Cassandra and Octavius and I have to be chorus, and then we all have supper. Oh, my dear Claudilla, you should be here because I have no one to laugh with; they are all so serious about these things. For me it is very very funny when my husband starts roaring and when Cleopatra goes mad.

Really, I rather like the Queen. Of course, she's not like you and me. I used to think she was quite ugly but sometimes she is almost beautiful. But, really, I am not the least bit jealous. My husband doesn't behave to her any differently than he behaves to Aunt Julia.

Yesterday, the Queen of Egypt asked my husband when you were coming back. She said that she hoped you would come back soon, as you are her instructress for the rites. My husband said he did not know what your plans were, but that he assumed you would be back by December first.

Dearest, I saw your brother, the younger one I mean; he came up to me on his horse while I was on the road to Lake Nemi. He looks so like you that I am always astonished. People say that he is a bad man, and even you say so, but I know he is not. You must not take that attitude to him, Claudilla, dear. Anyone would be bad, if you told them all the time that they were bad.

From this letter you must think that I am very happy, but I am not. I almost never go out of the house and no one I wish to see ever comes into it. I went to the Queen of Egypt's once; I went to pay a confinement call on Porcia, Brutus's wife. Sometimes I just sit and wish I were dead. What I think is that if one doesn't live when one's young, when do you live? I adore my husband and he adores me, but I like *people* and he doesn't.

I've just heard that my call on Porcia was simply wasted; word has just come that she's had a miscarriage, so I needn't have gone at all.

LIII   Cytheris to Lucius Mamilius Turrinus, on the Island of Capri.

[*November 25.*]

The air of Rome, my dear friend, is uneasy and fretful; its tongues are growing sharp and satirical, without laughter; one hears stories daily of behavior and crimes that are not so much passionate as erratic and illogical. For a time I thought that this malaise lay only within myself, but now all are remarking it. Our Master is busier

159

than ever; edicts fall about us daily. Regulations are laid down for usury and every man must clean the street in front of his door; a great map of the world has been set into the pavement before the law courts, picked out in golden eagles which denote the location of new cities. Young husbands stand before it, stroking their chins, trying to decide whether they shall set up a new home in ice and sleet or under a burning sun.

I was about to accept your invitation to come to Capri at once, when this Master requested that I come to his house to instruct his wife and his royal guest in the ceremonial that will be required of them in early December. We have had eight sessions, frequently concluded by readings from the tragedies in which we all take part, including Caesar himself. I find myself moving in a tragedy within a tragedy.

I am coming to understand that mystery, Caesar's marriage. I see that it is not based on any morbid inclination toward very young girls, as so many sneering tongues have held. Caesar is a teacher; it is a sort of fury in him. He can only love where he can instruct; the return he asks is progress and enlightenment. Of these young girls he asks only what Pygmalion asked of marble. I gather that he has been three times rewarded—by Cornelia, by his daughter, and by the Queen of Egypt; and many times resisted. The resistance he is now meeting is enormous and crushing. Pompeia is not an unintelligent girl, but his method toward her is so unintelligent that he is frightening and starving whatever intelligence she has. Love as education is one of the great powers of the world, but it hangs in a delicate suspension; it achieves its harmony as seldom as does love by the senses. Frustrated, it creates even greater havoc, for like all love it is a madness. On the one hand he loves her as a delicate growing thing and as a woman (and Caesar's glance resting on a woman is like no other man's), and on the other hand he loves her for the potentiality she may possess to be an Aurelia, a Julia Marcia. In his mind Rome is a woman; he married Pompeia to shape her into one more of those living statues of the great Roman matron.

Cleopatra has disappointed him also. One can only guess how intoxicatingly she must first have filled the requirements of a beloved pupil. She still is. I worship this colossus, but I am an old woman; I am no longer educable. Yet I understand well the eager rapture with which she receives every word that falls from his lips. He discovered, however, that he could teach her nothing essential, for the essence of what he has to teach is moral, is responsibility; and Cleopatra has not the dimmest sense of what is right and wrong. Caesar does not know that he has this passion for teaching; all that has for him the invisibility of things which are self-evident. Hence he is a very bad teacher. He assumes that all men are both teachers and voracious learners; that everyone is vibrant with moral life. Women are more subtle teachers than men.

I shall never cease to be moved by the view we occasionally have of great men trying to make a marriage where no marriage can be, continuing to expend a defeated tenderness on ill-compounded wives. The patience they acquire is a very different thing from the patience that wives exhibit toward husbands; that is in the natural order of things and should no more be singled out for praise than the honesty of the honest. One has seen these insulted husbands finally withdrawing into themselves; they have learned the basic solitude of man as their happier brothers will never know it.

Such a husband is Caesar. His other bride is Rome. To both he is a bad husband, but from an excess of conjugal love.

Let me go on a moment more.

I have only recently come to understand some words that you let fall years ago, that "wickedness may be the exploration of one's liberty"——have I got that right?——and that "it can be the search for a limit that one can respect." How stupid I am not to have digested that before, my dear prince; I could have played it into my Medea and into my Clytemnestra. Yes, in the light of that thought, can't we say that a great deal of what we call "wickedness" is the very principle of virtue exploring the laws of its own nature? Isn't that what Antigone, my Antigone, our Antigone, meant when she said: [*In Sophocles's play, in reply to Creon's assertion that her slain "good" brother would not wish her wicked brother to receive an honorable burial*] "Who can say but that in the underworld his [*wicked*] deeds may seem to be blameless?" Yes, there lies the interpretation of Clodia's disorders and unless Caesar is watchful, Pompeia will journey out in search of a limitation to her curiosities. Nature affords them to our senses: fire burns our fingers and the action of our hearts prevents our running up mountainsides; but

161

only the Gods have put a veto on the adventures of our minds. If They do not choose to intervene, we are condemned to fashion our own laws or to wander in fright through the pathless wastes of our terrifying liberty, seeking even the reassurance of a barred gate, of a forbidding wall. It is a recurrent joke among writers of farces that wives rejoice in being beaten by their husbands. It reflects, however, an eternal truth—that there is a great comfort in knowing that those who love you love you enough to take the responsibility for marking out the permissible. Husbands often err—but in both directions. Caesar is a tyrant—both as husband and as ruler. It is not that, like other tyrants, he is chary of according liberty to others; it is that, loftily free himself, he has lost all touch with the way freedom operates and is developed in others; always mistaken, he accords too little or he accords too much.

LIV   Clodia to her brother.
       [*From Nettuno.*]
       [*Selections from almost daily letters throughout November.*]

Don't come here, Brainless. I don't wish to see anyone.

I am completely happy as I am. Cicero is next door, repining and writing those doleful insincerities he calls philosophy. We met several times, but are now reduced to sending each other gifts of fruit or pastry. He could not interest me in philosophy and I could not interest him in mathematics. He's a very witty man, but for some reason he's never witty to me. I dry him up.

I do nothing all day and would be very bad company for you. I study numbers and can forget anything else for days at a time. There are properties in the study of infinity that no one has ever dreamed of. I have frightened Sosigenes with them. He says they are dangerous.

I am very angry with you for appealing to old Eaglebeak to close that play. Any mortification only begins for us from the moment we take any notice of such things. When will you learn that the enjoyment of the malicious is doubled when they learn that we have been wounded by their remarks?

As you say, it is vexatious to be charged with a thousand crimes that one never got around to committing. I certainly left my dear parents as soon as I could, but I never lifted a hand to annoy them. Not only did I not kill my poor husband, but I got down on my knees and begged him not to kill himself with overeating. I have never felt a tremor of passion for you or for Dodo; in fact, I have too often gazed with astonishment at the starved water rats that committed themselves to finding you attractive.

As to this last matter [*the death of Catullus?*], I don't wish you ever to mention it again. It is all so complicated; no one else will ever understand it. I don't wish to hear it mentioned.

The worst of being charged with crimes, however, is that it makes one restless to deserve all that censure. But, of course, only something enormous would do. Something to darken the sun.

Of course, I am angry that people should be saying that *he* directed me to go into the country. Although it's utter nonsense, it's more exasperating than all the other lies put together. But I shall not come into town merely to refute it.

[*November 27.*]
Come to Nettuno, Publius. I cannot endure this any longer, but I am not yet ready to come into town.

For the sake of heaven, come and don't bring anyone with you.

The worst about inactivity is that it sets one brooding about the passing of time. And it has set me to remembering, as though I were an old woman. Last night I could not sleep; I got up and burned all my mathematical notebooks; then I threw in all the letters I have received for ten years. Sosigenes danced around like an old moth trying to restrain me.

Start the minute you receive this letter. I have an idea. Marc Antony failed to complete "the most daring feat ever seen in Rome." Well, I know another.

Mopsa is here making me a new robe and turban for the Lalalala games.

[*November 28.*]
I hope this letter fails to reach you and that you are already on your way. If not, start at once.

I have just received a letter from the Dictator requesting me to return to Rome to take up my instruction for the Queen of Egypt. He has asked me to dinner on the second.

LV   Cleopatra to Caesar.
[December 5.]

I send you the following information, great Caesar, knowing well that my motives may be misunderstood by you. A month and a half ago I would have told it to you at once; that thought has decided me now.

The Lady Clodia Pulcher has had two robes and turbans made for the ceremonies on the night of December 11th. She intends to dress her brother in one of them and introduce him into your house. Your wife is aware of this, as a letter from her, now in my possession, shows.

LV-A   Caesar to Cleopatra.
[By return messenger.]
I thank you, great Queen. I am indebted to you for many things. I regret that this sorry matter to which you have called my attention should be among them.

LVI   Alina, wife of Cornelius Nepos, to her sister Postumia, wife of Publius Ceccinius of Verona.
[December 13.]

Just a word in haste, dearest Postumia. Rome is standing on its head. There has never been such an uproar. Public offices have been closed and most of the shopkeepers don't even open the shops. Word must have reached you before this: that Clodia Pulcher introduced her brother dressed as a votary into the Ceremonies of the Good Goddess. I was standing a few feet from him when he was discovered. They say it was the Lady Julia Marcia who called attention to it. Our singing had been going on for an hour, and the responses. Some women flew at him and tore off the turban and the bands. Such screaming you never heard. Soon women were striking him from all sides as hard as they could; others dashed about covering up the sacred things. Of course, there wasn't any other man within shouting distance; but presently some guards came

164

and picked him up, bleeding and groaning, and dragged him off.

This is the end; really, I don't know what to say. Everybody says, This is the end. People are even saying, Now let Caesar move Rome to Byzantium. In a moment I must hurry down to the trial. Cicero made a terrible and wonderful speech against Clodius and Clodia yesterday. All sorts of people are being called to testify and rumors are flying about. Some think that the Queen of Egypt had a hand in it, because Clodia served as her instructress; but the Queen was indisposed and did not even go to the rites.

The strangest thing of all is the behavior of Caesar. As Supreme Pontiff he should be directing the inquiry. But from the beginning he's refused to have anything to do with it. There's no doubt that his wife is as guilty as they are. Isn't it awful, awful, awful?

My husband has just come in. He says that Pompeia's family—twenty of them—went to Caesar last night to urge him to speak in her defense. It seems that he was very quiet and listened to them for an hour. Then he rose and said he had no intention of appearing at the trial; that it was possible that Pompeia was not implicated in this matter, but that it was not difficult for a woman in her position so to conduct her life that such a suspicion would never fall upon her; that the suspicion was damaging enough, and that he was divorcing her the very next day—that is today.

I'm hurrying to the trial, dear. I may have to give evidence. It is a strange feeling to be hurrying through the streets of this city! It's as though the city itself were in disgrace and that we all ought to move out of it.

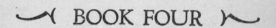

BOOK FOUR

LVII   Servilia in Rome to her son Marcus Junius Brutus.
       [*August 18. This letter reached Brutus at Mar-
       seilles as he was about to return to Rome con-
       cluding his governorship of Hither Gaul.*]

Return, Marcus, return to the city which is bending all
its eyes upon you.

The hero whose name you bear [*Junius Brutus who had
expelled the Tarquins*] lives in you, by spirit if not by blood,
and his task is on your shoulders.

Return to the city whose health is your own health and
whose freedom is your own freedom. Romans are again
calling on the name of Brutus and all eyes are bent on
you.

The man against whom Rome's rage is directed is no little man. The man who now stifles Rome is great in all
things and greatest in error. The murderer must be of equal
stature with the murdered of Rome is twice enslaved.
There is only one Roman at that height and all eyes are
bent on you. The hand that strikes him down must be
passionless as justice. The tyrannicide's task is a holy task;
it is remembered with grateful tears by generations unborn.

Come look on him; give him the honor that is his due;
look on him as a great son looks on a great father, and
with the blow not of one man but of ten thousand thousands—slay him.

Thinking of the child soon to be born to you, raise up
your hand and strike.

LVII-A   Brutus to Servilia.
         [*Returning the letter to her.*]

This letter is yours. That I have read it does not make
it mine.

The words with which you direct me to murder a friend

169

and benefactor are clear enough. The words with which you call my parentage in question are not clear.

By the age of twenty, madam, every man should be sufficiently his own father. His father by the body is of large, though lesser, importance. Those who call that parentage in question, however, should do so only under oath and under the most solemn oath and with the most absolute clearness.

This you have not done. Thereby I have lost, in two ways, a measure of the respect I am bound to owe you.

LVII-B   Cornelius Nepos: Commonplace Book.
[*Notes on Cicero's conversation.*]

I thought the moment propitious for asking the question which all Rome had wished to put to him for thirty years. "Tell me, my friend, what is your opinion—is Marcus Junius Brutus the son of Julius Caesar?"

He sobered at once.

"Cornelius," he said, "we must be careful how we use the word 'opinion.' With much evidence I venture to say that I know a thing; with a more limited amount I venture to say that I have an opinion on it; with less still I venture a conjecture. In a matter of this kind I have not sufficient even for a conjecture. Suppose, however, that I felt I had a conjecture—should I give it to *you*, you who will undoubtedly put it in a book? In a book, conjectures have a way of looming larger than facts. Facts can be controverted; a gloss can nullify them; but conjectures are not easily dismissed. The histories we read are little more than processions of conjectures pretending they are facts.

"Is Marcus Junius Brutus the son of Caesar? Put it this way: do I know, or have I any opinion as to whether this relationship is believed to exist by Brutus, by Caesar, or by Servilia?

"Brutus is among my best friends. Caesar is ... Caesar is the man whom I have observed most attentively for thirty, for forty, years. Servilia—well, overtures were once made that I should marry Servilia. Let us weigh this matter.

"I have seen the first two together many, many times and I can affirm to you that I have never seen any faintest sign pass between them that could be interpreted as an acknowledgement of such a relationship. Caesar holds Brutus in high regard. He has for him the affection, the tacit

170

affection, of an older man for a younger man of notable capability. Perhaps I should say grudging affection—that is to say, something like a fear of him, or at least a ... come now, Cornelius, do we seniors always rejoice in the knowledge that there will be brilliant historians and orators in the generations that follow us? Do we not feel that it is the duty of our successors to be inferior? Moreover, Caesar has always maintained his distance from all men of incorruptible independence—from all twelve of them, from all six of them. It cannot be said too often that Caesar is unhappy in the society of capable men—or, rather, of men who are possessed of both ability and high character. Oh, yes, he is; oh, yes, he is. He likes ability if it's unscrupulous, and likes high character if it's impractical, but he cannot endure both in one man. He's surrounded himself with scoundrels; he likes the talk of scoundrels; he likes their jokes—Oppius, Mammurra, Milo—scoundrels all of them. When he works, he works with people like Asinius Pollio, honest, loyal, and a mediocrity.

"Now Brutus's deportment to Caesar differs at no point from his deportment to any of us seniors. Brutus feels affection for no one, never has, and never will—except, of course, for his wife, and perhaps because of her, a little for his father-in-law. You know that impassive and handsome face, that deliberate utterance, that austere courtesy. If he thought that Caesar were, or even might be, his father—no, I cannot believe it! I have seen him thank Caesar for favors; I have seen him disagree with Caesar; why, I have seen him present his wife to Caesar. Caesar is all actor and we shall never know what he thinks, but Brutus is no part an actor and I would take my oath that he has never considered this possibility.

"There remains our conjecture as to what Servilia thinks.

"But before I come to that, there is one thing more that should be said: thirty years ago this relationship was firmly believed by many to be an undoubted fact. The dates, as one might say, support this paternity. At that time Caesar was consolidating his political advancement by a calculated succession of double adulteries. Women then played a far greater part in the life of the Republic and Servilia had one of the most brilliant political heads, male or female, in the entire aristocracy. She could sway the policies of twenty stupid and wavering multimillionaires; all she had to do was to tell them *what to be*

171

afraid of next. Do not judge the Servilia of those years by the Servilia of today. Today she is merely a frantic intriguing woman, floundering amid preposterous and conflicting principles and flooding the city with anonymous but transparent letters. The weather of Rome has deteriorated for women. Do not even judge the Clodia of ten years ago by the Clodia of today. Rome twenty and thirty years ago was an arena of forceful women—think of Caesar's mother, Pompey's mother, and Caesar's aunt. They thought of little else than politics and did not permit their husbands, lovers, guests, and children to think of anything else. People affect now to be shocked by the fact that their mothers and grandmothers appear to have been repeatedly married and divorced simply for reasons of political expediency. They forget that this was not only because these brides brought with them wealth and family connections—everyone knew that the bride was in herself a political general. Why, as the struggle between Sulla and Marius came to a head, poisoning was so frequent an occurrence that one thought twice before dining at the home of one's own sister.

"You can imagine what art it required of Caesar to glide in and out of the beds of these warring Clytemnestras! The story has never been told. The prodigy of it lies in the fact that each of his successive paramours worships him to this day. How often, finding myself in the company of one or other of our aging matrons, I have turned the conversation to praise of this man, only to discover that I am being listened to by a breathless and half-swooning girl, convinced that she was the only inspiratrix of that parded career."

Here Cicero fell to laughing and choking again and had to be beaten encouragingly on the back.

"Now, notice," he continued, "Caesar who in wedlock has only been able to achieve one child, outside wedlock went far toward justifying his appellation of 'the Father of his Country.' I think there is little doubt that he made every effort to bind these influential paramours to him by the bond of a child. Furthermore, it was often observed that when the woman of his attentions announced to him that she was pregnant ... are you following me? ... and when he was convinced that he was indeed the father of this ... this expectation, he invariably made a very handsome return; he presented the lady with a gift, and with no mean gift.

172

"During the years we are speaking of, however, never forget that Caesar was penniless. Yes, throughout the twenty most critical years of his career, Caesar was ... spendthrift without income and lavish with another's gold.

[*Here follows Cicero's digression on Caesar and money, already given in Document XII.*]

At all events, Caesar rescued from inactivity enough of his friends' money to present Volumnia with the "Andromache" of Apelles (fit subject for an adulteress), the greatest painting in the world, though a fading relic of its former self. Can you doubt that her twin daughters are the daughters of Caesar? Isn't that the *nose*—the nose, twice? And to Servilia he gave the rose-colored pearl that she wears so religiously at every celebration of the Founding of the City. That is the first pearl in the world and at the time it was the most talked-of object in Rome. The unappetizing bosom on which it now reposes, my friend (in defiance of the sumptuary laws) was once as beautiful as itself. Is it the reward for bearing Marcus Junius Brutus? We shall never know, we shall never know."

LVIII   Caesar, in Rome, to Brutus, at Marseilles.
        [*August 17.*]
        [*By private courier.*]

I do not have to tell you with what satisfaction I have received reports from many sources of the exemplary manner in which you have fulfilled your high office. I trust that my commendation is a satisfaction to you for two reasons; the lesser reason is that it comes from a friend who takes pride and pleasure in all you do; the greater reason is that I, too, am a servant of the Roman state and suffer when she is injured and rejoice when she is nobly served. By the immortal Gods I would that from all the provinces I heard news of such justice, such tireless concern for all her subjects, and such energy in the execution of her laws. To thousands awaking from the sleep of barbarism you have made Rome loved and honored; you have made her feared only so far as equity should be feared by us all.

Return, my dear young man, to the country which asks increasingly greater labors of you.

The letter I now write you is for your eyes alone and I

direct you to destroy it when it has been read. Take what time you wish to write me a reply; my courier will await your convenience.

I do not believe that in a republic it is among the responsibilities of a leader to indicate or appoint his successor. Similarly, I do not believe that the head of a republic should be invested with dictatorial powers. Yet I am Dictator, and I am convinced that the powers I have been obliged to assume are necessary for the State and I am convinced that only my appointment of a successor can save that State from another long and exhausting civil war. You and I have had many long conversations concerning the nature of government and the degree to which our Roman citizens at this time can be left to govern themselves. We have not always been in agreement as to the extent to which they are capable of governing themselves. I appointed you to the post which you are now leaving in order that you might learn through the daily exercise of administration the enormous extent to which the rank and file of men are dependent on those placed over them. I now wish you to hold a similar position in the capital and to discover for yourself a similar truth concerning our citizens in Italy.

I wish you to serve as Praetor. I am appointing your brother-in-law [*Cassius*] to serve with you. I wish you to be Praetor of the City; of the two offices it is the more difficult, the one more exposed to the public view, and the one closer to my self.

As I have said above, I believe that, given the disposition of our citizens and the political situation in the Peninsula, it is my duty to appoint my successor. It is true that a man in my position can only appoint a successor; he cannot confirm him. There is one thing of which all men are equally ignorant and that is the future. A successor must confirm himself. There are ways, however, in which, living and dead, I may still render aid to the man who follows me. One such aid is to introduce him to the methods by which the world is administered and to share with him information and experience which is not elsewhere obtainable. As Praetor of the City these would be at your disposal.

I am made aware daily that my life may be cut short at any time. I do not choose to employ those safeguards against my enemies which might secure my bodily safety at the cost of encumbering my movements and alarming

174

my mind. There are many hours during the day when it would not be difficult for an assassin to destroy me. The recognition of these dangers has impelled me to give thought to my succession. In dying I shall leave no sons behind me. Even though I had sons I do not believe that leadership is transmitted by paternity. Leadership is for those who love the public good and are endowed and trained to administer it. I believe that you possess that love and are so endowed; the training I have been in a position to secure for you. The decision as to whether you wish to assume the supreme command is open to you.

I ask you to send me your thoughts on this matter.

LVIII-A   Brutus to Caesar.
        [*By immediate return.*

I thank you for your commendation. I thank you for the assistance you gave to me throughout the duration of my office. I accept the Praetorship of the City and shall hope to fill it in a manner that will retain the good opinion which moved you to confer it upon me.

The further office which you designate I do not wish to consider. My reasons for refusing it are contained in your own letter. Permit me to cite your words: I do not believe that in a republic it is among the responsibilities of a leader to indicate or appoint his successor. Caesar's position only a Caesar can fill; should it fall vacant, that office and that concentration of power must necessarily come to an end. May the Immortal Gods long preserve you to direct the state in the manner that you alone can perform; when you depart from that office may They preserve us from civil war.

My further reasons for refusing this office are private to myself. With each succeeding year I feel myself more and more drawn to the study of philosophy. When I have served you and the State for a time as Praetor of the City I shall call upon you to release me in order that I may devote myself exclusively to such studies. In them I hope to leave behind me a monument not unworthy of our Roman spirit and of your good opinion.

LIX   Caesar to Porcia, wife of M. Junius Brutus, in Rome.
        [*August 18.*]

I cannot deny myself the pleasure of telling you that some days ago I recalled your husband to this City. It was not without regret, Madam, that I recalled him, for those who love Rome could well wish him to remain forever in Hither Gaul, continuing the notable services that he is there rendering Her. Permit me to repeat to you the words which I have recently written to him:

"By the immortal Gods, I would that from all the Provinces I heard news of such justice, such tireless concern for all her subjects, and such energy in the execution of her laws."

Allow me to say that there is nothing which touches your house which does not affect me also. No differences of opinion have shaken the profound respect which I bear to those most closely associated with you. [*Porcia was the daughter of the Younger Cato.*] The word has reached me that you are awaiting the birth of a child. Not you alone, Madam, but all Rome awaits the child of so noble a heritage. I rejoice to think that the child's father will be present in that auspicious hour.

LIX-A   Porcia to Caesar.
         [*August 19.*]

Porcia, wife of Marcus Junius Brutus, sends many thanks to Caius Julius Caesar, Dictator, for the kindness of his letter and for his part in the most welcome news which it contains.

LIX-B   Caesar's Journal—Letter to Lucius Mamilius Turrinus on Capri.
         [*About August 21.*]

947.   No man is free of envy. I harbor three envious impulses, if that name can be given to three subjects of admiring meditation. I envy you your soul, Catullus his song, and Brutus his new wife. Of the first two I have spoken to you at some length, though not for the last time.

The third is not a new arrival to my thoughts. Even while she was the wife of my Vainglorious and incompetent friend [*M. Calpurnius*] Bibulus I had remarked her. How extraordinarily silence becomes a woman, not a silence which is an absence and vacancy—though that is uncommon enough—but a silence which is all attention. Such graced my Cornelia whom I called "my speaking silence"; and such my Julia, long silent and silent even in my dreams; such Cato's Porcia.

And yet when they were moved to speak, what eloquence or wit could rival it? They could speak of the smallest things in the ordering of the household and Cicero in full Senate could not so enthrall the ears. My envious meditations have instructed me why. The trivial is only unendurable from the lips of those who put an importance upon it. Yet our lives are immersed in the trivial; the significant comes to us enwrapped in multitudinous details of the trivial; the trivial has this dignity that it exists and is omnipresent. By their very nature women are the custodians of an immense amount of such consequential insignificance. To a man the rearing of children appears to be a servitude more harassing than the rearing of animals and more exasperating than bivouacking among the gnats of the Egyptian desert. A silent woman is one who has distinguished in her mind the detail which must fly to oblivion and the detail which merits a second attention.

Envy of another man's wife is not generally thought to have this pacific character; but such has been mine. While Bibulus was alive, I was often in the house and saw and envied him his return in the evening to that judicious tranquility. When Bibulus died I took to long thoughts, but a move seemed out of the question. Long thoughts had Brutus also, no doubt; he was much censured for divorcing Claudia [*daughter of Appius Claudius, a distant cousin of Clodia*] after so long a married life; but I could understand it and all Rome is aware of a happiness that even the grimmest stoic must envy, and even the watchful dictator condone. [*The marriage reinforced the only party of opposition among the aristocrats which could be said to have the wide support of popular opinion. Brutus married his cousin, his monther Servilia being the sister of Porcia's father, the Younger Cato; Cassius and Lepidus were married to half-sisters of Brutus, daughters of Servilia by her earlier marriage to the Consul Silenus; both were women of extremely bad reputation.*] Is she on a par with your mother and mine and with my aunt?—I do not know. It may be that her virtues have that inflexibility that mars those of her husband and her father, joyless men. One cannot but deplore an austerity which came into being through revulsion against a flagrant environment; it is not slow to adopt censoriousness and complacency. I take some pleasure in remembering that my young friend Brutus was not always so marble a philosopher. He languished for a time beside the Incomparable [*Cytheris the actress*] and he made his fortune by grinding the faces of the Cappadocians and the Cyprians; I, being Consul that year, barely saved him from a clamorous trial for extortion.

Yes, these moralists are virtuous by revulsion, hence their rigidity. May this "speaking silence" have a beneficent effect on the noble and handsome Brutus. [*This is a play on words, for* brutus *means both brutish and ugly.*]

LX   The Broadsides of Conspiracy.
> [*The following broadside or chain letter was circulated throughout the Peninsula by the thousands during the first weeks of September 45. This first one appeared in Rome September 1.*]

The Council of Twenty to every Roman worthy of his ancestors: Prepare to shake off the Tyranny under which our Republic groans. Our fathers died to acquire those liberties of which One Man now is robbing us. A Council of Twenty has been formed; it has taken oaths before the altars; it has received assurance from the Gods that its course is just and will succeed. Every Roman who receives this bulletin is enjoined to make five copies of it. With all secrecy, see that these copies reach the hands of five men, Romans likely to be of this opinion or to be so persuaded; they in turn are enjoined to make further copies.

Other bulletins will follow. By degrees their measures will become more definite.

Death to Caesar. For our country and our Gods. Silence and Resolution.
> The Council of Twenty

LX-A   Asinius Pollio to Caesar.
> [*This is the conclusion of Pollio's report to Caesar from Naples on September 18, given as our Document XIV.*]

I forward to my General the thirteen copies of the broadside which were sent to me during the last six days—three at my lodgings in Posilipo, ten here. My General will notice that five of them appear to have been written by the same hand which has, however, attempted to disguise itself. Quintus Cotta received 16; Lucius Mela, 10.

A corresponding movement has been set in motion in these parts for the common people, that is for those who cannot read and write. Pebbles and shells are being circulated on which are written: XX/C/M [for Death]. My orderly has collected a number of these. He assures me that they cause more indignation than enthusiasm and provoked the circulation of other stones marker XX/M. Both inscriptions can be found scrawled on the pavements, walls, etc.

I do not venture to submit suggestions to my General as to measures calculated to counteract this activity. I give, however, the results of a discussion on the matter held in our offices by Cotta, Mela, Annius Turbatius and myself.

1. The movement started in Rome. It's first appearance here was fifteen days later.

2. Three slaves were apprehended while delivering these letters. They were subjected to torture. Two declared that they had found the broadsides, addressed to us, in public places (an old woman found one on the tray of figs she was selling) and then delivered them in the hope of attaining a reward. The whole circulation depends on the custom of giving fees to the bringers of messages. The third slave said that the letter, addressed to me, had been given him for delivery with a fee by a veiled woman on the waterfront.

3. The initiators of this activity do not appear to be the Clodius Pulcher group, as lacking the astuteness and patience, nor the Cassius-Casca malcontents, who would think only in terms of a small group. The desire to enlist wide adherence, the relative absence of incitation to violence, together with the claims to religious approval suggest a studious and perhaps elderly group. We do not exclude the possibility of a Cicero or Cato arriving at this type of measure.

4. It is difficult to see how a chain letter movement could transfer itself from negative to positive action. We are agreed, however, that the movement could achieve results detrimental to good government and await whatever instructions may be issued to counteract it.

LX-B   Second Broadside.
    [This broadside achieved even wider circulation
179

The Council of Twenty to every Roman worthy of his ancestors: second bulletin. Every Roman who receives this bulletin is enjoined to make five copies of it and with all secrecy to see that they reach the hands of the five men to whom they forwarded the preceding one.

Herewith is our directive:

Beginning on the sixteenth of this month September, every Roman as far as possible will see that himself and his household will make their purchases in the city, present themselves before the Courts, and engage in all activities of public life on the even days of the month only.

In addition, those in Rome will render themselves ostentatiously assiduous in acclaiming the appearances of the Dictator and in accompanying his train at all public appearances. In conversation they will declare themselves enthusiastically in favor of all projects which he entertains, particularly the transference of the capital to the East, a military campaign to India, and a restoration of the Kingdom.

Our next bulletin will contain still more definite measures.

Death to Caesar. For our country and our Gods. Silence and Resolution.

The Council of Twenty

LX-C The Commonplace Book of Cornelius Nepos.
     [*This entry was written after Caesar's Death.*]

Throughout the Fall of 45, the principal subjects of conversation were so-called chain letters and the visit of Cleopatra. In fact, the initiation of the chain letters was ascribed by many to the Queen of Egypt, as they were thought to have a devious oriental cast, such as would not have occurred to a Roman. The injunction to perform one's public business on the even days of the month was watched by the public with breathless interest. At first it was noticed that a preponderance of activity was taking place on the uneven days. This gradually relaxed and the reverse became apparent.

[Enclosing a copy of the first broadsides of the conspiracy.]
[September 8–20.]

979. Someone has thought up a new way to prepare the people for an overturn of the State and for my death by assassination.

I enclose a copy of one of these public notices. They are circulating throughout Italy by the thousands.

Scarcely a day has passed during the last year when I have not received new detailed evidence of one or other of these conspiratorial movements. I am brought lists of names and accoutns of their reunions. I intercept letters. The majority of such groups are unbelievably maladept. Their membership generally includes one who is eager to sell his information for money or favor.

Each new conspiracy awakens in me a great interest—I was going to say "a happy interest," soon disappointed.

In the first place, I have little doubt that, soon or late, I shall die by the hand of a tyrannicide. I have not chosen to encumber my life with the constant protection of armed guards nor my mind with the practice of vigilant anxiety. I could wish that it were the dagger of a patriot that strikes me down, but I am equally exposed to those of the madman and the envious. In the meantime, by incarceration, exile, admonition, and exposure, I have arrested such plots as have come to my notice.

As I say, I have followed them with interest. It is always possible that among those who plan my death I shall find the man who is right in the matters where I am wrong. There are many better men in the world than I am, but I have not yet seen the man who could be a better ruler of our State. If he exists I think he would now be planning my death. Rome as I have shaped it, as I have had to shape it, is not a comfortable place for a man whose genius is the genius for ruling at the top: if I were not Caesar now, I would be Caesar's assassin. (That thought had not occurred to me until this moment, but I see it is true; it is one of the many discoveries that come to me from the practice of writing letters to you.)

But there is an even profounder reason why I should wish to know something about the man who slays me, even though that knowledge is mine only during the last moment of my life. This brings me back to that inquiry which, as you know, occupies me increasingly: Is there a Mind in or above the universe which is watching us?

I am often called "Destiny's favorite." If the Gods exist they placed me where I am. They placed every man where he is, but the man who fills my seat is among the more conspicuous of Their appointments—as, in his way, the poet Catullus is; as you are; as Pompey was. The man who slays me would perhaps afford us some light upon Their nature—Their selected instrument. But even as I write this my pen falls from my hand. I shall probably die by the dagger of a madman. The Gods hide themselves even in their choice of instrument. We are all at the mercy of a falling tile. We are left with the picture of Jupiter going about dislodging tiles which fall upon a lemonade vendor or upon Caesar. The jury that condemned Socrates to death were not august instruments; nor were the eagle and the tortoise that slew Aeschylus. It is probable that my last moment of consciousness will be filled with the last of many confirmations that the affairs of the world proceed with that senselessness with which a stream carries leaves upon its tide.

There is another element in the eagerness with which I inquire into each new conspiracy. Would it not be a wonderful discovery to find that I am hated to the death by a man whose hatred is disinterested? It is rare enough to find a disinterested love; so far among those that hate me I have uncovered nothing beyond the promptings of envy, of self-advancing ambition, or of self-consoling destructiveness. It may be that in that last moment I may be permitted to look into the face of a man whose only thought is Rome and whose only thought is that I am the enemy of Rome.

980–982. [*Already given in Document VIII.*]

983. [*On the weather.*]

984. [*On the increasing divergence between written and spoken Latin and the decay of case endings and the subjunctive in popular speech.*]

985. [*Again, on primogeniture and the inheritance of property.*]

986. [*Accompanying the second broadside.*]

I enclose the second public notice of the Committee of Twenty. I have not yet learned who are the initiators of this series. It smacks of some new kind of malcontent.

Since childhood I have been attentive to the attitude

which men bear to those who have been placed over them and who are in a position to restrict their movements. What deference and loyalty masking what contempt and hatred! The deference and loyalty proceeds from a man's gratitude that his superior relieves him of responsibility and from the terrors of weighty decisions; the contempt and hatred from his resentment against the man who limits his freedom. During a part of every day and night even the mildest men is, however obscurely, the murderer of those who can command his obedience. In my youth I was often filled with consternation to discover that, waking or sleeping, I was prone to dream the death of my father, my tutors, and my governors toward whom I often bore a real, if intermittent, love. It was, therefore, with a kind of pleasure that I used to listen to the songs which my soldiers sang about their campfires; for every four songs that elevated me to the Gods there was a fifth that diminished me to idiocy, senile vice, and decay. These last they sang loudest and the woods rang with glee at my death. I found in myself no anger, but only a little laughter and a few accelerated steps toward old age when I discovered that even Marc Antony and Dolabella had for a time joined with a group which was plotting my death; for a time the master they loved had merged with all the masters they had hated. It is only dogs that never bite their masters.

This combination of impulses is a part of the movement of the world and is not for us to approve or disapprove, for like all the fundamental impulses it produces both good and ill. And from it I draw confirmation of my conviction that the central movement of the mind is the desire for unrestricted liberty and that this movement is invariably accompanied by its opposite, a dread of the consequences of liberty.

LXII   Notes by Catullus, found by Caesar's Secret Police.
       [*These reached the Dictator on September 27.*]
       [*These rough drafts were on the reverse of leaves
       containing fragments of poetry or on slates. In
       both cases they had been negligently erased.*]

. . . . A Committee of Ten has been formed. . . .

. . . . This Committee of Twenty, having taken oaths before the altars of the Gods . . .

. . . . beginning on the twelfth of next month, September . . .

. . . . on the uneven days of the month will refrain from all . . .

. . . . assiduous attendance at the public appearance of the Dictator . . . acclamations of profuse flattery . . .

LXII-A   Caesar to Catullus.
         [*September 27.*]

It has been brought to my attention that certain friends of yours have initiated a series of documents designed to overturn the government of this Republic.

I regard these measures as childish and mistaken rather than criminal. Your friends will have observed the means I have already taken to render them harmless and ridiculous. Pressure is being brought upon me, however, to inflict public punishment on their perpetrators.

I find it difficult to believe that you had any hand in so inept an excursion into public affairs; but there is evidence to show that you were at least aware of it.

For the sake of my long friendship with your father I am willing to deal leniently with these mistaken young men. I place their fortunes in your hands. If you are able to inform me that their part in the circulation of these letters will cease, I shall regard the matter as closed.

I do not wish to hear any defense of their action. An affirmative word from you will be sufficient. That word you can give me day after tomorrow when I shall meet you, I am told, at the dinner being given by C. Publius Clodius and the Lady Clodia Pulcher.

LXII-B   Catullus to Caesar.
         [*September 28.*]

The letters of which you speak were planned by me alone and the first copies of them were sent out by me alone. There is no Committee of Twenty.

The means I have employed to remind Romans of their shrinking liberties may well seem inept to a Dictator. His powers are unlimited, as is his jealousy of any liberty other than his own. His powers extend to ransacking the private papers of the citizens.

The composition of these letters by me has already ceased, since their efficacy is at an end.

LXII-C Third Broadside of Conspiracy, written by Julius Caesar.

> [*By "their efficacy is at an end" Catullus meant that the country was now so flooded by letters written in imitation of his own that the movement was soon dissipated in the bewilderment and flagging interest of the citizens. This Third Broadside which appeared a few days after the Second received the widest circulation of all of them.*]

The Council of Twenty to every Roman worthy of his ancestors, this third bulletin.

The Council of Twenty now feels that these letters have received a sufficiently wide circulation. Hundreds of thousands have been aroused to a patriotic hatred of the oppressor and to an eager expectation of his death.

In the meantime you are instructed to prepare the people for this happy event. Hence, lose no opportunity to ridicule the so-called achievements of the tyrant.

Belittle his conquests. Remember that the territory was conquered by the Generals working under him to whom he denied all merit. He is called Unconquered, but it is well known that he suffered many costly defeats which were concealed from the Roman people. Spread about many stories of his personal cowardice before the enemy.

Remember the Civil Wars; remember Pompey. Remind the people of the brilliance of his circuses.

The distribution of lands: enlarge upon the injustice done to the large landholders. Intimate that the veterans received only stony or marshy land.

The Council of Twenty has drawn up detailed plans for the control of public order and finance. The senile edicts of the Dictator will be revoked at once: the sumptuary laws, the reform in the calendar, the new currency, the ten-head system of distribution grain, the senseless expenditure of public funds on irrigation and the control of waterways. Prosperity and plenty will reign.

Death to Caesar. For our country and our Gods. Silence and resolution.

The Council of Twenty

LXIII   Caius Cassius at Palestrina to his mother-in-law,
Servilia, in Rome.
            [*November 3.*]
            [*Reading between the lines, the following letter
            discusses opportunities for assassinating Caesar
            and means of inducing Brutus to join the con-
            spiracy.*]

    The company which is seeking to do honor to our
friend is increasing daily. There are many whose names
we do not know. Our efforts to learn those of the admirers
last month [*Query: Those who attacked Caesar on September 27?*] have been unavailing.
    It is difficult to find an occasion when an honor of this
sort may be conferred, for it must both come as a surprise
to the recipient and at the same time make as strong and
agreeable an impression as possible upon the bystanders.
Plans were well advanced to effect this at the conclusion
of the Queen of Egypt's reception. Our guest of honor
mysteriously disappeared from the assembly, however, and
it was thought that he had received some intimation of the
ovation that was to be accorded him.
    I am increasingly of the opinion that this gratifying
event should be delayed until at least one more of our
friend's closest associates be included among those conferring this honor. We are deeply indebted to you for your
efforts toward this end. The person I have in mind has
avoided my company and has even sent excuses that he is
unable to see me in his home.
    We understand all the weight, honored Madam, of your
arguments urging haste. We also are alarmed at the possibility that others may forestall us in this laudable enter-
prise, and with results that could only be disastrous. I
hope to call upon you when next I come to the City.
    Long life and health to the Dictator.

LXIV   Porcia, wife of M. Junius Brutus, to her aunt and
mother-in-law, Servilia.
            [*November 26.*]

    It is with respect but firmness, Madam, that I must
ask you to cease to pay visits to this house. My husband

has not concealed from me the reluctance he has to receive you and the relief that he feels at your departure. You will not have failed to remark that he never calls upon you in your home; you may infer from that that he receives you here only from a sense of filial duty. His agitated behavior and his troubled sleep following your visits have led me to take this action. I might well have taken it earlier, for I feel it unsuitable that I, as his wife, should be sent out of the room at each of your interviews.

You have known me for many years. You know that I am not a contentious woman and that I have previously acknowledged many an indebtedness to you. That my sisters have also been obliged to take this same action does not render it easier for me [*i.e. her sisters-in-law; apparently the wives of Cassius and Lentulus had also closed their doors to their mother*].

My husband does not know that I am writing this letter to you. I am not averse to his knowing it, if you wish to tell him so.

I thank you for your letter of sympathy on my great loss [*her miscarriage*]. I would have been more sensible of your expressions of affection and esteem, had you elsewhere shown me that I was sufficiently a member of this household to be included in your agitating interviews with my husband.

LXIV-A Inscription.
[*The following words were inscribed on a tablet of gold which, among other similar memorial tablets, were set into the wall behind the household altars of the Porcian and Junian families where they remained until the destruction of Rome.*]

Porcia, daughter of Marcus Porcius Cato of Utica, being married to Marcus Junius Brutus the tyrannicide, was aware that her husband was concealing from her the plans that he was then evolving for the liberation of the Roman people. On a night she plunged a dagger deep into her thigh. For many hours she gave no groan nor any sign of the great pain that consumed her. In the morning she showed her husband this wound, saying: If I have kept silent about this thing, can I not be trusted to keep the counsels of my lord? Thereupon her husband embraced

187

her weeping and communicated all the thoughts that he
had kept hidden in his soul.

LXV   The Lady Julia Marcia from the Dictator's House
in Rome to Lucius Mamilius Turrinus on the Island of
Capri.

[December 20.]

We have been going through a distressing time, my dear
boy. You will forgive me, if I do not go into it at length.
This terrible event [the profanation of the rites of the
Good Goddess] has stricken us all. We leave the house as
seldom as we can. We look into one another's faces, like
ghosts. We are expecting some punishment—I was about
to say: we wish for some punishment. But, of course, we
are punished already. As you can imagine it has robbed
Rome of all joy in the Feast of Saturn [the Saturnalia began on December 17] and my bailiff writes me that a
shadow has even fallen across our hill villages. I grieve
particularly for the children and the slaves, for whom this
season has always been the crown of the year.

The latest news fills me with no less alarm than the
scandal itself. The wicked couple has been acquitted.
There is no doubt that the judges were bribed with enormous sums by Clodius. What is there to say? We must live
in a city where public opinion is overridden by money.
They tell me that crowds gather all day before the houses
of the judges and stand spitting against the walls and door-
posts. I had a few words with Cicero this morning. He is
overwhelmed with despair. His speech at the trial was the
greatest he has ever made. I told him so, but he only
waved his hands in the air and the tears streamed down
his face.

My nephew's refusal to prosecute the matter is under-
standable, though I regret it profoundly. What he shrank
from doing as a husband, he was not absolved of doing as
the Supreme Pontiff. There is one detail about all this
I feel I must tell, though in great confidence. My nephew
knew in advance that that dreadful man was coming to
the rites. He could have had him seized at the door, but
Caesar wished that the matter be exposed in the way
it was done.

How I wish you were here, my dear Lucius. He is not

himself. He has asked me to stay with him for a while. At my urging we have remained in the Public House. [*A Supreme Pontiff generally lived in the Public House on the Sacred Way, placed at his disposal by the State. Caesar, following on his wife's implication in the scandal, would have preferred to move to his house on the Palatine Hill*] He has plunged even more deeply into work. It seems certain now that we are to go to war with the Parthians. The Isthmus of Corinth is to be pierced with a canal. The Field of Mars is to be transferred to the region at the foot of the Vatican Hill and the present Field is to contain a vast housing project. Libraries for the people are to be opened, six of them in various parts of the City. This is our tabletalk at dinner, but these are not the subjects weighing on his heart. Oh, that he had some friend here with whom he could be at ease. He does not invite his convivial companions. From time to time we are joined by Decimus Brutus and the other Brutus, but the evenings are not successful. Our friend can only extend friendship to those who first extend it warmly to him. As my husband used to say of certain people: "bold-in-love is shy-in-friendship."

Let me share another secret with you. Advance warning of Clodius's sacrilegious effrontery came to us from—of all persons—the Queen of Egypt. It is widely believed in the City that he will marry her. That possibly would furnish ample motivation for her exposure of the dreadful plan. You have my complete assurance, however, that there is no truth in that rumor. Something happened between them; I do not know what it was. I think it plays a large part in his present dejection; I know that she is suffering. It is generally believed that we older women are very clever at divining the sentimental histories that are being lived in our vicinity. Not I. All I can say is that some stupid impediment arose to interrupt a most happy conversation. I observe that my great-nephew [*Marc Antony*] has made a journey to the east coast.

It is absurd that Caesar live here alone. We have been talking it over. The season of pretty young girls has passed. Who would be more suitable as a wife for him than our good Calpurnia, whom we have all known so long and who has carried herself with such quiet dignity through so many difficult circumstances? I think you will soon hear that she has moved into this house after the quietest of weddings.

The dogs are barking. He has just returned. I hear him greeting the household. Only one who loves him deeply can know that the good cheer in his voice is assumed. I am astonished at myself: I have loved and lost many in my long life, but never have I felt so great a helplessness before another's suffering. I do not even know its spring—or of its many possible springs, the principal one.

The next day.

This is written in haste, my dear Lucius. To whom can I speak but to you?

Strange things are happening. He too could not contain himself and spoke of it to me, with a feigned lightness. He was speaking of the many conspiracies that are continually being uncovered, plots to overturn the State and to assassinate him. He was folding and unfolding some papers in his hand. "Last year it was Marc Antony," he said. "Now it appears that Junius Brutus is thinking of these things." I drew back with horror. He leaned over me and said with a strange smile: "He cannot wait until these old bones are quiet."

Oh, that you were with us here.

LXVI   Cleopatra to the Lady Julia Marcia, on her farm in the Alban Hills.
   [January 13.]

Your assurance to me that you are completely recovered of your indisposition has given me great joy. I trust that the messengers I sent daily to your door did not become a burden to those who were attending you.

I have waited for your restoration to health to lay before you a most urgent question. I am surrounded by a wall of enemies; I am fortunate in this, however, that you are not only the sole person to whom I can turn, but that you are the person best fitted to advise me.

Gracious lady, I came to Rome in order to further the interests of the great country over which I rule. I came here as a stranger ignorant of the customs of the Romans and exposed to the danger of making errors which might jeopardize my entire mission. To protect myself I organized a system of observers whereby I might be kept informed of much that was passing in the City. At no time have I used the information which I have received in any way that might disturb the best interests of the citizens; on a number of occasions I have been able to serve the public order.

Through diligence and good fortune I am in a position to follow most closely the plans of a group which designs to overturn the state and assassinate the Dictator. The group I speak of is not the first that has been brought to my attention; it is the most determined. It is not advisable that I include the names of these conspirators in this letter.

Most gracious lady, it would be difficult for me to lay my information before the Dictator at this time. In the first place, he might well be vexed that for a second time a woman and a foreigner should be informing him of a matter that so closely concerns him. In the second place, a grievous mischance has separated me from his trust and confidence. My only consolation is that he knows that my loyalty to his position in the Roman Republic is unshaken and unshakable.

The conspiratorial group to which I refer planned to murder the Dictator as he returned at midnight on January 6 from supervising the elections of the aldermen. Their plan was to lie in wait about and under the bridge that crosses the rivulet by the shrine of Tebetta. On that occasion I sent anonymous letters to four of their members telling them that Caesar was aware of their intentions. They now plan to attack him as he leaves the games on 28th of January. You can understand that it would be unwise for me again to write to the conspirators and I have promised my informant who is enrolled in their number that I shall not do so.

I most urgently ask your advice on this matter, noble lady. The most obvious recourse, I realize, would be to submit this information to the head of the Dictator's confidential police. That I cannot do, however. I am only too well aware of the incompetence of that organization. It submits reports to the Dictator wherein misrepresentation masks negligence and private prejudice is set forth as assertion, important information is withheld, and trifles are enlarged.

Let me hear from you.

LXVI-A   The Lady Julia Marcia to Cleopatra.
         [*By return messenger.*]

I thank you, great Queen, for your letters and again for the many marks of your concern for me during my illness.

Of this last letter: my nephew is aware in general terms of the group that you speak of. That it is the same organization and that he knows their names I am assured by the fact that he discussed the ambush at the bridge. I have no doubt, however, that your information is more detailed than his and that it is of the greatest importance. It has been a constant anxiety with me, great Queen, that he does not bring to the suppression of such conspiracies the energy and attention which he devotes to the dangers to the State.

I shall see that he learns of the plans drawn up for an attack on his life to be made on the 28th. When a suitable moment presents itself I shall let him know that we are indebted to you for this warning.

The season we are going through has been filled with so many reasons for distress and confusion that the happy hour I spent with you seems to have taken place many years ago. May the Immortal Gods soon restore to Rome a measure of tranquility and may they avert from us Their just anger.

LXVII   Caesar's Journal—Letter to Lucius Mamilius Turrinus on the Island of Capri.
         [*The following entries appear to have been written throughout January and February.*]

1017.   [*Arguments for and against constructing a canal across the Isthmus of Corinth.*]

1018.   [*On the increasing demand for Roman luxuries in the cities of Gaul.*]

1019.   [*Request for volumes to stock the new public libraries.*]

1020.   You once asked me, laughing, whether I had ever experienced the dream of the void. I told you I had, and I have dreamed it since.

It is perhaps occasioned by a chance posture of the sleeping body or by some indigestion or derangement within us, but the terror in the mind is no less real for that. It is not, as I once thought, the image of death and the grin of the skull. It is the state in which one divines the end of all things. This nothingness, however, does not present itself to us as a blank and a quiet, but as a total evil unmasked. It is at once laughter and menace. It turns into ridicule all delights and sears and shrivels all endeavor. This dream is the counterpart of that other vision which comes to me in the paroxysm of my illness. Then I seem to grasp the fair harmony of the world. I am filled with unspeakable happiness and confidence. I wish to cry out to all the living and all the dead that there is no part of the universe that is untouched by bliss.

[*The entry continues in Greek.*]

Both states arise from vapors in the body, yet of both of them the mind says: henceforth this I know. They cannot be dismissed as illusions. To each our memory brings many a radiant and many a woeful corroboration. We cannot disown the one without disowning the other, nor would I—like a village peacemaker reconciling the differences of two contending parties—accord to each a shrunken measure of the right.

These last weeks, not my dream, but my waking state has been the contemplation of futility and the collapse of all belief. Oh, worse than that: my dead call to me in mockery from their grave clothes and generations still unborn cry out, asking to be spared the clownish parade of a mortal life. Yet even in my last bitterness I cannot disavow the memory of bliss.

Life, life has this mystery that we dare not say the last word about it, that it is good or bad, that it is senseless, or that it is ordered. That all these things have been said of it is evidence only that all these things are in us. This "life" in which we move has no color and it gives no sign. As you once said: the universe is not aware that we are here.

Let me then banish from my mind the childish thought that it is among my duties to find some last answer concerning the nature of life. Let me distrust all impulses within me to say at any moment that it is cruel or kind, for it is no less ignoble from a situation of misery to pronounce life evil than from one of happienss to call it good. Let me not be the dupe of well-being or content, but welcome all experience that reminds me of the myriad cries of execration and of delight that have been wrung from men in every time.

From whom better than from you could I have learnt

this? Who ever so constantly invoked the extremest ranges of yea and nay—who, but Sophocles, known throughout his ninety years as the happiest man in Greece, and yet from whom no dark secrets were hid?

Life has no meaning save that which we may confer upon it. It neither supports man nor humiliates him. Agony of mind and uttermost joy we cannot escape, but those states have, of themselves, nothing to say to us; those heavens and hells await the sense we give to them, as all living things awaited, incult and abashed, the names that Deucalion and Pyrrha pronounced over them. With this thought I dare at last to gather about me those blessed shades of my past whom hitherto I had thought of as victims of life's incoherence. I dare to ask that from my good Calpurnia a child may arise to say: On the Meaningless I choose to press a meaning and in the wastes of the Unknowable I choose to be known.

The Rome upon which I have built my life does not exist in itself save as an agglomeration of structures larger or less large than another, of citizens more or less industrious than those of another city. Flood or folly, fire or madness may destroy it at any time. I thought myself to be attached to it by inheritance and upbringing, but such attachments have no more meaning than the beard that I shave from my face. I was called to its defense by the Senate and the Consuls; so Vercingetorix defended Gaul. No, Rome became a city for me only when I chose, as did many before me, to give it a sense and for me Rome can exist only in so far as I have shaped it to my idea. I now see that for years I childishly believed that I loved Rome and that it was my duty to love Rome because I was a Roman—as though it were possible or worthy of respect to love accumulations of stones and throngs of men and women. We are not in relationship to anything until we have enwrapped it in a meaning, nor do we know for certainty what that meaning is until we have costingly labored to impress it upon the object.

1021. [*On the rebuilding of Carthage and the construction of a mole in the Bay of Tunis.*]

1022. I was told today that a woman was waiting to see me. She entered my offices entirely veiled and not until I had dismissed my secretaries was I permitted to know that this was Clodia Pulcher.

She came to warn me that there was a conspiracy afoot to take my life and to assure me that neither herself nor

194

her brother had any part in it. She then began to give me the names of these agitators and to tell me the days that were being selected for their attempts.

By the immortal Gods, these conspirators failed to take into account that I am the darling of women. No day goes by without new aid from these fair informers.

I was on the point of telling my visitor that I knew all this already, but I held my tongue. I saw her as an old woman sitting by the fire and remembering that she had saved the State.

There was one new fact that she was able to impart to me: these men are meditating the assassination of Marc Antony also. If that is true, they are even more inept than I had thought.

From day to day I postpone measures to frighten these tyrannicides, nor can I make up my mind what should be done with them. It has been my practice hitherto to encourage all nuisance to come to a head; it is the deed itself and not the punishment that is instructive to the public. I know not what to do.

Our friends have chosen an ill-judged moment to raise their hands against me. The City is already filling up with my veterans [*re-enlisting for the Parthian War*]. They follow me about the streets with shouts. They cup their hands before their mouths and joyously call out the names of battles we won, as though they had been carefree foot races. I ordered them into every danger and I drove them mercilessly.

These conspirators I have only overwhelmed with kindness. The majority of them I have already pardoned once. They crept back to me from the skirts of Pompey and kissed my hand in gratitude for their lives. Gratitude sours in the belly of a small man and he must puke it up. By the rivers of hell, I know not what to do with them, and I do not care. They gaze piously at the images of Harmodius and Aristogiton [*the "classic" tyrannicides of Greek history*]—but I am wasting your time.

LXVIII   Inscriptions in Public Places.
          [*Cards bearing the following words were found attached to the statue of Junius Brutus, the Elder.*]

Oh, that thou wert with us now, Brutus!

Oh, that Brutus were alive!
> [*The following were found propped against the chair reserved for Brutus as Praetor of the City.*]

Brutus! Are you sleeping?

You are no Brutus!

LXVIII-A   The Commonplace Book of Cornelius Nepos.
> [*From December forward Nepos entered all matters, even those dealing with early Roman history, in cypher.*]

Fr. An agitated visit. He says that he has been approached by Longshanks [*Trebonius? Decimus Brutus?*] It was impossible to discuss the basic madness of the project. I limited myself to giving him a sound drubbing and to turning the conspiracy to ridicule. I pointed out to him that there was not a name among the agitators that was not known to my wife and to her friends; that any conspiracy which sought his adherence was bound to fail, for he was known to be a man who could not hold his tongue; that his visit to *me* was evidence that he had not sufficient conviction in the aims of such an uprising to have any part in it; that he had nothing to contribute to it but his wealth and that a conspiracy that required wealth was a failure in advance, for money has never yet bought secrecy, courage, nor fidelity; that should this conspiracy succeed his fortune would be wiped out in five days; that there was little doubt that Caesar was in possession of the most detailed particulars and that we may expect to hear momently that the hotheads will be dragged from their homes and locked up in the caves under the Aventine Hill; and that the great man whom they are attempting to remove will probably not deign to execute them, but will send them to the shores of the Black Sea, where they can lie awake nights remembering the tumult of high noon on the Appian Way and the smell of roasting chestnuts on the steps of the Capitol. Yes, and the look on the face of the man they thought they could replace, as he mounts the

196

steps to the platform and turns to address the guardians of Rome.

The City held its breath. The seventeenth [*of February*] has passed without event.

Every public event is now read in one light. The people are again paying the closest attention to the daily omens. Cicero is back in the City. He was seen to speak rudely to Longshanks and to pass the Blacksmith without greeting.

Since Caesar's remarriage the Queen of Egypt is suddenly very popular. Odes to her are displayed in public places. Her departure has been announced, but deputations of the citizens present themselves at her door, urging her to prolong her visit.

The tide of rumors has abated. A new chief and a stricter discipline? The influx of veterans?

LXIX   Caesar's Journal—Letter to Lucius Mamilius Turrinus on the Island of Capri.

1023.   By the immortal Gods, I am angry and I shall take pleasure in my anger.

The charge that I am the enemy of liberty was never brought against me while I commanded the armies of Rome, though, by Hercules, I so limited their movements that they could not walk a mile from their tents. They rose in the morning when I told them to and they lay down to sleep at my direction; and no one protested. The word freedom is in everyone's mouth, though in the sense that it is being used no one has ever been free or ever will be free.

In the eyes of my enemies I sit clothed in the liberties which I have stolen from others. I am a tyrant and they liken me to the potentates and satraps of the East. They cannot say that I have robbed any man of money, of land, or of occupation. I have robbed them of liberty. I have not robbed them of their voice and their opinion. I am not oriental and have not kept the people in ignorance of what they should know, nor have I lied to them. The wits of Rome declare that the people are weary of the information with which I flood the country. Cicero calls me the

Schoolmaster, but he has not charged me with distorting my lessons. They are not in the slavery of ignorance nor under the tyranny of deception. I have robbed them of their liberty.

But there is no liberty save in responsibility. That I cannot rob them of because they have not got it. I have never ceased from placing before them the opportunity to assume it, but as my predecessors learned before me, they know not where to grasp it. I rejoice at the extent to which the outposts of Gaul have shouldered the burdensome freedom which I have accorded them. It is Rome which has been corrupted. The Romans have become skilled in the subtle resources for avoiding the commitment and the price of political freedom. They have become parasites upon that freedom which I gladly exercise—my willingness to arrive at a decision and to sustain it—and which I am willing to share with every man who will assume its burden. I have been watching my Praetors [*Cassius and Brutus*]. They fulfill their duties with clerklike diligence; they mutter "freedom, freedom," but not once have they raised their eyes and voices toward a greater Rome. On the contrary, they have laid before me sheaves of suggestions that would at the same time reinforce their little dignity and diminish Her greatness. Cassius wishes me to silence the enthusiasts who day by day in public places rail against me and our edicts. Brutus wishes to safeguard the purity of our Roman blood by limiting the right to citizenship. By the immersions of Castor and Pollux, his African doorman knows better than that. That is the refusal of freedom, for it is by taking a leap into the unknown that we know we are free. The unmistakable sign of those who have refused their freedom is envy; it is the jaundice of the eye that cannot rest until it has ascribed base motives to those who do not receive but who make their freedom.

But I have reminded myself that the mind is free and my anger has passed. The mind is easily wearied and easily frightened; but there is no limit to the pictures it makes; and toward those pictures we stumble. I have often remarked that whereas men say there is a limit beyond which a man may not run or swim, may not raise a tower or dig a pit, I have never heard it said that there is a limit to wisdom. The way is open to better poets than Homer and to better rulers than Caesar. No bounds have been conceived for crime and folly. In this also I rejoice and I

198

call it a mystery. This also prevents me from reaching any summary conclusion concerning our human condition. Where there is an unknowable there is a promise.

LXX   Caesar to Brutus: Memorandum.
      [*March 7.*]
      [*In a secretary's hand.*]

The following dates are now established:

I shall leave on the seventeenth [*for the Parthian War*].

I shall return to Rome for three days on the twenty-second, should it appear advisable, to address the Senate on the electoral reform.

Billeting: the numbers [*of recruits and veterans joining up*] are exceeding my expectations. The eight temples [*assigned to them for lodging, in addition to the facilities afforded by the barracks*] may not be sufficient. Tomorrow we are moving from the Public House to the Palatine. The Public House should contain at least two hundred.

[*Caesar continues in his own hand.*]

Calpurnia and I hope that you and Porcia will dine with us, on the Hill, on the afternoon of the fifteenth, for my leavetaking. We are asking Cicero, the two Marcuses [*Antony and Lepidus*], Cassius, Decimus, Trebonius, and their wives, that have them. The Queen of Egypt will be with us after dinner.

So great is the pleasure that I take in your company, and in that of Porcia, that I could wish that you alone were our guests at that time. Since there will be others present, let me avail myself of this opportunity to lay upon you an injunction justified by our long friendship and by the kind offers of service which you have frequently made to me.

The separation from my dear wife will be hard for me; it will be hard for her. I shall rejoin her for a short time next autumn in Dalmatia or—without public notice—at Capri. In the meantime, I could know no greater consolation than to be assured that you and Porcia were holding her in your loves. To Porcia she has been bound by a close friendship since childhood; to you she bears the esteem which your character and your loyalty to me deserve. There is no second home that she could frequent with more profit and none to which my thoughts would more frequently have preceded her.

LXX-A   Brutus to Caesar.
        [*March 8.*]
        [*The following is the unfinished draft of a letter which was not sent.*]

I have taken note of the arrangements you have reported to me.

It is with regret that I must say that I shall not be able to be among your guests on the fifteenth. It has more and more become my practice to devote to study the few hours remaining to me at the close of the day.

I shall indeed, during your absence, seek to be useful to Calpurnia Piso in every way that I can. I think it well, however, that you consign her to the particular attention of others than myself, more active in the social life and less preoccupied by public business.

Your letter speaks, great Caesar, of my loyalty to you. I am glad you have done so, for it makes clear to me that you accord to loyalty the same meaning that I do. You will not have forgotten that I took up arms against you and received your pardon and that you have permitted me on many occasions to express opinions contrary to your own. From this I assume that you accept the loyalty of those who are first loyal to themselves and that you recognize that such loyalties may often come into conflict.

Your letter speaks, great Caesar, of my loyalty to you. That you have done so is——

It is with regret that I must reply to you that my wife's ill-health will prevent our——

... before your departure, to express a measure of the gratitude I bear to you. That indebtedness I cannot repay. Since earliest childhood I have received——

I have taken note of the arrangements you have reported to me.

INGRATITUDE BASEST OF ALL THOUGHTS AND AC

*[The following phrases are in early Latin. They
appear to be an oath used in courts of law.]*

"Oh, Jupiter, unseen and all-seeing, who readest the
hearts of men, witness now that what I declare is true,
and if there be any fault in it, may . . ."

Three yards of wool, medium weight, finished in the
manner of Corinth; one stylus, trimmed fine; three broad
lamp wicks.

My wife and I shall, indeed, with pleasure, that so great
an oak, not forgetting him on whom shall rest the last
glance of those great eyes, not without surprise and never
to be forgotten so.

LXX-B   Brutus to Caesar.
        [As sent.]

I have taken note of the arrangements you have reported to me.

Porcia and I shall come to you with pleasure on the fifteenth.

Rest assured, great Caesar, that for her own sake and
for yours, we love Calpurnia no less than ourselves and
that we shall not be happy until she looks upon our home
as her own.

LXXI   Caesar's Journal—Letter to Lucius Mamilius Turrinus on the Island of Capri.

1023.   I have been remiss in writing to you. The days
have been filled with preparations for my departure.

I am impatient to be off. My absence will constitute no
inconsiderable gift to the City which is as harassed as I
am by the continual rumors of sedition. It is ironical, is it
not, that in my absence these men are powerless to alter
the government and that when I have passed the Caspian
Sea they have no choice but to return to their proper
duties.

Their number appears to include some fifty members of
the Senate, many of them holding the highest positions in
the City. I have given that fact the grave consideration it
deserves and I remain unshaken.

The Athenians passed a vote of censure on Pericles. Aristides and Themistocles were driven by them into exile.

In the meantime, I guard myself, within reason, and I continue my occupations.

My son [*i.e., his nephew Octavius, formally adopted in his will which was written in September but not yet made public*] returns to Rome soon after my departure. He is an excellent young man. I particularly rejoice that he has written me of his high regard for Calpurnia. I have told her that he will afford her the companionship of an older brother, nay, of an uncle. Octavius traversed his youth in a year and is now well advanced into his middle age. His letters are not less sententious than those in *The Correspondence of Telemachus* [*a "model letter writer" widely used in schools*].

The great Queen of Egypt is returning to her country, having learned more about us than many who have spent a lifetime here. To what uses she will put that knowledge, to what uses she will put her ever-astonishing self it would be hard to say. There is a gulf between men and animals; I have always thought it to be narrower than many suppose. She possesses the rarest endowments of the animal and the rarest endowments of the human being; but of that quality that separates us from the swiftest horse, the proudest lion, and the shrewdest serpent she has no inkling: she knows not what to do with what she has. Too wise to be gratified by vanity; too strong to be content with ruling; too large for wife. With one greatness she is in perfect harmony and on that score I did her a great injustice. I should have permitted her to bring her children here. She does not know it yet to the full; she is that figure which all countries have elevated to the highest honor and awe: she is the mother as goddess. Hence those wonderful traits that I was so long in explaining to myself—her lack of malice, and her lack of that fretful unease to which we are so wearisomely accustomed in beautiful women.

I bring my precious Calpurnia to you next autumn.

LXXII   Calpurnia to her sister Lucia.
         [*March 15.*]

Each day, before this departure, grows more precious. I am ashamed that I had not realized before more clearly the fortitude that is required of a soldier's wife.

202

Yesterday afternoon we dined with Lepidus and Sextilia. Cicero was there and the company was very merry. Later my husband said he had never felt such friendship for Cicero, or from him; and this in spite of the fact that they baited one another with such sharpness that Lepidus did not know where to rest his eyes. My husband gave an account of the revolution of Catiline as though it had been a rebellion of mice against a worried cat called Cicero. He rose from the table and darted about the room peering into the wrong corners. Sextilia was laughing so that she got a stitch in her side. I find a new husband every day.

We came away early and before dark. My husband asked if I would let him show me some places that he loved. I was anxious to be off the streets, as you may well imagine, but I have learned not to urge caution on him. I know that he is well aware of the danger and chooses these risks in all consciousness. He walked beside my litter, followed by a few guards. I called his attention to an enormous Ethiopian who seemed also to be following us. He explained that he had once promised the Queen of Egypt that he would never object to the presence of this attendant who has since appeared and disappeared mysteriously, sometimes standing all night before our house and sometimes following him about for three days at a time. He is, indeed, a terrifying figure, but my husband appears to be very fond of him and was continually addressing remarks to him.

The high wind was rising that was soon to turn to storm. We went down the hill and into the Forum, stopping, dear Lucia, at this and that while he recalled a moment in history and in his own life. How he rests his hands on what he loves and how he gazes into my eyes to make sure that I am sharing his memory! We went into little dark streets and he put his hand against the house where he had lived for ten years as a young man. We stood at the foot of the Capitol. Even when the storm broke and the passersby fled by us like leaves, he would not hasten his steps. He made me drink from the spring of Rhea [*reputed to insure fecundity*]. How is it that I can be the happiest of women, and yet so filled with foreboding?

Our little trip was all unwise. We both passed a most disturbed night. I dreamed that the pediment of the house had been lifted in the storm and dashed upon the pavement. I awoke to find him groaning beside me. He awoke and flung his arms about me and I could feel the loud beating of his heart.

Oh, may the Immortal Gods watch over us.

This morning he is not well. He was fully dressed and ready to set out for the Senate when he changed his mind. He returned to his desk for a moment and has fallen asleep there, which his secretaries tell me has never happened before.

Now he has awakened and gone off, after all. I must hurry and prepare for the guests this evening. I am ashamed of this letter, so womanish.

Suetonius: The Lives of the Caesars: Book One.
    [*Probably written some seventy-five years later.*]

When he sat down, the conspirators thronged about him and Tillius Cimber, who had put himself at the head of them, came close to him as though he were about to ask a question. When Caesar with a gesture tried to hold him at a distance, Cimber seized hold of his toga at both shoulders. As Caesar exclaimed: "Then this is violence!" one of the Cascas, standing at his side, plunged a dagger into him, just below the throat. Caesar caught hold of Casca's arm and ran his pen through it; but as he tried to rise to his feet he was held down by another stab. When he saw that he was surrounded on all sides by drawn daggers, he wrapped his head in his robe at the same time drawing its folds about his feet with his left hand so that when he fell the lower part of his body would be decorously covered.

In this manner then he was stabbed twenty-three times. He said no word, merely groaned at the first stroke, though certain writers have said that when Marcus Brutus fell upon him he said in Greek, "You, too, my son!"

All the conspirators took themselves off and left him lying there dead for some time. Finally three common slaves put him on a litter and carried him home, one arm hanging down over the side.

Antistius the physician said that of all those wounds only the second one in the breast would have proved fatal.

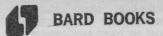 **BARD BOOKS**

the classics, poetry, drama and distinguished modern fiction

FICTION

ACT OF DARKNESS John Peale Bishop	10827	1.25
ALL HALLOW'S EVE Charles Williams	11213	1.45
AMERICAN VOICES, AMERICAN WOMEN Lee R. Edwards and Arlyn Diamond, Eds.	17871	1.95
AUTO-DA-FE Elias Canetti	11197	1.45
THE AWAKENING Kate Chopin	07419	.95
THE BAG Sol Yurick	20891	1.95
THE BENEFACTOR Susan Sontag	11221	1.45
BETRAYED BY RITA HAYWORTH Manuel Puig	15206	1.65
BILLIARDS AT HALF-PAST NINE Heinrich Böll	23390	1.75
THE CABALA Thornton Wilder	24653	1.75
CALL IT SLEEP Henry Roth	10777	1.25
THE CASE HISTORY OF COMRADE V. James Park Sloan	15362	1.65
THE CLOWN Heinrich Böll	24471	1.75
A COOL MILLION and **THE DREAM LIFE OF** **BALSO SNELL** Nathanael West	15115	1.65
DANGLING MAN Saul Bellow	24463	1.65
THE DOLLMAKER Harriette Arnow	11676	1.50
THE ENCOUNTER Crawford Power	10785	1.25
THE EYE OF THE HEART Barbara Howes, Ed.	20883	2.25
THE FAMILY OF PASCUAL DUARTE Camilo José Cela	11247	1.45
GABRIELA, CLOVE AND CINNAMON Jorge Amado	18275	1.95
A GENEROUS MAN Reynolds Price	15123	1.65
GOING NOWHERE Alvin Greenberg	15081	1.65
THE GREATER TRUMPS Charles Williams	11205	1.45
THE GREEN HOUSE Mario Vargas Llosa	15099	1.65
HEAVEN'S MY DESTINATION Thornton Wilder	23416	1.65
HERMAPHRODEITY Alan Friedman	16865	2.45
HOUSE OF ALL NATIONS Christina Stead	18895	2.45
I THOUGHT OF DAISY Edmund Wilson	05256	.95

BD 7-75

IMAGINARY FRIENDS Alison Lurie	23762	1.65
JEWS WITHOUT MONEY Michael Gold	13953	.95
THE LANGUAGE OF CATS AND OTHER STORIES Spencer Holst	14381	1.65
LEAF STORM AND OTHER STORIES Gabriel García Márquez	17566	1.65
LES GUERILLERES Monique Wittig	14373	1.65
A LONG AND HAPPY LIFE Reynolds Price	17053	1.65
THE LOTTERY Shirley Jackson	08060	.95
LOVE AND FRIENDSHIP Alison Lurie	23739	1.65
THE MAGNIFICENT AMBERSONS Booth Tarkington	17236	1.50
THE MAN WHO LOVED CHILDREN Christina Stead	10744	1.25
THE MAN WHO WAS NOT WITH IT Herbert Gold	19356	1.65
THE MAZE MAKER Michael Ayrton	23648	1.65
MEMENTO MORI Muriel Spark	12237	1.65
NABOKOV'S DOZEN Vladimir Nabokov	15354	1.65
NO ONE WRITES TO THE COLONEL AND OTHER STORIES Gabriel García Márquez	14563	1.50
THE NOWHERE CITY Alison Lurie	23754	1.65
ONE HUNDRED YEARS OF SOLITUDE Gabriel García Márquez	16626	1.95
PATHS OF GLORY Humphrey Cobb	16758	1.65
PNIN Vladimir Nabokov	15800	1.65
REAL PEOPLE Alison Lurie	23747	1.65
THE RECOGNITIONS William Gaddis	18572	2.65
RITES OF PASSAGE Joanne Greenberg	15933	1.25
SUMMERING Joanne Greenberg	17798	1.65
62: A MODEL KIT Julio Cortázar	17558	1.65
THE UNCOMMON READER Alice Morris, Ed.	12245	1.65
THE VICTIM Saul Bellow	24273	1.95
WAR GAMES James Park Sloan	17335	1.65
WEEKEND IN DINLOCK Clancy Sigal	12229	1.65
WHAT HAPPENS NEXT? Gilbert Rogin	17806	1.65
THE WOMAN OF ANDROS Thornton Wilder	23416	1.65

Where better paperbacks are sold, or directly from the publisher. Include 25¢ per copy for mailing; allow three weeks for delivery.

Avon Books, Mail Order Dept.
250 West 55th Street, New York, N.Y. 10019

BD 7-75

 **BARD BOOKS**

distinguished poetry

EVANGELINE Henry Wadsworth Longfellow	01669	.60
LEAVES OF GRASS Walt Whitman	02154	.60
THE RIME OF THE ANCIENT MARINER Samuel Taylor Coleridge	24331	.95
THE RUBAIYAT OF OMAR KHAYYAM Edward Fitzgerald	18770	.70
SHAKESPEARE'S SONNETS Ed. by Barbara Herrnstein Smith	08904	1.25
A SHROPSHIRE LAD A. E. Housman	02139	.60
SONGS OF INNOCENCE AND OF EXPERIENCE William Blake	18762	.70
SONNETS FROM THE PORTUGUESE Elizabeth B. Browning	19836	.75
YEVTUSHENKO'S READER Yevgeny Yevtushenko	14811	1.45